Red
The Forgotten

Printed in the United States of America

Publishers Cataloging-in-Publication Data

Witt, Amanda Beth.
  The Forgotten / Amanda Witt.
  pages cm.
  Series : The Red Series.
  ISBN 978-0-9965761-3-0

1. Totalitarianism--Fiction. 2. Dystopias. 3. Dystopian fiction. 4. Science fiction. I. Series. II. Title.

PS3623.I8765 W38 2015
813.4 --dc23   2015945738

River Jude Press
www.riverjudepress.com

Cover Image Pixabay, MysticsArtDesign

This is a work of fiction. Any resemblance to persons living or dead is purely coincidental.

For my father, who was always there
with lots and lots of books

The Forgotten

Book Four in *The Red Series*

Amanda Witt

River Jude Press

Chapter 1

My hair blew back from my face, twisting and whipping in the wind. The sea spray dampened it, making it curl and tangle, and when I licked my lips they tasted of salt.

We were going fast, cutting cleanly through the moonlit waves, and no one was having to row. Mal called this a cat-boat, but it didn't seem to have anything to do with cats, only with sails.

Mal was in the back of the boat holding the tiller and calling, now and then, for us to do something. Usually it was just to move out of the way of the sail, which wasn't always easy to do. Seven of us in a smallish boat wasn't ideal. But Mal insisted his boat was strong and stable, and we were traveling light.

"So they planned to go straight to the stockade," Earl said, speaking to Mal.

"That is right."

"Then we'll head for the stockade, too. Our first order of business is joining up with the others."

That wasn't my first order of business.

"There's no time," I said. "Meritt's in trouble and he might not even know it. And anyway we don't know how to get to the stockade."

Rain threw me a flat-eyed look and spoke to Earl as if I'd

said nothing. "Wonderful," she said. "It'll be just like home. Dad can boss me around and forbid me to do anything useful."

"You might end up taking orders from my father instead," Fiona said sweetly.

Rain scowled at her. I was beginning to see how the family feud had persisted all those years.

"My father and my Uncle Eric are two peas in a pod," Rain said. "Though they'd never admit it. And I don't intend to take orders from anyone who didn't want me along."

"So you would take orders from someone else?" Mal said, and I looked at him in surprise. Did Mal actually banter?

Rain stared at him as if he'd grown an extra head.

"Perhaps it is me," Mal said, smiling at her. "Perhaps you will take orders from me."

Rain's stare grew cold. "Why on earth would I take orders from you?"

"Because I am the one making it possible for you to reach Optica." He gestured to his bare chest. "And because you like my designs."

Rain looked nonplussed.

Earl sighed.

"I know nothing about you," Rain said, recovering. "Boats and battles are completely different skill sets."

"Getting to the battle is half the battle," Mal said.

"Clever," Rain said. "But can you fight?"

"I believe I am fighting now." He winked at her.

At another time I might have enjoyed watching Rain be disconcerted, but I had to talk sense into the lot of them, and time was short.

"I'm not going to the stockade," I said, raising my voice to be clearly heard over the shushing water and the wind. "Meritt doesn't know he's in trouble. I have to tell him."

Everyone looked at me, and every face showed some degree of disagreement.

"But Red," Fiona said hesitantly. "It'll be so dangerous over there."

My sister hadn't exactly had good luck with her adventures thus far. She'd been drugged by Eric Alleyn the night before and drugged by the Dream Recorder that morning, and she wanted her Papa and her brothers. I could understand that, so I tried to speak gently.

"Of course it's dangerous," I said. "That's the point. That's why we're going."

Fiona ducked her head and I felt bad, but not bad enough to relent. "Meritt needs help," I said. "And no one else is willing to help him."

"I'm willing," Michael Alleyn said, and my heart lifted. If the watchmaker would take my side, Meritt might stand a chance.

Unfortunately, Michael's offer wasn't unconditional. "First, however, I must speak with your old Guardian. With luck he can help me fine-tune a few matters. And I will also need to enlist the aid of your brothers—people the Watchers presumably won't recognize—in order to make my plan work."

"What is your plan?"

The old watchmaker shook his head. "Not yet," he said. "Let me speak first with the Guardian, and take advice from him."

I didn't know this man well at all—we had only just found him—and I was hesitant to argue with him, given who he was. Still, Meritt had no one but me looking out for his interests.

"While you go find Sir Tom and my brothers, I'll go into the city to warn Meritt," I said. "He's in terrible danger, immediate danger. There's no time to waste."

Michael Alleyn gave me a long thoughtful look, saying nothing, but Earl shook his head. "Gabriel hits hard and he hits fast," he said. "Eric Alleyn is the same. And they're a full day ahead of us. What's going to happen if they make their move sooner than you expect, and you're trapped behind enemy lines?"

"What if they make their move, and Meritt gets killed behind enemy lines?"

Rain gave an exasperated sigh. "I hate to be the one to break it to you, but the world does not revolve around Meritt. Don't be so stubborn."

I gave her a scathing look, but I didn't argue. There was no point. They wouldn't listen. As for being stubborn—well, I wasn't Eric Alleyn's daughter for nothing. I knew what was right and what was wrong.

"We'll all go to the stockade," Earl said, in a tone of finality.

For a time we skimmed across the dark water in silence. Michael Alleyn gazed out across the waves, his face unreadable. Fiona stared fixedly at him, as if he might vanish at any moment. Rain watched Mal at the tiller, more or less surreptitiously, and Earl watched Rain with a mixture of resignation and amusement. Will Bright, bizarrely, was looking downright happy. Once or twice he actually broke out in a cheery whistle.

After awhile Fiona turned to me. "I wonder what the others will think when they see us?" she said.

Rain snorted. "They'll be mad at Mal."

He smiled without looking away from the horizon. The moon was dropping rapidly—soon we'd be in complete darkness, save for whatever starlight penetrated the spotty clouds. Could Mal navigate by starlight?

"Gabriel won't blame Mal," Earl said pointedly.

Rain threw him a cool look, but then seemed to think

better of it. "Maybe you could explain," she said. "He listens to you. You could go in first, and explain that we came because we had to bring the watchmaker."

Michael Alleyn smiled faintly.

Earl leaned forward and rested his elbows on his knees, making the muscles in his arms bulge. "How many years have I been bodyguard for your family?" he said to Rain.

"All my life."

"And how many times in nineteen years have I interceded with Gabriel for you?"

Rain's face softened. "Only once a week or so."

"And how many times have I helped you directly disobey his wishes in a matter of life and death?"

Rain frowned. "This is the first time," she said. "But I'm not a child any longer. I'm old enough to decide what I want to risk, and when."

Earl nodded. "Agreed. That's why I let you come. I could have stopped you."

I expected Rain to deny it, but she merely nodded.

"All right," she said. "I get the point. If I'm old enough to risk my life, I'm old enough to tell my father."

I was still mad at Earl—and everyone else who had left us in the dark about the group slipping away in Mal's first boat—but I had to admit he was pretty decent. His wife had died a long time ago, and the Drewbloods were as close as he had to family. I guessed he was a sort of an honorary uncle.

Which reminded me of my uncle Rafe.

I listened to the waves slapping against the boat and thought about him, wishing I could tell him everything I'd learned in the few short days since his death. It seemed unfair that I knew about our family, about the other island, about the experiment, and he didn't. It seemed unfair that he had laid so much of the groundwork, and wouldn't get to see the end.

And what would he have thought of his brother and his parents? For a time I entertained myself with bittersweet imaginings, picturing a family gathering with Rafe sitting beside Gabriel at the table, our mother smiling and leaning down between them, setting out platters of food. Three Drewblood siblings, now lost to each other. Three siblings, and only one left to carry on the family memories and the family name.

Mal's sail, full of wind, pulled us speedily along beneath the setting moon. Sooner than I would have thought possible, the island where I'd grown up was rising in the distance.

"Is the island bigger on the other side?" Will said, studying the coastline.

"No," I said. "It's much smaller than your island, and it's almost a perfect circle."

I spent a few minutes describing the city's layout, the streets that stretched out from the watchtower like spokes from a wheel, the location of the Watcher compound.

"The stockade is somewhere north of the compound," I concluded. "Somewhere back in the woods."

Earl spoke. "Approximately how far is it from the north beach to the stockade?"

Carefully, I kept triumph out of my voice. "I don't know."

"*Approximately* means make your best guess," Rain said.

"I can't. I tried to tell you earlier, but nobody would listen. I've never been to the stockade."

Silence met that announcement. Then Rain flung out her hands. "So how will we find it?"

"Well, I have a sort of general idea of where it is," I said.

Will Bright gave me a look that said he knew I was enjoying this, but he didn't speak. Neither did Michael Alleyn.

"How general is general?" Fiona said. "How long do you think it will take to find it?"

"I don't know, since I don't know where it is. And we can't go in a straight line. The wilderland has a lot of big rocks and fallen trees we'll have to go around, and in some places the underbrush is so thick you can hardly walk. We'll have to keep an eye out for the wild men, of course. And Sir Tom sets booby traps. I don't know where all of them are."

Their faces turned toward the moon, which was falling fast toward the horizon; it would be completely gone by the time we reached land.

It took all my self-control, but I didn't say anything else. I'd given them enough to think about.

As we drew nearer, the tree line rose dark and threatening over the pale strip of sandy beach, and the moon vanished below the horizon.

Mal began to furl the sail. "We will paddle from here," he said.

"This is the beach where Sir Tom's cave is," I remarked, trying to sound casual. "That's where I stayed the first time I left the city. It's safe and has a bed and supplies."

Michael Alleyn eyed me speculatively.

"All right," Earl said, his tone telling me I wasn't getting away with anything. "We can go to this cave tonight, and then on to the stockade at daybreak. You're sure you can find this cave?"

"I think so. There's a giant tree near it—Jensen shot at us from there."

"Quiet now," Mal said, tying off the sail. "Sound carries over water."

We drifted nearer and nearer. Mal pulled on his shirt and began to paddle, and the swishing of the oars was soft, obscured by the shushing of the sea. We were almost perfectly silent, almost perfectly invisible.

The night was very dark, even with the stars, but by peering hard into the darkness, I finally made out what I was sure was the giant tree. I touched Mal and pointed in its direction and he turned the nose of the boat toward it. We slipped closer and closer, and now I could hear the waves lapping on the shore. I could only guess how far the cave was from that tree, but surely even in the dark we could find Sir Tom's hiding place. His beach had been flat, tilting gently down to the water. So the cave had to be somewhere between the two steeper areas in front of us.

We ran aground a few feet from the shore and, climbing out, quietly pulled the boat beyond the tide line and into the shadows of a stand of trees. I didn't see the other boat; the men must have landed somewhere else, closer to the stockade. Surely they had—surely they weren't lost at sea.

Pushing that thought away, I helped the others unload our supplies—mostly food—and divide them up. Everyone was silent; Fiona looked nervous but determined.

I was glad that thanks to the heavy rain that morning we'd both put on pants, instead of Fiona's usual dresses. Even so, except for Earl we were an unlikely group of warriors— three girls, two old men, and the ever-strange Mal. At least Fiona had her gun, but all I had was a handcuff key and a bottle of Dream Drops, Ezzie's gifts to me. A lot of good those would do.

But brute strength wasn't all that mattered in this fight. We would be clever, and we would certainly be unexpected.

"Thank you," I murmured, leaning close to Mal.

"The directions were good ones," he replied, in an almost soundless voice. "And the wind was in our favor, and my boat handled very well. She is a good boat." With this burst of unusual chattiness—he must be very pleased to successfully have sailed all the way across the sea—he turned away. To check on Rain, I noticed.

I started off across the sand, looking for the large boulder that held the cave. Unfortunately, there were plenty of large boulders, all hugging the tree line where the cave would be, and we had to inspect each one or risk missing the crevice in the dark. This took time, moving through the soft shifting sand, and I was a little worried about Will Bright. He was probably about the same age as Michael, but he didn't look anywhere near as fit. The old watchmaker sure had fortunate genes.

I led, and Earl brought up the rear. The wind sighed and stirred my hair. The sea whispered. No one questioned me, but I began to wonder uneasily whether I'd been wrong. Had I picked the wrong tree as a landmark? Was the one Jensen had climbed somewhere further down the shoreline?

I had almost given up hope when Mal touched my hand. I looked in the direction of his gaze.

At first I saw nothing. Then it came again—the tiniest flicker of light, deep in a dark rocky cleft.

It was the cave, and someone was in it.

Chapter 2

A ngel had to be staying somewhere out here, now that Sir
Tom had control of the stockade. I hoped Angel wasn't
the one in the cave. I wanted to find him—surely he at least
would want to help Meritt—but I didn't want to find him
tonight. Will Bright and Michael Alleyn were both tired, I
knew, though they'd made no complaint; and I wasn't sure
Angel would take us in or that we'd be safe if he did.

I looked at Earl. "I'll go see if I can tell who it is."

His gaze ran over me and I knew he was checking my
clothes—they were dark and wouldn't catch anyone's eye.
Then he nodded. "Take Mal with you," he said.

Fiona moved close. "And take my gun," she said, her
voice thin and pinched sounding.

I reached for it, but then stopped. "You keep it. I'm a
terrible shot."

It was true, and I didn't want to accidentally shoot Mal
while aiming at an enemy—but also, my sister was scared to
death. She needed the reassurance of her birthday present far
more than I did.

While Earl guided the others a little deeper into the
trees, Mal and I set our bags down and slipped silently
forward. We hadn't gone far before Rain was beside us.

"You might need me," she breathed in my ear.

I didn't care whether she came or stayed, as long as she didn't do anything stupid.

"Stay behind me," I said, and—for once in her life obedient—Rain dropped back to walk beside Mal.

We went on. I thought back to my time in the cave, to its angles and contours, trying to figure out where I'd need to be to see inside from as far away as possible. I didn't want to be silhouetted against the stars, and I didn't want motion to catch anyone's eye.

Deciding on an angle, I dropped into a crouch and crept forward. Just behind me Mal and Rain followed my lead, and slowly we moved off the sand and onto the stubbly grass that bridged the space between the beach and the dense woods.

The light in the cave was steady. Someone had been moving around, but now had set the lantern down.

Gesturing to the others to stay put, I crept a little closer. Then I stopped, waiting for someone to move across the cave opening. If no one did I'd eventually have to creep closer— but if I went any closer Angel would certainly be able to catch me, if he was the one in there. If he came after me I'd have to hope Rain and Mal had the sense to leave me and get back to the group. Angel was less likely to hurt me than them. I thought.

Inside the cave someone's back came into view. Whoever it was had on Optica gray. I moved a little closer, a little to one side. I didn't make any noise but still the person turned and looked out into the darkness, toward us.

It was Shawna.

I was relieved, not just because she wasn't Angel, but because the last time I'd seen Shawna she had been tending Ezzie's injuries, and since then I'd become afraid that she might have gotten infected from such close contact with him. She looked fine, though. A little tense, but fine.

I didn't want to jump up and startle her, so I called her

name softly. Her head turned and she looked puzzled, as if she hadn't quite heard me. Behind her in the cave I could see someone's legs, someone lying down.

"Shawna!" I called a little more loudly. "It's me. Red."

She came to the cave opening. "Red?"

I stood up and went closer. Shawna saw me and came to meet me, her eyes round with surprise. "Where did you come from?" she said.

Behind her Farrell Dean's mother, Alice, was lying on a pallet on the floor. She sat up, looking startled, and when she saw me she got to her feet and hurried forward, hope in her eyes.

"Where's Farrell Dean?" she said.

"He's fine," I said instantly, hoping it was true, not wanting her to worry, though my own heart gave a worried stutter. "He came last night. He should be at the stockade by now—you haven't seen him?"

She shook her head. "We've been out here since yesterday evening."

Surely he'd made it—he had an engine, and my brothers, and he'd made the trip across the sea before.

"Where have you been?" Shawna said. "Did you really go to another island—" She saw Rain and gave a little jump, then saw something else that made her eyes go wider still.

I turned. It was Mal, standing just behind Rain. He looked very exotic, what with the dozens of long honey-colored braids, the gold rings in his earlobe, and the black designs running out his rolled-up scarlet sleeve and down to his fingertips.

"Go get the others," I told him. "It's okay. These are friends."

From Sir Tom's bed, Joe called softly, "Hey, Red." A thick white bandage ran around his chest and looped around his shoulder, and against his dark hair his face was very pale.

He looked small and broken—he'd never been a big guy, but he'd been strong and quick, good at climbing trees and cutting wood.

Seeing him like this made my heart hurt. I went to him, kneeling beside him on the dirt floor. "Are you going to be all right?" I said.

"Eventually." He smiled but I could tell he was in pain, and he kept his eyes warily on Rain.

"This is my cousin," I said, gesturing to her. "Her name is Rain. I have a whole family on that other island. They've come back with us to help."

"How many?" Joe said. His dark hair looked stiff with sweat and I wondered whether he'd been feverish.

"There are nine in the other group, counting Farrell Dean and Ezzie," I said. "Although Ezzie's hurt. And there are six others with me. And we brought guns and ammunition and supplies—the other group did, I mean."

Behind me Alice gave a sharp gasp, and Shawna called my name faintly, as if she hadn't enough air.

When I turned they were paper white, staring at Fiona.

"It's all right," Fiona said, casting a reproving look my way. "She should have warned you. I'm her sister. Her identical twin."

Joe was struggling to raise up on his elbows.

"Stay put," Shawna told him. "You'll pull it open again."

"Louie," Alice said, moving forward. "How did you find us? What's happening in the city?"

"I'm not Louie," Will said. "I'm his brother. I live on the other island."

There was a confused rush of noise as everyone talked and I made introductions.

Earl was scanning the cave. "It's small," he said. "But for the rest of tonight it will do."

A low hum of conversation filled the cave. Alice was

talking animatedly with Will; Rain and Fiona were examining Sir Tom's supplies; and Michael Alleyn bent over Joe, talking with Shawna about his injury, while Mal and Earl listened to Joe's description of recent events.

"They wanted to get us out of the way in case they lost the stockade," he was saying. "It's been pretty bad there. The wardens keep sending one group right after another. We haven't been able to let down our guard even for a minute, not until a lull yesterday just after nightfall. That's when Sir Tom brought us here and then went straight back. We haven't heard anything since."

His face was even paler now and I hoped we weren't wearing him out. "If they'd hit my left arm I'd have stayed," he said. "But I'm no good at all with my right arm out of commission. Shawna's a decent shot but they made her come, too, even though Alice can take care of me now that Shawna's sewn me up, and even though they might need a medic back there."

Alice interrupted her conversation with Will to comment on that. "Harding wanted her safely out of it, and I can't blame him one bit," she said. Shawna's cheeks went pink, but she didn't comment.

Michael Alleyn was studying the bandage around Joe's chest and shoulder. "Would you allow me to take a look?" he said, and Joe nodded.

"How is everyone else?" I asked.

"Okay."

Joe winced as Michael peeled away the bandage, but he kept talking. "They're all tired, of course. Cline's holding up best. He's unreal. I don't think he's slept in three days, but he's still going strong."

"What about Judd?"

Joe looked away, just for a second, and then met my eyes again. "He's fine," he said, but his tone said different. "Liza's watching his back. He can be a little random. He wants to be a hero. You know, to make up for Petey."

"And have you seen my brother?" Will asked. "Or any of the older people? Some of them escaped from the city a couple of nights ago." He didn't explain how we knew that.

Joe shook his head, and Alice suddenly looked worried. "We haven't seen anyone but wardens, not for days. Not since Meritt brought the transmitter." Her eyes went to me. "It was so good to hear you made it to the other island safely," she said, and I knew she was thinking of her son. Had I even mentioned him, when I talked to Sir Tom? I was such an idiot—I should have realized his mother would be worried.

"Farrell Dean helped rig an engine so they could get back here," I said. To Mal I added, "This is his mother."

"Farrell Dean is very good with his hands," Mal told her.

She nodded, smiling at him. "Thank you. How is his back?"

"It's much better," I said. I didn't tell her it had been several days since I'd seen him.

"Alice?" Shawna said. "Didn't we bring some tablets?"

She was rummaging in a box of what must have been medical supplies, Michael Alleyn leaning over her. Alice stepped forward, pointing toward another box in the corner, and Rain and Fiona shifted to let her past. Earl was showing Will a gun, and Will was nodding, cracking it open, while Joe watched with interest.

It was the moment I'd been waiting for. Everyone was busy; no one was looking at me.

As casually as I could, I edged toward the door and slipped out into the cool dark night.

Chapter 3

B lindly I stumbled into the woods and then stood still, waiting for my eyes to adjust to the darkness. It wouldn't be long before someone noticed I was gone—though with luck they'd think for a few minutes that Fiona was both of us. And a few minutes was all I needed. No one would venture into the dangerous woods to find me, not in the dark, and not a one of them knew the way from the cave to the city.

As my eyes adjusted the sky emerged, a lighter dark than the rest of the world. Trees began to take shape. When I could see the paler areas of earth among the tangled undergrowth, I began to move.

"Wait," someone breathed from behind me.

I thought about making a run for it, but I didn't want to do anything to attract the attention of the wild men.

"I will go with you," the voice said in my ear. It was Mal.

We didn't talk any more. We moved quickly and carefully through the dark woods, avoiding Sir Tom's traps, keeping a close watch for wild men, for Jensen and Angel, for wardens. It was easier to walk in the dark wilderland now that I was wearing shoes that protected me from sharp rocks and thorns. I thought of Ezzie carrying me on his back the night he got hurt, the night we first left the city, and then I had to blink away tears.

Mal moved even more quietly than I did. Once or twice I heard a leaf rustle, but it wasn't because of us. Each time we froze in place, easing down so that we might be mistaken for bushes or the shadows of rocks, counting to three hundred before moving on again.

We made it to the southern gap in the city wall without incident, stopping at the edge of the woods just before the wasteland. I tucked my hair under my black cap, and Mal pulled a dark square of cloth from his pocket and tied it over his pale honey-colored hair. Then he tied another piece of fabric over the lower half of his face, so that only his eyes showed, and handed one to me, gesturing that I should cover my face too.

He seemed a little too prepared for this sort of thing.

We edged closer to the city. A small glowing ember marked where a warden stood smoking a cigarette just inside the gap. I couldn't tell whether he was alone, and I didn't know how I was going to get past him.

Maybe I should have taken Fiona's gun, after all.

Mal bent and pulled up his pants leg. A leather sheath was tied to his calf by two thin leather straps. It held a knife, its blade six or seven inches long.

Mal untied the sheath from his leg, pulled up my pants leg, and tied the sheath to me. The knife ran most of the length of my calf, and I was glad it was safely wrapped in leather; otherwise I'd probably manage to stab myself in the ankle. Just to be safe I flexed and then straightened my leg. The knife stayed where Mal had tied it.

Mal leaned against me and breathed in my ear, his words so quiet they might have been the sighing of the trees in the wind. "For emergencies," he said. "Do not slash. Too easy to block. Instead, stab. Underhand, not overhand. Keep it close to your body and aim for the center. Do it very hard and very fast."

Trying not to imagine how it would feel to stab a man—much less how he would feel—I nodded again.

"I will distract the wardens so you can get in," Mal said, looking up at the stars as if they told him something. "When dawn comes I will create a distraction so you can get out, but I will do this at the western gap. An hour later, I will make a distraction here. Then the western again, back and forth every hour until you get out. You see?"

I nodded, but we both knew it would be best if I made it out the first time, at dawn. Every subsequent attempt would be increasingly dangerous for both of us.

Could I find Meritt by dawn? Now that it was November, dawn came late—I had two hours, maybe longer. That wasn't very long, but it was at the best time of the night, the time when everyone asleep slept hard, and anyone still on guard was likely to be bleary-eyed and inattentive.

"Once you are out, do not wait for me," Mal murmured. "I will find you. If not, I will meet you back at the cave."

"Thank you," I whispered. I felt like I should explain—I owed Meritt something, I loved him, I couldn't bear the way everyone kept setting him aside as irrelevant or dangerous—but I didn't know how to say it succinctly or quietly. I thought saying it might make me cry.

Mal was unusual, though. Maybe he understood.

"Best wishes to you," he breathed. Then he was gone, melting into the dark shadows of the tall pine trees, and I was alone.

I should have been nervous. I was sneaking back into Optica, a place I'd risked my life to escape because staying inside would mean certain death. I should have been petrified, but I wasn't. I felt calm and clear-headed. I could do this. I had to do it—there was no one else. Meritt needed me.

In the dark woods far to my right a strange sound rose, making the hair on the back of my neck stand up. It was an unnerving cross between a howl and a laugh, and more unnerving as it faded away than when it began.

At the gap in the city wall the small ember arced to the ground as the warden dropped his cigarette. A shadow eased out into the wasteland.

The laughing howl rose again, and this time a voice rose in response. Mal. He sounded frightened. "No!" he said. "Get back! Help—warden—help me!"

I took an instinctive step toward him and then froze. They hadn't come at the same time, the howl and Mal's yell. They hadn't overlapped. It was Mal, all of it.

I hoped.

The dark form of the warden moved cautiously out into the wasteland. I began to edge in from the other direction. Mal yelled again, sounding further away. The warden wasn't conferring with anyone; he must be the only one out here. He took three more steps in Mal's direction and I ran flat out, crossing the exposed wasteland behind him, slipping into the gap and pressing my body against the wall, in its familiar shadows.

Had the warden seen me? Was he coming back into the city? I didn't know, and I didn't look to find out. I hurried up the dark sidewalk, staying close to the wall. If the warden called for backup they'd come in patrol cars, on the streets lit by electric blue lights. Here on the shadowed sidewalk I was invisible unless I walked right into someone.

Quickly I bent, untied my shoes, and pulled them off. Knotting the laces I tucked the shoes under one arm and began to run swiftly and silently through the deserted city. The cinderblock houses were dark. In the distance the watchtower rose up straight and tall in the middle of the city. Every few minutes its spotlight flashed in my eyes, following its circular path around the city. Soon I'd be close enough that I'd be in its range and I'd have to take care to avoid it, just in case the warden in the tower was standing at the telescope and actually paying attention.

My old world felt smaller than I remembered. The wall was protection, but it made me feel claustrophobic, too. Or maybe that was Optica itself, encircling me, staring at me. It had felt so strange when I'd walked across the other island with Tor, finding no boundaries other than natural ones like rivers and hills. How could I not be cramped and stunted, growing up in a place like this?

I shoved that thought away. Of course Optica was horrid. That was why we'd come back—we had to destroy it. We had to make sure no one else got wrapped in its suffocating layers.

Still, a feeling that was almost happiness filled me. I knew this place, this dark sidewalk, the electric blue streets. I knew this city, and I was running toward Meritt.

Where would he be?

Not at his dormitory. They'd started grooming Meritt to be a Watcher, so he wouldn't be in his regular place with regular people. The Watchers kept themselves isolated. They wanted us to think they were special.

But surely he wouldn't be at the Watcher compound, not if they were doubting him, asking questions about him. They wouldn't want him to have such ready access to their private quarters.

That left the prison. But that would tip their hand; it would tell the whole city—and Meritt himself—that they didn't trust him. Were they ready to do that?

Maybe instead they'd put him in one of the adult houses. Maybe a warden was keeping an eye on him there. Yes, that was the most likely scenario. But there were hundreds of houses—how could I guess which one?

A few dry leaves drifted across my path. An abandoned bicycle made me swerve away from the sheltering wall, and then quickly I pressed back into its shadow, slowing to a jog as an idea struck me. That last night when Meritt and I had been running, the night Rafe had been taken ... where exactly had I been when the patrol car found me? I'd been just outside my own area, near the girls' dormitories, the cafeteria, the schoolhouse.

Speeding up again, I headed for the place where I'd been captured. When I drew close I stopped and pressed back against the wall, listening, letting myself catch my breath, waiting.

After a time I began to feel cold. Then a muscle in my leg began twitching in an irritating way. A rat scurried by, not afraid, not even pausing to consider my presence. When would the wardens come by on patrol? At least it wasn't raining.

Finally I heard footsteps. Was it one set or two? I couldn't tell.

Very slowly I slid down into a crouch, making myself as small as possible. Very slowly I eased out a tiny bit, trying to see the blue-lit street, and then a tiny bit more.

Then I saw him. In the light of the electric blue street-lamps I saw him clearly. He was walking toward me with a slow, deliberate tread. His black warden clothes made his face and hands stand out sharply in pale contrast. His right hand was on his stunner, but casually, as if he didn't expect to need to use it. His left hand held his radio. His face was young, hard, and had an ugly scar running through the upper lip.

Slowly I eased back into the deeper shadows. Karl's partner was here, but where was Karl?

I thought I could make a good guess. I stayed where I was until the sound of the warden's footsteps died away in the distance, and then I slipped toward the center of the city.

No one was guarding the circle. Usually at least one warden stood outside the prison house, in the shadow of the tower, keeping track of who went in and out. Maybe tonight they were all out dealing with the rebels in the woods.

With one last glance around, I sped silently to the base of the watchtower, opened the prison house door, and slipped inside.

Chapter 4

The tiled floor was cold beneath my bare feet. The hallway was only dimly lit, and no bars of light shone from beneath the doors of any of the cells or interrogation rooms. That was no good. I'd hoped to be able to hear Karl interrogating someone, as I had been interrogated. I'd hoped that was why he wasn't out patrolling with his partner. Without Karl, how could I get a lead on where Meritt was?

To my left a short hallway doglegged. I thought it might lead to the prison offices. Was Karl there? It didn't matter if he was, because I couldn't exactly go open the office door and see who was inside.

As I hesitated, I heard the sound of a door opening somewhere down that hallway. Hurriedly I yanked open the first unbolted door, hoping that no lock meant no prisoner who might yell and attract attention.

The room was pitch black. I eased the door shut and stood pressed against the wall beside it.

Distant voices spoke. Then footsteps moved in my direction. Was it Warden Karl? Maybe I'd recognize his voice—though I couldn't call out to him, not if he was with someone else. All I could do was stand there holding my breath as the footsteps came closer, and closer, then drew even with my door, then went on past.

I pictured the long hallway. Surely I had time, before they turned around and came back my way.

Carefully I eased the door open a tiny crack. I could still hear the footsteps moving steadily away, so I opened the door a bit more and peeked out.

It was only one man, and it wasn't Karl but his partner, the one with the scar through his lip—the one who had wanted me to "buy" his protection. He was not, needless to say, a person I wanted to bump into.

I eased the door shut and stood there in the dark, cursing my luck. Minutes were ticking by. Dawn would come, and what would I do if I hadn't found Meritt? Leave without him? That would mean another day lost, another risky entry later, more danger for Mal as well as for myself.

I had to find him.

The warden took forever getting to the end of the hallway, turning, coming back. He was making rounds, I guessed. Finally his footsteps passed my door and covered the short remaining distance to the end of the hall, where it turned and led to the offices.

Carefully I eased the door open and listened. Nothing. I eased the door open a little more, but before I could peek out, an arm grabbed it and threw it wide open, jerking it out of my grasp, and someone crowded in against me, grabbing me, groping for my face and putting a hand over my mouth, backing me farther into the room.

I dropped my shoes and struggled, twisted, tried everything I knew to get free. The door swung shut. The warden was looming over me, taller than I'd expected, but then everyone loomed over me and it was dark, I had to get his hand off my face and yell, but if I yelled and brought other wardens running then I'd never get away, and maybe I could get away from him, just one warden, a young one and fit, but only one.

I tried to double over, leaning hard on the arm that was

pinning me. I wanted to get to Mal's knife. But the warden pulled me back upright, catching me hard under my ribs and knocking the wind out of me, and I made some sort of soft noise.

A hand yanked my cap off and at the same time the warden turned me around to face him, and I cursed my hair for catching his attention in the first place, for giving him a reason to watch me.

Frantically I grabbed at Mal's knife but the warden was too close, was pulling me up against him, and I struggled and kicked with all my might because this was not going to happen, I wouldn't let it happen—

"Red!" he breathed in my ear. "Is that you?"

Terror evaporated like mist; relief made me weak. If he hadn't held me up I would have fallen. It was Meritt.

"Are you all right?" he whispered against my ear, and I nodded. I was better than all right. He was alive—he was safe—I couldn't believe it. I clutched at his arms, reached up and touched his face. It was really him. He was here and he was solid and definitely alive.

My heart was pounding furiously and I was shaking with adrenaline, and he laughed softly and ran a hand over my hair.

"You almost gave me a heart attack," he said. "Come on. Let's get out of here."

Quietly he eased open the door and checked both ways, then ran silently down the hall to the prison door. I crammed my feet into my shoes and followed, staying right on his heels, pulling on my cap as I ran, feeling as if I'd wandered into a dream.

The light in the hallway was dim, but as best as I could tell Meritt was unharmed. From the back, at least, he looked like he'd always looked, tall and straight. He ran the way he always ran and moved the way he always moved, and when at the door he turned to make sure I was there, his gray eyes looked the same, his dark hair was the same, and he flashed me a grin and it felt as if the past month with all its horrors had never happened; and then we were outside in the darkness and the sharp cool air.

We slipped around the corner toward the dark cafeteria, then on through the empty streets, staying in the shadows and on the sidewalk, away from the blue lights, and the whole time I kept my eyes on Meritt. I couldn't believe I'd found him—or rather that he'd found me—and now we were running through the dark deserted streets as we'd done a hundred times before.

Meritt ran straight toward the least-watched area of town, the bee meadows behind the girls' dormitories, and I followed. From there we went on, out to the orchard where I had waited for him the night we escaped from Optica, the night the Watchers had almost killed Farrell Dean in the city meeting, the night the wild man had mauled Ezzie.

I wanted to keep running, to hurry to the gap and wait until Mal distracted the warden and let us out, but in the shadows of the twisted apple trees Meritt finally came to a stop and swung around to face me.

"What are you doing here?" he said, and the challenge in his tone took me aback. "I told you to stay away."

"You did not," I said. "You said you needed me here to help with Sir Tom."

"I said the currents were too dangerous."

"Obviously they weren't."

Meritt made an indecipherable gesture. "If you're here to help with Tommy, why aren't you at the stockade?"

"Because I had to find you first," I said. "The Watchers know about you, Meritt. I came to tell you. You have to get out. They know you're working against them."

He said nothing. I strained to make out his expression,

but the night was too dark, so I kept on talking, trying to make sure he understood.

"Cynda told them you've been disabling cameras," I said. "They've been questioning Louie, too, trying to find out what else you've done."

I paused, trying to think of a quick way to explain how I knew all that, wishing I could be certain Angel wasn't spying on us even then. Even if we could safely talk, I didn't know how much Meritt already knew, and it wasn't a story I could tell quickly.

Before I could even decide how to begin, what to risk saying, Meritt shifted away from me, and suddenly I was afraid he'd turn around and go straight back in. He was acting odd enough to do just that.

"You can't go back," I said hurriedly. "You have to come with me now, out of Optica, before they arrest you."

He didn't answer, though he did stop moving.

"Meritt," I said sharply.

"I heard you."

He didn't say anything else, and I began to feel as if I couldn't breathe. What was going on? In the prison he'd seemed glad to see me, but now he was angry and terse and I didn't understand why. "Meritt?" I said.

He turned around. "It's too late," he said. "I have to stay. I've started something and I have to finish it. I'm the only one who can."

"What is it?"

Again he shifted away from me.

"This is no time for secrets." I had to struggle to keep my voice even. "People are dying. Joe's been shot."

"Joe's dead?"

"No, but some of the old people are."

"I know that. I did my best, all right? I got some of them out. But I can't save everyone."

"The ones who got out—where are they now?"

"Aren't they with Tommy?"

"I don't know," I said. "And do you know why I don't know? Because the second I set foot on this island, I came to find you, to warn you, and now you won't come with me and you won't even tell me why."

One hand went to his head, and even in the dark I knew that gesture. His hair was in his face and he was pushing it away, as he always did when he was troubled, when he was frustrated.

The familiarity of it made my throat close up. If it hadn't—if I'd been able to speak—I'd have thrown caution to the wind. I'd have asked him about Rafe—not to accuse, only to question, to ask for his help, to tell him everyone misunderstood, everyone thought Meritt was on the side of the Watchers, and if he'd only explain to me why he'd been out there, if he'd only trust me, then I could defend him. Because they had arguments and logic and details, and all I had was my faith in him and they didn't care about that.

But even to mention Rafe's death would have been unforgivable; even to mention it would be to concede, somehow, that I wasn't certain. And so it was good that I couldn't speak, and I stood there, getting control of myself, reminding myself not to say words that could never be taken back, and Meritt half turned away from me.

"You were easier when you were younger," he said.

That surprised a pained sort of laugh out of me. "You mean back when your father gave me to you as a pet?"

"It wasn't like that."

It took a moment to sink in.

"You knew." I couldn't believe it.

The spotlight flashed toward us, slicing white through the tangled trees, throwing stark shadows. It didn't quite reach us, and even if it had I wouldn't have cared.

"You knew all along that your father had abducted me?"

"Abduction's a strong word—"

"You knew where my family was. You knew all along and you never told me. How could you not tell me?"

In the darkness Meritt shrugged. "It was complicated," he said.

I stared at his profile, waiting for him to say something more, anything more, but he looked out at the darkness, at the maze of trees, and didn't say another word.

It was complicated.

His father had kidnapped me, brought me here, put me in this awful city, and all those years Meritt had known and never told me. Even though he knew how lonely I was, even though he knew I felt like a freak, a mutant, all alone in the world. He *knew* how desperately I wanted to belong to someone, anyone. And all he could say now was *it was complicated?*

I was turning to walk away when he spoke.

"Look, Red, I'm sorry."

If he hadn't spoken then, I would have walked away and left him there. I'd have walked away and never looked back, and then everything would have been different.

But he spoke and I stopped, one hand on the rough bark of a tree, feeling the need to somehow ground myself because in my mind the earth had shifted under my feet. He had known all along, and he had never told me.

It was complicated.

"I'm sorry," Meritt said again. "It scared me, finding you like that in the prison. I could have hurt you."

For a moment I was too disoriented to make sense of his words. Then I got it: he wasn't apologizing for keeping secrets all my life, about my life; he was apologizing for being mad at me just now.

"I thought you were one of the wardens," he said.

"They've been following me around—they think they're sneaky but I always spot them—and I couldn't afford to get caught right then, so I grabbed you. But you were a girl, and you were small, and you—well, you were you. But you were supposed to be all the way across the sea. I couldn't believe it was really you, right there in the prison."

I turned around. "Why were you there?" I said.

He knew it was an ultimatum. In the darkness he moved again, shifted. He'd always been fidgety, but that night he was really keyed up.

But he answered. "I was there because I'd been up in the watchtower to see what the spy cams had caught."

"Did you drug Warden Zee again?"

He didn't answer for a long moment. Then he said, "No. I killed him."

I blinked.

He said it again, as if I might not have understood. "I killed him. You're determined to know everything, so there you go. Right before I found you, I killed him. I broke his neck. It wasn't hard." He sounded faintly surprised. "My father told me how, and it worked exactly like he said it would. All you do is—"

"Why didn't you use the sedatives?"

"I didn't have time. I can't always get out. I'm not a prisoner but they do keep my door locked at night. I mean, they know who my father is, after all. So sometimes Marta comes and unlocks my door, but I never know when that will be, and I always have to be back by dawn to lock myself in again. So I couldn't drug him."

"You did what you had to do." I tried to sound more nonchalant than I felt. "So what did you learn?"

"Nothing." The wind had all gone out of him. "I killed him, and I didn't learn a thing."

Now I understood why he'd been so angry with me—

he'd killed a man and then someone else had been there, someone he thought was watching him. And Meritt had gone after him.

After me.

Meritt had almost killed me.

For a long moment we were silent. Through a thin layer of clouds the stars above twinkled—more faintly now that dawn was near—and I had a wild thought that if I wished on them, perhaps they'd brighten again, wind back the clock until the previous day, and this time through I wouldn't be fooled into getting left behind. I'd get here in time to keep Meritt from going up into that tower.

"I never knew what to do with you," he said, and in the quietness of the orchard I could hear every nuance of his voice, his natural confidence, his strength, and the tremor that ate at the edges.

"I thought it would be safer if you didn't know where you came from, and I thought it would be safer for you to be with me than not. But how could I know for sure? I never knew. I still don't know. But I know you're not safe with me now." He gave a short unhappy laugh. "That's pretty clear. So I tried to get you to stay away, over and over, in every way I knew how, but you just don't listen. Not to me, not to Tommy. You used to listen, Red. You used to pay attention. Why aren't you listening to me anymore?"

I could feel strain coming off him like heat, waves of it. "I'm listening now," I said, as calmly as I could.

He didn't answer.

"You ought to come with me," I said finally. "You need to get out of the city. If they figure out you killed Zee, you'll be in even worse trouble than you already are."

"I'll be locked in my room. They won't know it was me."

"And you said there's something else you have to do."

"That's right." He took a deep breath, held it. Then he

said, "I'm going to tell you, Red, because … I'm just going to, that's all. Not because you're hassling me but because I want you to know. But don't tell anyone, especially him." He sounded very young, and I knew he was talking about Angel. "It's a secret, it's dangerous, and if he found out he'd—"

He stopped.

"I can keep a secret," I said. "Especially from Angel."

"I've looked at it from a million different angles, and this is the only surefire way," he said. "There's a tunnel that goes from the Watcher compound to the stockade. But it's coded, and the Guardian who knew the codes isn't in his right mind."

"Jensen?"

"You know their real names? He won't use them. Says it wakes sleeping dragons."

"He calls Jensen 'Caliban.' I don't know the names of the others."

Meritt nodded. "He's the one. Caliban used to know the passage codes. None of the other Guardians did—I'm not sure they even knew about the passage. But that's what I'm doing—I have to figure out the code so we can get the passage open."

"To get the rest of the old people out?" I felt vindicated. No matter what Sir Tom and Rain and the others said, Meritt was on our side. Not on the Watchers' side, not on Angel's side, but ours. He was risking his life to help my old people.

"Why can't you do it from the stockade?" I said. "Break the code from there?"

"That won't work."

"Why not?"

"Well, because—it's the doors. They're double coded. They won't swing the right way unless you have the code for that direction, so if I worked from that end I'd have to break two codes."

I thought about this. "So if you knew the code in the stockade, you could get into Optica, but you couldn't get back out."

"Right. I need the code for leaving Optica, and I'm working on it. I think I can get it."

"And then you'll come out? Through the tunnel?"

"Yes," he said, "I will." He said it with such finality that I knew, this time, I could take him at his word. "Once I know the code, it'll all be over."

"Good. Then I'll be waiting for you at the stockade."

For some reason that made him laugh. "I won't hold you to that," he said. "You know me. Deadlines make me go all to pieces."

He laughed again, jaggedly, and now he was scaring me. I thought he was probably scaring himself. And anyway it wasn't true—he worked great under pressure.

"Just focus on what you need to do," I said, trying for a practical tone.

That stopped his unnerving laughter, anyway.

"Just focus," he said after a moment. "That's exactly what Rafe used to say. Focus on the thing at hand. Well, Rafe focused like a laser. And now he's dead."

My throat felt thick with tears.

"You thought I was heartless when you told me," he said. "You told me about watching him die and you didn't like the way I reacted. You thought I was cold-blooded."

I had, but I couldn't say so now.

"The whole thing was so unreal." He ran a hand through his hair. "We went to meet him and then they arrested him and then he was dead. Just like that. I never expected Rafe to die."

"Me either." I was only half listening to his words. Dawn was coming and I had to get out of the city, but I couldn't go until I got Meritt calmed down, and that was not something

I'd ever had to do before. Meritt was always full of energy but relaxed, nonchalant. Not like this.

Maybe if I gave him something concrete and immediate to think about …

"What are you going to do about Cynda?" I said.

"About Cynda." He said it as if he had no idea what I was talking about.

"She told them you'd been sabotaging cameras. She told the wardens. They know you're working against the Watchers."

"Cynda's scared," he said.

"I know. But still—"

"They probably took her to the prison and interrogated her about you, since you were friends and all that. She probably traded information about me for a promise that they wouldn't kill her or let her starve. Not that their promises mean anything."

"In any case, she's put you in danger," I said. "How can you stay here now?"

"I'll find some way around it."

"But how? What will you do, exactly?"

"I'll … I'll make a preemptory strike, confess to disabling the cameras before they accuse me of it. I'll say that my father wanted the wild men to be able to sneak in unseen, so they could terrorize the city. I'll say I went along with him because I thought a fear of things outside the wall would make everyone more dependent on the Watchers."

"And you could say you were scared of Angel," I said, keeping my voice low. "You could tell them you were scared to cross him."

Meritt took a deep breath, let it out.

"That would work," he said, sounding more like himself. "That would make sense to them."

"I hope so. But Meritt, please be careful. If something

happened to you …" I didn't know what I'd do if something happened to him, especially now, when we were so close to being free.

He came close to me, then, and touched me softly on the shoulder. "I'll be careful," he said, and now he sounded like his old self. "And listen, Red. Even though I wish you weren't here, I'm glad to see you. I've missed you."

A lump rose in my throat. "I've missed you, too," I said, and his hands tightened on my shoulders and he leaned in and I thought he was going to kiss me, and it was all wrong, he was half distraught over what he'd done and almost done. He'd killed a man with his bare hands and he'd have killed me, too, if I had been the spy he'd thought I was. He'd have broken my neck just as he'd broken the warden's.

I didn't flinch—at least I don't think I did—but Meritt abruptly released me, stepping back, putting yards of empty space between us.

"It's getting late," he said. "I have to go." And it was true—the darkness in the eastern sky was thinning dangerously.

"I'll go part way with you." There was time. I could go with him to the edge of the city proper and still be back at the western gap by true dawn. Mal would know I'd need as much time as possible —he wouldn't rush the exit strategy.

Together Meritt and I walked through the orchard and the bee meadows, moving carefully, watching our steps, and the darkness continued to thin. After a few minutes I held out my hand and he took it, and it didn't feel like it felt when I held hands with Farrell Dean. It felt like I was lost, and Meritt was lost, and that by holding hands we could at least be lost together.

At the edge of the city proper Meritt stopped and turned toward me.

"No matter what happens, don't come into the city

again," he said, reaching for my other hand. I could see him better now, washed colorless by the gray dawn, his skin pale against his dark hair, his gray eyes serious. "It's too dangerous," he said. "Stay with Tommy. And stay away from Angel. Don't trust him."

"I thought he was helping us."

"Not you. He hates you. It's not your fault, but he does." As he spoke he shifted, and from the corner of my eye I saw two wardens coming around the corner of the cafeteria, patrolling where wardens never bothered to patrol because there wasn't much mischief anyone could get into out there with the bees. But now they were there and they were close, only fifty feet or so away.

"I think he's jealous," Meritt went on, and gripping his hands I pulled him back toward the shadows of the meadows and the trees, but I moved too quickly or maybe we just had bad luck because the wardens looked up, both of them, and saw us. They started toward us, reaching for their guns, their footsteps loud and distinct on the pavement.

Meritt glanced over his shoulder and I knew with perfect clarity that my mistake was surely fatal—maybe not for me because I was behind him, they hadn't gotten a good look at me, I might still get away, but for Meritt there was no time, no way to pretend he hadn't been out, hadn't killed Warden Zee. Then something even worse hit me and I felt the ground giving way.

This was my nightmare.

This was the moment Meritt was backed against a wall and I was at hand, I was here, I was the pawn that would save him and save Optica.

I couldn't bear it—I couldn't let him do it—he'd hate himself if he did—but if he didn't do it he'd die. There was no way out.

No—there was a way.

If I'd had more time to think I'd never have had the nerve to do what I did, but I didn't have time. The wardens were almost upon us. I grabbed Meritt's arm and said clearly, "But I thought you loved me!" It was easy to sound upset.

Meritt didn't pretend to not understand.

"Stop it," he hissed, and shoved me hard toward the orchards. "Go, Red. Now!" But it was too late. The wardens were right behind him, and besides I knew this was his only chance.

"If you take me to the Watchers they'll kill me," I said, focusing on his face as if I had no time for anyone else, as if I didn't care who was coming, who heard. "How can you say you love me—"

Then the wardens flanked us and shone their bright lights in our faces. Meritt's was white, reproving, stricken, and I didn't want the wardens to think about why, so I slapped him, hard, across the face.

One of the wardens laughed and the other grabbed me by both arms.

"No more of that," he said, twisting my wrists behind my back and clamping handcuffs on me so tight they cut into my flesh.

"Good work," the other warden said to Meritt. "We'll take it from here. This one's a firebrand, I'll give her that."

"Better search her," the one holding me said, but when the other warden moved toward me Meritt cut him off.

"Don't touch her," he said. "I'll do it."

The warden laughed again. "I guess you've earned it," he said. I didn't like the way he looked me up and down, but he backed off.

Meritt didn't meet my eyes as he patted me down. He didn't flinch or slow when he felt my pockets, though he surely felt the little bottle and the key. Nor did he react when he ran his hands down my legs and over the knife.

"Nothing," he said to the wardens, straightening up. "Let's go."

The wardens pulled me through the streets toward the prison. Now and then I lost my balance—it was surprisingly hard to walk with my hands bound behind me.

"Go easy," Meritt snapped at the wardens, and his tone was so imperious that I glanced up in surprise. One warden cast a cold look in Meritt's direction, but the other made more of an effort to help me walk.

As we went the sky lightened bit by bit, showing the gray cinderblock buildings in all their ugly sullen sameness. The blue lights clicked off. A cold breeze began to blow, bringing with it the smell of burned toast.

Somewhere in the distance an eerie howl rose up, mournful and angry and violent, tapering off into a lunatic chattering laugh.

Chapter 5

They put me in the same cell Farrell Dean had been in, the one way back toward the staircase that led to the watchtower. They pushed me in, shut the door before I could even turn around to get one last glimpse of Meritt, and locked the door.

They hadn't chained me to the wall, as Farrell Dean had been chained, and they didn't turn off the lights—the switches were out in the hallway—so I stood in the middle of the small room and looked around my prison.

It didn't take long. There wasn't much to see. Besides the ring and chain set into the back wall on the left, there was only a low cot with a bare mattress against the far right wall. No windows. Nothing.

I went to the corner where Farrell Dean had lain all bloody and beaten. There were no traces of his presence, not a single hair, not a drop of blood. Still I almost could see him there, and when I turned around I had the strangest feeling, as if I could almost see all the other people who had been imprisoned in this room before me, some chained, some pacing back and forth, weeping, cursing, hoping this room wasn't the end.

Beginning to feel queasy, I went to the cot and sat down. It was awkward, because my hands were still cuffed together behind my back. Maybe that meant I wouldn't be waiting long.

Maybe that meant I would die soon.

That thought brought me back to my feet. I tried to reach my front pants pocket, where the handcuff key Ezzie had given me was stashed. At first I thought it was impossible, but I twisted and craned and finally managed to snake one finger in and hook the contents out.

The key and little bottle fell on the floor. I squatted and felt for them, hoping the wardens wouldn't choose this moment to return. When I found the bottle of Dream Drops I shoved it under the thin mattress. When I found the key I tried to get it into the lock, but the angle was impossible.

If I could just get my arms in front of me, maybe I could manage the key. I arched my back and tried to hook my foot through the circle of my bound hands. I could catch my big toe, but though I strained and fought, I couldn't arch back far enough to get my leg through. I made one last desperate attempt, lost my balance, and fell against the cot. It clanged noisily against the wall and I froze, listening, afraid I'd attracted attention to myself. But no one came.

Then I hunched forward and pulled my arms down behind me as far as I could, but—I never thought I'd say this—my hips were too big. Though I twisted and craned, I just couldn't get my rear end through the circle of my arms. My wrists were cuffed too closely together. And I couldn't get my legs through without getting my hips through first.

When my back screamed for mercy I finally gave up. I picked up the key and began working behind my back again. I tried again and again to get it into the lock on the cuffs, but I kept dropping it and having to grope behind my back for it again. Pretty soon I sat down on the cot so at least it would fall closer to my hands.

After a time my wrists began to burn—the cuffs were

tight and I'd been twisting so much—and I decided to take a little rest. Briefly I considered trying to reach Mal's knife, but I didn't think I could, and anyway what would I do with it? Run backwards to attack a warden?

At least if Meritt managed to come for me, he could use the key to get me loose. If it fit these cuffs, anyway. In the meantime, all I could do was sit there.

Footsteps went down the hall, but they didn't pause at my door. Five minutes or so later they came back, at a run. Maybe that meant someone had discovered Zee's body.

Sure enough, many people passed my door shortly after that, walking with hurried steps. A long time later they came back, walking more slowly, and now they were talking in angry upset voices but I couldn't make out any words.

Then someone slammed a fist against my door, or kicked it, and I jumped. Then a horrible possibility occurred to me: What if they thought *I* had killed Zee?

That thought scared me, but not as much as I might have expected. Might as well be hung for a sheep as for a lamb—that was something Louie used to say. If they blamed me, at least it would keep Meritt out of trouble.

And anyway this was all my fault; Meritt had tried to keep me out of it. He'd tried and tried to make me stay away. He'd tried, but I hadn't been listening, that was what he'd said.

He'd also said I hadn't been listening to Sir Tom either. What was that supposed to mean?

I thought it all over, replaying in my mind the conversation I'd had with Meritt over the transmitter, the one when he'd tried to get me to stay away, using—I now saw—the sea currents as an excuse.

Something struck me. I had been the one to bring up the possibility of my talking to Sir Tom on the transmitter—but it was Meritt who had hinted and hinted until I'd finally voiced the idea. But why? Sir Tom hadn't told me not to come back. Sir Tom had said …

Sir Tom had told me not to trust Meritt. And Meritt had known he'd say that—Meritt had been trying to protect me by making me distrust him.

And it wasn't the first time he'd used that strategy. Hadn't I wondered why he'd brought wardens, that day on the cliff? Farrell Dean had thought he was trying to catch me, and I'd said no, Meritt didn't need wardens to capture me because if Meritt called, I'd go straight to him. Meritt knew that.

That was why he brought the wardens. He hadn't been trying to catch me, he'd been doing the exact opposite—trying to scare me away, to make me distrust him. So I'd be safe.

On the beach Angel had offered to take me to Meritt.

Don't trust him, Meritt had said in the orchard.

No wonder Meritt was wound so tight—he was all alone, deliberately alone, and walking a tightrope with enemies on every side.

My shoulders began to ache, and in an attempt to find relief I lay down on one side. My arms still hurt, but it felt good to lie down. I was so tired, and I was still recovering from being sick.

Anxious though I was, frightened at being locked in the prison, my eyelids began to droop.

I was almost gone when a sudden thought hit me. Struggling to sit up again I felt under the mattress for the little bottle. This would be tricky. I didn't want to spill it all.

Getting down on the floor on my knees, I craned around so I could see my hands and the bottle. Carefully I opened it. Carefully I squeezed the dropper and let one drop fall onto the tile floor.

I thought a second, then dropped two more onto the

tiles. Then I screwed the cap back down firmly, and bent and licked the Dream Drops from the ground.

Rain was angry.

"Blast it! What sort of idiot is she?"

Mal's expression turned disapproving. "She is not an idiot," he said. "She did what she set out to do. She warned him, because no one else would."

Rain snorted. "She just had to go warn the traitor who got my Uncle Rafe killed. He was probably thrilled she showed up—now he's back in good with the Watchers."

"But he let her keep the knife," Mal said reasonably.

"Because he's still playing her," Rain said. "He probably can't help himself—he's probably one of those guys who has to make every girl love him."

"Or else he was trying to help her."

"If he'd really wanted to help her, he'd have gotten her back out of the city. But no, he had to stand around chatting, waiting for the wardens to show up. He probably knew exactly when they'd be coming around on patrol. And you let him get away with it!"

"There was nothing I could do," Mal said. "Not then. If they had seen me, they would be forewarned that people from the other island had arrived."

Rain conceded the point by not arguing.

"I should not have gone into the city at all," Mal said.

Rain frowned. "At least we know what happened to her," she said. Then she pressed her palms against the sides of her head. "This is terrible. They don't even know we're here, much less that we've lost her again. I can't bear the thought of telling Uncle Eric."

"We should talk to Michael. He will know what to do."

Rain dropped her hands. "Do you know his plan?"

Mal shook his head.

"I wonder how much time she has," Rain said. "Alice says it's a pretty long way to the stockade, and we'll have to talk her or Shawna into showing us the way. If we get lost or run into trouble with Angel or the wild things, that'll slow us down even more."

Slowly, Mal nodded. "And when Eric sees that Michael is not dead, he will have questions. It will be hard to move quickly."

Rain thought for a moment. "We have Earl," she said. "He won't like it, but he'll help us get her out."

Then she turned her head and looked straight at me. "It's your call," she said. "Do we go tell our fathers what has happened, or do we try to do this ourselves?"

Chapter 6

The sound of the door opening woke me. I sat up, momentarily disoriented, and stared at the bald, bearded man in the doorway. Warden Karl.

"Rise and shine," he said, but his tone was grim. He didn't smile or let on that he knew me.

The Dream Drops were still in my left hand. As I struggled to rise I remembered the key. I felt for it, found it, palmed it in my right hand as I stood.

"You're a lucky girl," he said, and I perked up, but then he went on, "You get to use the real bathroom. Most prisoners get buckets in the cells."

He led me midway down the hallway to a closed door. He turned me around and unlocked my cuffs, and I hoped he wouldn't notice my clenched fists, hoped it wouldn't matter if he did.

"Get cleaned up and change clothes," he said. "You have a ten a.m. appointment with the Watchers."

The door locked with a snap behind me, and I looked around the small bathroom, hoping he had given me some means of escape. Toilet, sink. No window, no mirror. One towel on the back of the toilet, along with a set of clothes in Optica gray.

My wrists stung when the water hit them. They were

raw in places and bruises had begun to form. I splashed my face and ran wet fingers through my hair, wishing I could have a real bath. At least I was fully awake by the time I'd finished. The Dream Drops—or the short sleep—had left me feeling groggy, and that wouldn't do if I were to have any hope of escaping.

I changed clothes—hating it, not wanting to put back on Optica gray, but afraid to disobey—and transferred the key, the Dream Drops, and my black cap to my pocket. The clothes were a little too big and I had to roll the sleeves and pants cuffs. If I got a chance to run, I didn't want to be tripping over my own clothes.

When I rapped on the door Warden Karl opened it instantly. Looking at my wrists, he said, "You have to be cuffed again."

He cuffed my hands in front of me, meeting my eyes deliberately as he did so, then shooting a sidelong glance down the hall. I understood. We might be overheard.

Silently we left the prison and walked through the streets toward my fields, beyond which lay the Watcher compound.

Quite a few people were out and about—it must be late morning by now—and I was surprised by how industrious everyone seemed. Maybe they were trying to make up for our losses, I thought; maybe the threat of starvation had motivated them.

I should have known better, though, and when I glanced back over my shoulder, I realized my mistake. I was walking with a warden; I was seeing Optica from a warden's eyes. And I knew from long experience that my field workers always got moving when a warden was in sight. Everyone did, and when the warden was gone, everyone slacked off.

Almost everyone, that is. Everyone but a few old people and my friends, and now maybe that made sense. People like

Louie with half-buried memories of other places, and the people who'd been more or less raised by Rafe—we were the ones who worked.

My cap was in my pocket, and my hair shone like a beacon as we crossed the city and then the fields. People stopped to stare at me, then leaned towards each other to whisper, and my cheeks flamed. Why hadn't Warden Karl brought me to the Watchers in a patrol car? Had they ordered this public march through town?

As we drew near to the Watcher compound my heart began to pound. This could be it, the last few minutes of my life. They could have me shot right now. I'd escaped from Tristan only to die in Optica. My father would think I was safe at home until someone told him I was here, dead. He'd be devastated, and he'd be furious. Everyone would be.

And they'd all blame Meritt.

Stop it, I told myself. Panicking wouldn't help. I needed my wits about me.

At least Warden Karl was here. He had gotten me out of tough places before, though never a place as bad as this one. And maybe Meritt would come up with something. He was good at getting out of bad situations.

The courtyard of the Watcher compound was surrounded by a tall cinderblock wall, a privacy wall, I supposed. We went through a gate and then up a set of shallow concrete steps to the door of the compound itself, which was covered by an overhang. Then there was a series of locked doors. They worked with codes, not keys.

The outside of the compound looked pretty much like all of Optica—gray, cinderblock, concrete, though it had fancy ridges and ledges and arches that no other place had. The windows were small and very high up. It looked more like a fortress than a dormitory or house, but it fit Optica.

The inside of the compound, however, didn't look like

Optica at all. The floors were not bare tile or concrete, but wood and soft colored rugs. The furniture was colorful, too, and comfortably padded. The walls were textured and painted, and hung with large colorful paintings. There were potted plants and mirrors. There was a shell-shaped fountain with real running water spraying up from it.

There were also a lot of wardens, all with their guns out and at the ready. How had Meritt gotten past them when he sneaked out at night? Had he made allies among the wardens?

Warden Karl led me to the conference room I'd seen on the monitor the night Meritt and I had spied on the Watchers. On the monitor I had only been able to see the large table and the bare walls. But now I could see that the table was a beautiful dark wood and the floor was covered by a deep blue rug.

The seven Watchers were already gathered. They were dressed all in white and all were seated on the far side of the table, facing me. Each Watcher had an assistant in gray standing behind his or her chair, and heavily armed wardens in black were sprinkled around the room. When I came in the wardens all pointed their guns at me. Maybe I was more threatening than I felt.

Warden Karl stood me in front of the conference table, facing the Watchers, and stepped back, leaving me alone in the long bare middle of the room. Only then did I notice that one of the wardens was the blonde woman who had kissed Meritt. Warden Rhoda. She looked through me as if I didn't exist, but her gun was pointed straight at my heart.

As I stood there with my hands cuffed in front of me, not knowing where to look, the door opened and Meritt came in. He was wearing Watcher white and looked completely calm and unconcerned.

The Watchers all stood up, and together they all

gestured toward an empty chair at the far end of the table. Meritt walked to it and they all sat down. An assistant I hadn't noticed before came forward and stood behind Meritt. It was Cynda.

I stared at her but she wouldn't make eye contact. What was she doing here? She was a relief worker. Had Meritt already made his preemptive strike? Maybe when he had, he'd requested her as his assistant; maybe he thought he'd be safer if he could keep an eye on her.

Or maybe she'd been ordered to keep an eye on him.

At some invisible signal the assistants handed their Watchers notepads and pens. Then they gave the Watchers glasses of something that was thin like water but a pale golden yellow color. They also gave them small pastries on delicate white plates.

Once the assistants were back in their places behind the Watchers, everyone looked at me.

I looked back at them, trying to keep my expression blank. I recognized them all from the spying we'd done. The short round-faced man was on my far left, then the long-faced man, then the very old man. The heavy-set man who narrated the city meetings sat in the middle—I thought of him as the Voice—and then came the creepily cheerful plump woman, the languid bored woman, and Marta.

Meritt was on the women's side of the table next to Marta; that must be the least prestigious seat.

"Let us proceed," the Voice said, and his voice unnerved me, took me back to the city meetings, to fear and confusion and death and Rafe's blood on my feet. But I made myself look at him and when I did, something in his face told me he knew the effect he had on me, and that he enjoyed it.

I lifted my chin and stared him straight in the eye.

He didn't ask my name or age or any of the usual things. Instead he got straight to business.

"You left this island," he said. "Why did you abandon Optica?"

I could tell the truth—that my friends thought they were saving me from Meritt—but I didn't want to say that. Even if it had been Meritt's intention to make us distrust him, I didn't want him to know he'd succeeded. Not when he was so tense and alone. Then I remembered what Ezzie had assumed about my departure, and what Meritt himself had said on the transmitter. That would work.

"I had to get Farrell Dean away from here," I said. "I didn't want you to kill him."

"That is direct rebellion," the Voice said, frowning. "You deliberately obstructed the course of justice."

"Yes," I said. "I know. But—"

I knew what I had to say and I started to say it, but my throat suddenly closed up. The words were there, but I couldn't say them, even though they were true. Because they were true.

The Voice chuckled, a low unpleasant sound. Then he turned to Meritt.

"It seems we have this Farrell Dean to thank for your change of heart," he said. "There's no point in protecting a girl who falls in love with your best friend, now is there?"

Meritt met his eyes coolly but didn't answer. I couldn't even begin to guess what he was thinking.

"If Meritt doesn't care for her any more, does it count that he turned her in?" the round-faced man asked. "He was supposed to bring us the one he loves most, but she has humiliated him. No doubt he now hates her."

"That's a good point," the long-faced man said. "Especially given that Meritt was the one who enabled this friend to escape the city meeting in the first place. Why should we allow him to release those he loves, and bring us only those he has come to hate?"

Meritt said nothing. His eyes were on me, gray and inscrutable.

The Voice leaned forward, his forearms resting on the tabletop.

"But note the irony," he said. "Meritt risks our displeasure to set his friend free, and his friend repays him by stealing away his girl."

He leaned back in his seat. "Everyone in the city knew how close they were, those three," he said. "Everyone we questioned said that Meritt was confident in their friendship, their loyalty to him. Now he has been blindsided by their betrayal. Can you feel the humiliation?"

The other Watchers nodded, the expressions on their faces ranging from discomfort—Marta—to pleasure—the creepy cheerful woman. I looked at Cynda, who had so often teased me about my interest in Meritt, and about Farrell Dean's attentions to me. Her eyes were carefully cast down.

"So now he craves the Watcher white," the Voice went on dreamily. "It is his salvation. For the city cannot mock him as a fool if he triumphs over those who deserted him."

It was ridiculous, all of it, and ridiculously insulting to Meritt. I looked at him and I knew my face was apologetic, embarrassed, but surely that was all right, that was the way they'd expect me to look. Meritt stared back at me, his face unreadable. He looked very handsome and aloof; he didn't look like someone who felt he had been made to look a fool.

The Voice studied me for a long moment; then he turned and spoke directly to Meritt.

"The pain will pass," he said. "You will get over her soon enough. We will see to that."

"Perhaps he has a comment," the very old man said. "Perhaps he would like to make a formal statement of intent."

"That would be fitting," the Voice said. "Meritt?"

In the split second it took for everyone to turn

expectantly toward Meritt, a flash of anger crossed his face, instantly replaced by the blank impenetrable mask.

"She is dead to me," he said, his unreadable eyes fixed on my face.

"Well said." The Voice turned toward me with an air of getting back to business.

"So, traitor," he said. "When you left our island, where did you go?"

"To another island."

The Watchers, all of them and almost imperceptibly, leaned forward in their seats.

But of course—they were starved for information. Apparently Angel—the only one who knew everything—had told no one, not on this island, not on the other island, about the end of the experimenters. How could I use that to my advantage?

"What did you find on this supposed other island?" the Voice said, carefully bland.

I didn't know Michael Alleyn's plan, or my father's. I could say that a huge army was coming, and the Watchers had better not mess with me or they'd be sorry, but they'd either think I was making it all up and kill me, or they'd be fortified and ready when my father struck. Or both. In short, I was afraid that anything I said would be the wrong thing.

So I shrugged. "Not much," I said.

"It is in your best interest to give me more detail than that," the Voice said.

"It's a big island," I said. "I think most people live on the other side from where we landed. We didn't exactly go exploring."

"And did this Farrell Dean come back with you?"

"No," I said, which technically was the truth.

The Voice knew I was hedging; I could see it in his face. Why did I have to be such a bad liar? I had to protect Farrell

Dean. I couldn't say anything that might make him a target, make the Watchers decide to hunt him down.

"I'm going to ask you one more time," the Voice said warningly. "Where is the boy?"

Cynda's long ago advice about lying, about going on the offensive, came back to me all in a rush and I glared at the Voice, which was easy to do.

"He died," I said, meaning to sound accusing, but the bare thought of Farrell Dean dying made my voice waver. "His back got infected. He had a fever, and I didn't have any medicine, and no one over there would help us."

Marta was watching me closely, concern mixed with doubt on her face. The others clearly couldn't care less about what might have happened to Farrell Dean. The plump and creepily cheery Watcher actually was smiling, nodding at me knowingly, as if to say I'd gotten what I deserved. The Voice was scarier than she was, but I disliked her most of all.

The Voice opened a large worn ledger and turned a few pages. I could see that each page held three columns. He read, flipped a page and read some more, then uncapped a black pen. "What was the date of his death?" he said without looking up.

"What day is today?" I had become totally unmoored from the calendar.

"Thursday, November the third."

It was my birthday—Fiona's and mine. We hadn't even realized.

Then I was remembering standing on the road to Doria being kissed by Farrell Dean, who had wanted out of Optica before he turned nineteen—

"We are waiting," the Voice said.

"Sunday," I said. "He died this past Sunday."

The Voice wrote something in the book, and then glanced up with a small smile.

"He died on his birthday," he said. "How pleasingly symmetrical."

Then he drew a firm dark line across the page, crossing out Farrell Dean's name, and a chill ran down my spine.

But Farrell Dean was fine—surely he was fine, he was at the stockade, he was safe. This book meant nothing. Though Farrell Dean and my family could have had trouble at sea … They weren't experienced sailors, and they didn't even have a sail, and what if the engine had died and they were drifting out there, lost?

"So Farrell Dean died, and you promptly came running back to Meritt," the plump creepy woman said, still with her cheery voice and inappropriate smile. "As if a Watcher would take leftovers."

She was insulting me and, worse, she was insulting Meritt, trying to hurt him. I lifted my chin and stared at her, letting her see every bit of the dislike and disdain I felt for her. She blinked back at me, her smile never wavering, but in the end she was the one who looked away, pretending she'd become distracted by something more worthy of her interest.

The Voice started to shut the book but paused, holding it open with one finger.

"No point in putting this away," he said softly, his eyes on me. "Not yet. Tell me, traitor, what would you prefer? Death by gunshot, drowning, hanging, or decapitation? And what shall we do with your body afterwards? We're a bit low on forage, so perhaps we'll feed you to the pigs. Or perhaps we'll hang you from the watchtower as a reminder of what happens to those who betray and abandon the Family."

"Stop tormenting the child," Marta said sharply. "If you're going to kill her, get it over with. Do it now and be done with it."

What?

"But we aren't finished with her yet," the oldest Watcher

said, and then I understood that they instinctively opposed whatever Marta said, and that she had counted on it.

"She has been very bad," the plump Watcher said, rubbing her hands together. "She attempted to intervene in an execution, and she left the city, and then she left the island and helped a convicted traitor escape as well. And on top of that she has been very rude."

"And she murdered a warden," the long-faced man said, steepling his hands together on the table in front of him.

"Ah, yes," the Voice said. "Warden Zee."

Deliberately I kept my eyes away from Meritt.

"I'm not convinced she's responsible for Zee," the languid woman said. "I mean, look at her. She's a tiny weak little thing, and Zee was fit."

The Voice nodded. "Then let us ask her. Traitor, did you kill Warden Zee?"

I wasn't a killer and I wanted to say so—it almost felt as if pretending to be a killer would make me the sort of person who could be one. And besides, they'd expect me to deny killing the warden, and would be suspicious if I didn't. On the other hand, if I denied it and convinced them of my innocence, then Meritt would be put in danger, because they knew he'd been out of his locked room last night.

So, basically, I had to deny it, but make them believe I was lying.

"I did not kill Warden Zee," I said firmly, and I looked fixedly at the Voice. "I never even went up there."

Meritt shut his eyes.

The Voice smiled. "Up where?" he said.

"Anywhere—I never went anywhere in the city." It wasn't hard to act flustered. "I was just out in the orchard, that's all."

"And yet you knew where Zee was when he died," the Voice said.

Liars give too many details, Cynda always said—liars talk too much and trip themselves up. "I heard," I said. "The wardens were talking about it when they caught me."

"The wardens didn't know about it until after you were locked up." The Voice looked up and down the table at the other Watchers. "That settles it, then."

Marta was frowning. She knew exactly what was going on, I thought; she knew there was no way to protect both me and Meritt.

"Still. I wouldn't have thought she'd be strong enough to break a grown man's neck," the languid woman said.

The Watchers were all eyeing me speculatively.

"She used his own weight against him," the long-faced man explained, leaning forward so he could see the woman who had raised the question. "No doubt she took him by surprise."

"Or else there was a scuffle and he fell and landed wrong," the very old man said. "The girl might simply have been lucky."

My relief was short lived.

"In any case, she killed him and so she must be executed," the plump woman said, in the tone of one anticipating a great treat. "But not immediately, and not in private."

"Agreed," said the long-faced man. "Let Optica anticipate her punishment. Let her be a lesson to them."

"Marta, you must not be squeamish," the languid woman said. "We must make the most of this opportunity."

The Voice had opened the ledger and was studying it again. Now he smiled.

"Speaking of birthdays," he said, "Tell me, traitor. When is yours?"

Obviously he knew, but he wanted me to say.

I lifted my chin a little higher. "Today," I said. "If today really is November the third."

"Today's her birthday?" said the creepy plump woman, clapping her hands. "But that's wonderful! So symmetrical!"

"It will be most effective if the city knows what's coming," the long-faced man said. "We must announce the event immediately."

"Yes," the Voice said. "We will do that. Word of her capture and arrest will already be out. All we must do now is give word of her sentence."

He looked pointedly at the wardens, who nodded. Then he bent his head and wrote something in the ledger—the date of my death, I supposed—and shut the book with a thud.

"The execution will be at six o'clock tonight," he said to his fellow Watchers. "That will be just after sunset, and it will interfere with their dinner hour."

"An additional disruption," the very old man said, nodding. "Very good. Minor indignities can be more demoralizing than major ones."

The Voice nodded in acknowledgement and stood up. "Remove the prisoner," he said, and as Karl led me to the door the other Watchers began to stand up.

In the doorway I glanced back. Cynda was staring after me, her face troubled. Meritt was standing by the Watchers' table, looking down at the blonde warden. She was talking, and when she put a hand on his arm he flashed her that dear familiar smile.

I knew he didn't mean it, but it made my heart contract all the same.

"One more item," the Voice said, and all faces turned toward him. "We will have the official swearing-in after our newest member has presented his completed offering."

Surely that couldn't mean what I thought it meant. Surely they wouldn't make Meritt be the one to pull the trigger.

But when I met Meritt's eyes I knew that was exactly what the Watchers intended.

Chapter 7

An afternoon. Seven hours, more or less. That was all that was left in my life.

I stumbled and would have fallen, but Karl pulled me upright. He wasn't rough with me, but he wasn't gentle either. Too many people were watching.

We made it through the city, past the workers in the fields, the gawkers in the streets. When we reached the prison and my cell, he ushered me in, then came in behind me and pulled the door closed.

"I sure wish you had stayed away," he said in an undertone, reaching for my wrists and unlocking the handcuffs.

"Sorry." My voice sounded feeble.

"So am I." Karl's face was grim. "They're counting on me to disable the wardens' weapons before they try to take the city. If I help you now and get caught, we'll be sunk."

I looked up at him sharply. "They? Who?"

"You know who. Your brothers and the rest."

Relief flooded through me, making me feel so weak I had to sit down on the little cot. Farrell Dean was alive, he was here, he and the rest of them—they'd made it. They hadn't been lost at sea.

"They're okay?" I said. "Farrell Dean, too?"

"Him too. They're fine."

"Where did you see them? What did they say? What were they doing?"

"I saw them last night. At least, I saw Farrell Dean and Judd."

"I'm sorry I left Judd," I said. "I didn't mean to, but I did. Leave him, I mean."

Karl nodded, running a hand over his short beard. "They told me what happened. Judd was hoping it meant you'd be safe." Again he gave me a reproving look.

"So what happened last night?"

"I was stationed at the eastern gap and those two were heading in to look for Meritt."

He gave me a long look. "I stopped them. Told them they couldn't reach him, not at night. He gets locked in."

"Sometimes he gets out. He was out last night."

Karl's expression hardened. "So the official story is true. He turned you in."

"It was an accident," I said. "My fault." I didn't want to explain further. "What else do you know?"

"Yesterday morning, early, Farrell Dean and your brothers shot down eight wardens so they could get to the stockade." Karl was speaking so softly I could barely hear him. "The other wardens are looking for revenge."

"They know it was Farrell Dean?"

"They know."

"Then the Watchers know I was lying. They know Farrell Dean is alive." It didn't matter to me—I was scheduled for execution anyway. But I didn't like the thought that the Watchers would be after Farrell Dean in particular.

Karl was shaking his head.

"They might not know," he said. "Not yet. The wardens who work in the compound don't mix much with us patrol wardens. They all think they're a notch above us. Eventually, though, word will get around. It will filter on up."

"But the patrol wardens are already after him?"

"After him and all the other rebels, yes. But the stockade is strong, and your brother Mick had an idea for disabling the guns. They'll still be outnumbered, your crew, but not out-gunned. Not if I do my job. And they sure can shoot. With them here we actually have a chance."

Then his face darkened and he frowned at me. Everyone had a chance but me, that was what we were both thinking.

I swallowed. "Don't do anything to endanger them," I said. "Take care of the guns. Maybe Meritt will find a way to get me out."

Karl frowned again, but said nothing. There was nothing to say.

When Karl had gone, I pulled out Mal's knife, still in the sheath strapped to my leg. It had a bone handle and its blade was more than six inches long and looked quite sharp. If I touched a hair on my arm, the blade cut it. That was hair, though. I didn't know how the blade would do with anything more substantial.

The thought made me cringe. Carefully, I tucked the knife back into its sheath and covered it with my pants leg.

Then I stared at the walls. They were gray and bare. I tried not to think about hanging, decapitation, shooting. Pig forage.

Out of habit I began to braid my hair, as I had done a thousand times before, but this time felt different. My fingers were clumsy and forgot their way; I had to think about what I was doing, and when I was finished, the braid felt uneven, insecure.

Maybe sitting still wasn't a good idea. It let me think too much.

I got down on the cold smooth floor and did some push-ups, as if building up a little extra muscle might do me some good. I did push-ups until my arms quivered and I couldn't raise myself one more time. Instead I rolled onto my back and stared at the ceiling, listening to my own breath, feeling my own heartbeat. I could blink; I could turn my head; I could clear my throat.

In a few hours I'd be unable to do any of those things.

There I went again, thinking too much.

What time was it? I had absolutely no idea. If this was to be my last afternoon alive, it should fly past, not crawl like it was doing, second by interminable second.

There were no cameras in the cell—at least none that I could see—but suddenly I wanted to hide. Sitting up, I un-braided my hair and shook it around my face.

Surely Fiona would tell Papa what had happened; surely she and Rain wouldn't try to rescue me alone. I wished I knew what Michael Alleyn's plan was. I wished I knew whether my being here messed it up. But Michael Alleyn was smart—even if I'd ruined his first plan, he'd think of something. And he had Earl, and Mal, and Rain could be good in a crisis. It was only when people underestimated her that she got weird.

I had almost managed to buck myself up when the next thought knocked me reeling. If their rescue of me went wrong, Eric Alleyn could lose his father and two daughters, all in one fell swoop.

Getting to my feet, I went to the corner where Farrell Dean had been chained. I lay down where he had lain, pressed my cheek against the floor where his had been, and held the chain in my hand as if it linked me to him.

If he knew I was in the prison, he'd find some way to help me, but he didn't know. And if Fiona voted to go tell him—if she took the time to find the stockade and explain everything to my father and the others—there was no way help could reach me in time. They couldn't just waltz in and get me.

The wardens would put me in the city circle with the whole city around me. The spotlight would shine on me as it had shone on Rafe and Petey and all the rest, and then Meritt would pull the trigger and I wouldn't be there anymore. Or Meritt wouldn't pull the trigger and the result would be the same, except that he'd be gone along with me.

Where would we be when we weren't here? Someplace else, or nowhere at all? I felt like Rafe was somewhere else, but I couldn't fathom where that might be.

Poor Meritt. What a terrible position I'd put him in. But what I'd told Angel was true—I didn't want Meritt to die trying to save me, even if by dying he could.

Angel was jealous of me, Meritt had said. Jealous, because Meritt loved me? I couldn't think of any other explanation.

For years I would have been thrilled to think Meritt loved me. Now I hoped it wasn't true. It would make everything so much harder for him if he loved me.

The floor was cold, and as I lay there the cold seemed to seep through my skin, deep into my bones. I stayed put, though, because it was where they had chained Farrell Dean. How many days had it been since I'd been here with him? How long had it been since I'd last seen him, there on the beach in Locria? He'd been so distant that day. Was Gabriel right? Was it because I'd been happy about talking to Meritt?

Farrell Dean and Meritt … what would they say to each other, afterwards? Nothing, if Meritt was dead, too. If he wouldn't shoot me, they'd kill us both.

Would they kill me first and make him watch, or would they kill him first to extend my punishment? He would fall and his limbs would go limp, and his blood would puddle like Rafe's had done, spreading out around his head. His eyes would turn empty and he would be gone, and I would follow but what if I couldn't find him, wherever we went?

What if I was somewhere but nowhere, empty, lost, always alone …

Locked in the prison I couldn't see the sky, the clouds or the sun, only the one bare bulb on the grim gray ceiling. When they led me out, the sun would already have set, and if the sky was covered with clouds, then I would never see the stars again either.

I began to breathe too fast. The stars—I couldn't see them—but they were there, they were always there, and even though I couldn't see them and might never see them again, I talked to them anyway, out loud, my voice echoing in the cold silent room.

"Please," I said. "Let someone find me, help me get out, make this all be a dream. Please—I don't want to die. I'm only seventeen."

No one answered; no one came.

But maybe the stars were listening after all, because my terrified heartbeat began to slow and my thoughts stilled and, after a time, I fell asleep.

My heart leapt up, though strangely it still beat in slow calm rhythm.

Farrell Dean was outside in strong clear light, his hair ruffling in a breeze I couldn't feel. He looked good. He looked strong and focused and capable.

But something was wrong. He was looking at me, looking straight into my eyes, but looking at me in a way he'd never done before, not even during those last odd hours in Locria. I couldn't quite pinpoint what was wrong, but the look in his eyes made goose bumps rise on my arms.

"She's been enchanted," I said. "I told her so, but she laughed at me."

It was the strangest thing. I could feel the vibration of my vocal cords, hear my voice from inside my skull, but I had no control over what words came out. And wasn't that the gazebo at my father's house? We were on Aislin, then. The Watchers, the prison cell—that was all a bad dream. We were safe. We were home.

But the distance in Farrell Dean's eyes cut like a knife. "She isn't enchanted, Fiona. He's a likeable guy. I like him myself."

Fiona? I'd been so sure he'd always recognize me. I felt like crying—somewhere I was crying—but at the same time my eyes stayed stubbornly dry, and when I spoke my voice came out clear and calm.

"It's a dangerous place, your Optica," I said. "And he's playing a dangerous game. Chances are—"

"Don't even say it."

"But if it happened to happen…"

"Then I'd lose a good friend and I'd lose her, too. I can't compete with a dead hero."

I couldn't pay close attention to his words, because he still had that remote look, as if there were a wall between us that kept him from really seeing me. I wanted him to look at me the way he usually did, I wanted to shake him and make him wake up, but I couldn't make myself move. My limbs had a mind of their own.

Maybe I was already dead.

The door to my cell opened and I jerked awake. My back was to the door and I rolled over and sat up, half expecting to see Farrell Dean.

Instead I saw the scarred warden. He looked just like he had the night he and Karl had caught me out on the streets, like he had that day in the cafeteria—muscular and predatory. His hair was cropped. The ugly puckered scar ran through his top lip. His eyes were pale and flat.

I wasn't dead. Not yet. If I were dead I wouldn't be frightened.

"It's almost six o'clock," the warden said, and smiled.

Chapter 8

The door swung closed with a thud. The cell felt colder than before, and smaller, and though there were no windows, the light in the room seemed to have dimmed.

I thought the warden would tell me to get up, to come with him, but seconds passed and he didn't. He leaned against the door, crossing his arms over his chest, and stared at me with those flat expressionless eyes, that faint unpleasant smirk. Maybe—just maybe—

"They're going to kill me," I said. My throat felt very dry and the words came out thin and cracked. "But you could stop them. You could help me. We could run away."

His eyes turned derisive. "You had your chance."

He still didn't move, and he didn't tell me to get up. He lounged against the door, not seeming to be in any hurry.

"I can take you to meet your brother—"

With an effort I made myself backtrack, explain. Make sense. "You have a brother. He lives on another island. He's your identical twin—he was born at the same time as you, and he looks just like you. He dreams about you. Do you ever dream about him?"

The warden's expression didn't change.

"You're not just a freak," he said, staring at me from across the small room. "You're a crazy freak."

"I'm telling you the truth. We're all an experiment. Me, you. Your brother, my sister. We're rats in a lab. I can prove it—I can show you books—your brother—"

He pushed away from the door and started toward me. I hadn't convinced him. He was going to yank me to my feet and handcuff me, and take me out to be executed by Meritt. This was it. This was the end.

Pulling my feet up onto the cot, I wrapped my arms around my knees, willing myself to be immovable, heavy. I would stay right here. I'd stay in prison—at least I was alive in prison—this was all a bad dream and I'd wake up and see Farrell Dean, rowing in the little boat—

The warden walked right up to me, stopping only when his legs pressed against the edge of the cot.

"Look at me," he said.

I did.

He stared down at me for a long time. Then he uncrossed his arms, reached out with one hand, and touched my hair. I forced myself not to move away from his hand. He was my only hope.

He leaned down until our eyes were level. "Somebody somewhere got hold of the wrong end of the stick," he said. "A few minutes ago I got a call from my partner telling me to go relieve one of the wardens at the gaps. No point in me standing around here, he said, since you'd already been picked up for transfer."

He waited for that to sink in, but I couldn't make sense of his words or his meaning—there had been a mix up—so was he saying he would help me after all? He still looked threatening, but maybe he couldn't help that.

Then he spelled it out.

"Officially I'm not here, and neither are you. We're ghosts. So I can do whatever I like. And what I'd like is to collect what you owe me."

My blood seemed to congeal in my veins.

"We're all alone," he said in a voice that was almost sing-song and, reaching forward, ran one finger down my cheek. This time, I flinched.

"What's the matter?" he said, his flat eyes narrowing. "Don't like my scar?"

Suddenly I was angry at being toyed with, now, when my life was almost over.

"The scar's fine," I said. "It's you I don't like."

The warden stared at me as if he might have misheard. Then his face hardened and he backhanded me sharply across the face.

My teeth cut the inside of my cheek and I tasted coppery salty blood. The warden stood back, looking at me as if assessing the effect of the blow. Blood was filling my mouth and I was afraid I'd gag if I tried to swallow, so I leaned forward and spat on the floor.

The warden's flat dead eyes came weirdly alight. He reached out and ran his thumb across the side of my mouth. It came away bloody and he smiled.

Then he began unbuckling his belt. There was no radio attached to it, no stunner, just the long black leather strip. He pulled it out of the belt loops and twisted it into a circle, sliding the tongue through the buckle.

"Get up and put your hands behind your back," he said.

This wasn't happening—

"Or I can chain you to the wall," he said. "I'll count to three. If you're not up with your hands behind your back, I'll take that to mean you want the chain."

Hurriedly I slid off the cot, bending forward from the hips as if keeping my balance, letting my hair fall down over my shoulders and arms, hiding me.

When my feet hit the floor I came up hard and fast. I did just as Mal had said. I kept the knife close and thrust it forward and up, putting all my weight behind it, thrusting it underhand, up and deep.

The warden grunted and grabbed at me and I wrenched away from him, still holding tight to the knife, and it came out and blood sprayed in my face, my eyes, and the warden swung wildly and caught me hard across the side of my head and I staggered but so did he.

I ran for the door and he was cursing and yelling and I expected to feel his hands grabbing me, stopping me, but then I was out. I was out and the hall was empty and I slammed the door and with shaking fingers slid the bolt home.

I was out. He was trapped and I was out.

But he was yelling, pounding on the locked door, and someone might hear him, someone might come.

So much adrenaline was pounding in my veins—I couldn't think—I had to think.

Get out, that was all I could come up with.

I ran down the hall to the outside door, and I wanted to fling open that door and keep running but I made myself stop and open the door just a crack and peek out. And it was good that I stopped, that I didn't go hurtling out into the circle, because the circle was filled with people—it was six o'clock, they were gathered as ordered, standing in rows, all dressed in gray, talking and looking around. Waiting for me.

And two wardens were crossing the circle, heading straight for the prison door.

What was I going to do? There was no other way out. If I hid in an empty cell they'd find me. That would be the first place they'd look once they freed the scarred warden. But I couldn't stay there by the door, not with the wardens coming.

I started down the hall at a sprint, and just as I passed the door to my cell the pounding and yelling stopped. The scarred warden said something—I couldn't tell what—and then he fell silent. Had he passed out? But there was blood on the door—even if he stayed quiet they'd see the blood on that door. Darting back, I scrubbed at it with my sleeve, wiping it mostly clean, then ran again.

At the end of the hall I opened the door leading up to the watchtower and slipped inside the stairwell and waited, listening, hoping the other wardens would go down the other hall, the short one that led to the offices.

No. They were coming this way. They were talking, not sounding alarmed, but they were coming in this direction. I should have gone into another cell, I should have hidden anywhere but here—

I started up the stairs, the knife still in my hand. The door at the bottom opened.

I ran faster, staying on the outside edge, against the wall, hoping I was far enough above them that they couldn't see me. I tried to run quietly because the stairs were metal, but I was going too fast for silence and a faint humming started, but the whole stairwell was echoing and the wardens were climbing, too, and they weren't trying to be quiet. Their footsteps were loud and their voices were loud, echoing in the stairwell. One of them laughed.

I was at the very top now. There was no place to hide, only that staircase leading down to the wardens who were climbing up. There was nowhere to go but into the Opticon.

Cautiously I cracked open the door. The monitors were lit, scrolling brightly through scene after scene, but I didn't see a warden. Surely they'd replaced Zee—someone had to monitor the screens.

There he was. I could just see the top of his head. He was in one of the comfortable chairs, facing a window.

Was he dead? Had Meritt been back up here yet again?

I didn't know, and I didn't have time to wonder for long. I could hear the wardens coming up the stairs outside the door. I sprang for another deep chair, a chair facing away from the door, toward the far wall of windows. I curled up tight in a ball, careful to keep my hair away from the arms where it might be seen. I'd almost not noticed the warden in his chair, and I was smaller than he was. Maybe it would work.

In any case there was nothing else to try.

The door opened. There was a long moment of silence.

"Where is he?" a man's voice said.

"Over there."

The second man sounded alarmed and I knew he was wondering, like me, whether the warden in the chair was dead. "Ross!"

Now a third voice spoke. "What are you trying to do, give me a heart attack?"

Warden Ross—which one was he? I had a vague memory of a burly man, brown hair—

"You're asleep on duty," one of the other wardens said, his tone equal parts exasperation and relief. "What do you think you're doing?"

"Surviving, that's all." Warden Ross didn't sound the least bit apologetic. "You get to move around—all I do is sit here, and that's after two back-to-back patrol shifts. I'm exhausted."

"At least you're not getting sent out into the wilderland," one of the other wardens said.

"Wish I were," Warden Ross retorted. "Those rebels can't shoot worth anything."

"They're getting better. Or else they've brought in reinforcements."

"What, field workers with pitch forks?"

"Rumor has it that the Guardians are helping them."

"Nobody's seen a Guardian," Ross said. "Not ever, as far as I can tell."

"Doesn't mean they don't exist," another warden said. "Somebody sure busted up Frank's crew."

"Yeah, well, Frank's going to be reassigned," the other said. "Once they release him from medical observation."

"Mental instability?"

"Yeah. Or lying to save his own skin. He swore the red-headed girl had gotten away in a boat, but she didn't go anywhere. She got away from Frank, that's all, and hid in the woods until Meritt lured her out last night."

I heard movement. "It's past six—why hasn't it started?" He was looking out the window, I guessed, or through the telescope.

"Who knows," one of the others said. "Maybe the Watchers changed their mind."

"Or maybe she got away again."

The other wardens laughed.

"Psychological torture, that's what it is," one said. "Make them wait, make them nervous. Make them miss their dinners."

"Nah. My bet's on the girl."

A radio crackled, blurred words I couldn't make out.

"Roger that," one warden said, serious again. "We're on our way." The radio went silent. "Someone's out in the woods by the southern gap. Let's go."

I heard the door open.

"Stay awake, Ross. If we need backup I don't want to have to be waiting for you to finish your beauty sleep before we get it."

Ross said something crude and the door closed.

The warden moved around, yawning loudly. I heard him clicking keys at the monitor, then nothing more.

What would I do if he came over here, if he found me? Could I get past him to the door? I was fast. I could try. I didn't want to stab anyone else, but I would if I had to.

But he didn't come. The room stayed silent. Had he put the headphones on? Was he sitting at the monitor bank? Was he standing at a telescope?

When the sound began I thought I was dreaming. It was too much to hope for, but it was true. The warden was snoring softly.

Very slowly, I uncoiled and peeked around the edge of the chair. He was in the same place as before—apparently it was his favorite chair.

Very slowly, I stood up. Very slowly, I crept across the room, glancing at the bank of monitors as I passed.

There was the cafeteria, completely empty. There was the schoolyard, also empty, and the outside of the food preservation building. A screen changed and I saw my own dormitory room. Kari was still there, and young Lea, crying. They were skipping my city meeting.

Another screen changed and there was a boys' dormitory, empty. One by one the screens kept flickering, scrolling through their endless cycles, showing only empty rooms. There was the city circle, full of people dressed in gray. They looked impatient, and frightened, and confused.

The scarred warden—he hadn't been sent to take me out to the circle to be executed. He was supposed to go somewhere else because I'd "already been picked up." What did that mean?

I couldn't make sense of it. What exactly had he said? That there was a mix-up, that his partner had called him and sent him—

I was an idiot, fear was making me stupid—*Karl* must have called him and told him I was gone. Maybe Karl had planned to come get me, once the coast was clear. Maybe he was down there right now looking for me.

But that didn't make sense either. If Karl was going to spirit me away, he'd only have had a tiny window of time—

the few minutes after the scarred warden left, and before the wardens in charge of my execution got impatient and came looking for me. So Karl should have turned up when the scarred warden was in my cell—he should have been there by the time I escaped. Because now it was too late. It was after six. The people were all out there in the circle, waiting for me to be brought out and executed. The wardens would be looking for me—they were probably down there looking for me right this minute.

I didn't know what to do.

I glanced at the warden asleep in the chair—he wasn't moving, and the snores were deeper now.

Careful not to make any sound, I put the knife on the desk, sat down in front of the monitors, and plugged the headphones in. I pictured Meritt's fingers on the keyboard, remembered how it felt to stand here and watch him, fascinated by what he was doing but distracted, too, trying to tell him that Farrell Dean was being flogged downstairs.

Very softly, very carefully, I pressed the series of keys. Last time, Meritt had shown me a scene that had been recorded. I wasn't sure how it worked—there was a loop, and some sort of timer or motion activation—but maybe I'd see something useful, something to tell me what to do next.

The empty cafeteria vanished. That screen went black, then flickered, and when it cleared it was showing the conference room in the Watcher compound. They were all there, all seven Watchers and Meritt, too. They were all in white, and they were sitting around the long table talking to each other.

I watched for a few minutes, listening to indeterminate murmurings, fragments of conversation that seemed to have nothing to do with anything important.

In the room with me, in the chair by the window, Warden Ross slept on. But he could wake at any moment, and anyway there was no guarantee that the recording had caught anything useful.

Just as I reached to remove the headphones, every face turned toward one side of the screen, and all the conversations stopped.

Then Michael Alleyn and Fiona walked into the room.

Chapter 9

"Your positions have been terminated," Michael Alleyn said to the assembled Watchers, with no preface. "You have ten minutes until departure."

The very old man clutched at his heart; the long-faced man turned white; the plump woman's eyes were popping out of her head. Even the Voice looked nonplussed.

Only Marta looked completely calm. She was eyeing Michael carefully and, as I watched, she leaned over and said something in Meritt's ear.

Without taking his eyes from the old man, Meritt nodded. His own expression was carefully blank, save for one quick flash of something that looked strangely like dislike. Then he turned his face toward Fiona, and frowned. Did he think she was me? I couldn't tell.

"Just like that?" the Voice said. His heavy-jowled face had turned a dark plum red. "We've invested our lives in this city, and now—after two decades of neglect—you show up and expect us to leave with no forewarning?"

Michael looked down at him. "You show a quick grasp of the situation," he said, and the casual deadliness of his tone made my skin crawl. I didn't know him well, but I'd sure never heard him sound like that.

"I apologize if that sounded discourteous." The Voice

seemed to be trying for respect, but it came out as thinly veiled anger. "I merely thought that for continuity's sake, we should perhaps consider a more incremental transition."

My grandfather looked at him without speaking.

"You should never argue with Meritt Alleyn," the very old man said to the Voice. "What can you possibly be thinking?"

Michael turned away from the Voice, as if the man were not worth any further attention. "The experiment has been compromised," he said to the other Watchers. "We are collating the information from the past fifty years, and will decide on our next step once all the data is analyzed. In the meantime, your services are no longer required."

"We will be debriefed on the mainland?" the long-faced man asked.

"That won't be necessary. Surely you don't think we are uninformed about your doings?"

The round man shot an uncomfortable look at the Voice.

Michael pulled something from his pocket, a small box, maybe a transmitter. "This has been an expensive operation," he said, glancing up at a corner of the room. "But it has provided ample data for a variety of lines of inquiry."

All eyes followed his. I could see nothing up there, but I knew what he was implying—a hidden camera, a hidden microphone. The Watchers knew, too. They stiffened and carefully didn't look at one another.

Through all this Fiona had been standing with her head down. She looked small and frightened, and she was wearing Optica gray. The clothes were too big on her; they must have belonged to Shawna or Alice.

"If you don't mind my asking, why have you collected the traitor?" The plump woman's sycophantic voice was at odds with the spiteful glance she threw at Fiona. "She's docketed for execution shortly. She has caused enormous trouble."

Michael didn't even bother to glance at the woman. "Of course she has," he said, tucking the small thing back in his pocket. "She's the watchmaker's granddaughter."

The shocked expressions told me no one had known.

Michael looked at each Watcher in turn. They all seemed to be paralyzed, even the Voice.

"I gave clear instructions that my brother and his family were to be left to me, and me alone." Now his voice wasn't dangerous and casual but dangerous and cold, as hard as flint. "You will answer for this."

"But we had no idea," the plump woman said, and some of the others joined in.

"Angel brought her here—"

"Should she never have been here at all? He didn't tell us—how could we have known?"

"We aren't criticizing Angel, of course—"

"We would never—the execution—it was only because—"

"Save it for the inquiry," Michael said, and the moment he spoke the Watchers went instantly and deferentially silent.

A shiver of doubt ran down my spine. This was really my grandfather, wasn't it?

Michael glanced at his watch. "Thanks to your mishandling of a fairly simple task," he said, "rabble from Aislin are swarming the beaches. You can stay here to greet them—which is what you deserve, given the havoc you have wreaked on my experiment—or you can be at the extraction point in six-and-a-half minutes."

He took Fiona's arm—none too gently—and started from the room, a hard man, a man accustomed to being obeyed.

And the Watchers obeyed him.

"Are we being airlifted out?" the very old man said to the long-faced one, as they all began to get to their feet.

"I don't know," the long-faced man said. "I didn't hear any helicopters."

"Perhaps there's new technology. They were working on sound-masking devices, back when first we came."

"He'll leave us if we're late," the plump woman said, heading for the door.

"After all this time, to so suddenly appear," the languid woman said, following her.

"The years have been remarkably kind to him." The plump woman spoke over her shoulder. "And the burn didn't even leave a scar."

The languid woman nodded. "It's a good thing he agreed to have it seen to on the mainland. We couldn't have done as good a job here."

The Voice frowned and looked in the direction Michael Alleyn had gone. He raised one hand and opened his mouth to speak, and at the same moment movement caught my eye—movement in the room with me. A few yards away from me the warden shifted in his chair, sat up.

Hurriedly I pulled off the headphones, hit a few keys. The Watcher compound vanished. Nothing else came up— the screen stayed black—but I didn't know what else to do and I sure didn't have time to experiment. The warden was stretching, his arms looking very long, very muscular. He was still facing the window.

I snatched up my knife, crept quickly to the door, pulled it open, and slipped out, my heart pounding so hard I could barely breathe, and began making my way downstairs. The stairwell was silent when I entered and stayed silent as I climbed the long winding way down.

At the bottom door I paused, pulled on my cap, and listened. I heard nothing, so cautiously I opened the door and peeked out. The long hall was empty and I heard no sound, no voices, no footsteps, no pounding from the cell where I'd killed the warden.

The outside door looked very far away. Once I was in the hallway I'd be completely exposed. If anyone opened that outside door, he'd see me instantly. If anyone came around the corner from the prison offices, he'd see me.

But I had to risk it. I couldn't just stand here waiting to get caught.

Taking a deep breath I ran down the hall, keeping as far to the left as I could, as far away as possible from the door to the cell where the scarred warden waited.

At the outside door I stopped, and in my head I was talking to the stars—please let it be dark enough now, please let the spotlight be on, please let it be pointed at the circle.

It was. A stream of bright light poured down on the center of circle, waiting for me. The faces nearest the center of the circle were shown clearly in its glow, but the ones further back were almost invisible in the dark misty twilight. And I was invisible too, hidden in the extra shadow of the watchtower.

Without pausing to think—if I thought, I'd be afraid to move—I slid out the door and around the building away from the circle, away from the muttering voices, the rising tide of anger and confusion.

No one called out. No one tried to stop me. As soon as the watchtower blocked me completely from view I cut down between two buildings, heading away from the circle and the people, staying close to the buildings and far from the live cameras, pausing only to slide the bloody knife into its sheath, making sure the black cap stayed securely over my hair as I ran.

It was almost dark, and almost everyone was confined to the circle, whispering about me and my arrest and execution.

They'd be talking about Meritt and what he had done and what he was going to do, and some would approve and some would be angry.

Where should I go now? Michael Alleyn must have a plan—he'd be expecting to find me at the prison, or for Karl to find me there—but I couldn't stay here, not with the dead warden, not knowing whether Michael had been found out.

I had to get out of the city. I had to get out and find out what was going on, and whether Michael and Fiona were safe, and if they weren't we'd have to come back for them.

Focus. I had to focus on getting out, and worry about everything else afterwards.

Without making any sort of conscious decision I found myself heading for the slaughterhouse, where Meritt and I had met so often. That was fine—that was as good a place as any. But how was I going to get out with the wardens on guard at the gaps? If only I could signal to Rufus or Mick or whoever was out there, if only I could get out of this city and never come back.

When I reached the back of the slaughterhouse, where the broken camera wouldn't give me away, I pressed back into the darkness of the doorway and caught my breath. I needed to catch my breath. I need to calm down and think clearly.

The eastern gap was only a few dozen feet away, just beyond the slaughter yard, but I didn't think the warden posted there would see me, not back in the shadowy doorway, not when he was supposed to be watching the wasteland and the woods beyond.

Karl had been stationed there last night, had talked to Farrell Dean and Judd right there, just a few feet from where I was hiding. But this wasn't Karl. He was too slender, too tall.

I tried to think of a way to get past him, to get out, but

there in the slaughter yard, with the smell of blood all around me, my mind kept returning to the feel of the knife as it plunged into a living man's belly, the faint resistance of the skin and the deeper resistance of the muscle, the blood spraying hot on my face.

Pulling my sleeve over my hand, I scrubbed at my skin. Then I spat on the hem of my shirt and raised it to my face, scrubbing some more. I couldn't get clean—I knew I couldn't get clean.

Then I took the knife and plunged it up and down in the muddy ground until surely most of the blood was gone, and then I wiped it on the grass and slid it back into the sheath tied to my calf, being very careful because now I knew it was razor sharp, for it had gone easily into a living man with only my strength behind it. It had gone up under his ribs, under his sternum, and then it had met resistance--gristle or muscle or bone, I didn't know which—

I didn't want to think about that. I couldn't fall apart, not now. I had to think good thoughts, calm thoughts.

Calm thoughts.

It was my grandfather, in the Watcher compound with Fiona, not Meritt Alleyn. And my grandfather hadn't known about his brother's burn, about whatever had happened that made Meritt Alleyn go to the mainland for treatment.

If Michael had talked to Sir Tom before he came in, like he'd intended to do before I messed things up, then probably he'd have known details like that. So apparently they had come straight to the Watcher compound without going to the stockade first.

Could Michael Alleyn talk his way out?

He was a doctor—he could make up something about a new burn treatment—but what if he failed? What if he and Fiona had been arrested—what if I got out, but then I had to tell my father that Michael and Fiona had been killed?

Calm thoughts.

I saw why my grandfather had needed Fiona to go in with him. The Watchers wouldn't start the execution with the prisoner apparently standing right in front of them, being guarded by Meritt Alleyn. And it had given him instant credibility, marching in with her as if the prison wardens had automatically given him whatever he wanted. Further, it had put the Watchers in the wrong, to be confronted with the watchmaker's granddaughter, who should never have been in Optica to begin with. It was a good visual aid. Fiona was a good visual aid. But it was so dangerous—too dangerous— what if they'd marched her straight to the circle and shot her as me? She could have been killed.

Calm thoughts.

But first I had to spit more blood. My face felt swollen where the scarred warden had hit me. One tooth on that side felt loose. Had the scarred warden's brother back on Aislin been watching us, seeing himself assaulting Fiona Alleyn, getting stabbed by her?

I hoped not. Surely he wouldn't be sleeping and dreaming now, at suppertime, and if the scarred warden finished dying before bedtime then maybe his brother would never know. I hoped he would never know. I hoped no one had seen what had happened to me, what I had done.

But I had seen things through Fiona's eyes that had happened in the past—I'd seen her talking with Farrell Dean, and that was a memory.

But if the warden was dead he'd have no memories for his brother to see—unless memories lived on, like ghosts, even after the person who made the memories was dead. It seemed possible, somehow. Actual events that happened surely didn't vanish, wiped out as if they'd never occurred. Even if people weren't watching, the stars were watching, and stars would never forget. They'd always know I stabbed a man. Maybe they'd see it happening over and over, always happening—

Think calm thoughts. I was out of the prison. I was out, and if the scarred warden was dead—

I couldn't help thinking about it. I had killed him. Meritt had killed a warden, and now I'd killed one too, and I'd have tried to kill another, if the warden in the watchtower had turned toward me as he awoke. And to think I'd flinched away from Meritt's hands.

Meritt had searched me when I was arrested, and now the wardens would know he'd left me a knife. He'd be in danger, worse danger even than before.

I should have played the hand out to the very end, let the scarred warden do whatever he wanted to do. He wasn't going to kill me, he had to let Meritt do that, and wasn't I willing to suffer a little to help my friends free Optica? Maybe Michael Alleyn was on his way right now to find me, and I wouldn't be there, and he wouldn't know where else to look, and it wouldn't be long before the Watchers realized his bluff, if they hadn't realized it already.

In the misty darkness I began to shiver harder, shaking uncontrollably, and then I began to cry, the hot salty tears mingling on my face with the traces of the warden's blood and my own.

I pulled the bottle of Dream Drops out of my pocket and held it in my hand, felt it tempt me, call to me, promise me comfort. I could go back to Doria and watch Fiona talking to Farrell Dean. I could be somewhere else, someone else.

But that would be one more foolish move, unless I intended to get myself caught again. I had to stay awake. I had to stay alert.

The cattle men came early to the pens, before breakfast even, sorting cattle to breed, cattle to slaughter, and the butchers sometimes met them. If I couldn't figure out a way to get past the wardens and out of the city tonight, I'd have to make my way back across to the western section, to the orchards that were largely abandoned this time of year, to the place where Karl might be on guard since he wasn't here. I'd have to go late, after everyone was asleep, and hide there among the twisted trees. Could I stay out of sight there? If I had to stay hidden in the city for days, could I find food and water?

Darkness closed in and the moon appeared, obscured by a veil of clouds. The air felt damp, the way it did just before a heavy fog moved in. I'd have to make a move, but not yet, not when I could hear a warden talking into his radio off and on.

Rain began to fall. The doorway protected me, mostly, but I reached out and let my sleeve get wet so I could scrub my face again.

After awhile the rain eased and the moon tried but failed to break free of the clouds, its light a feeble glow. Farrell Dean was outside the city, outside those walls. Meritt was inside, but even if I could get to him, he couldn't help me and I couldn't help him. He was walking too thin a line.

I knew he was simply playing the game. I did. I knew. But I kept seeing him smile at the blonde warden, and his words to the Watchers kept echoing in my head.

Dead to him. I was dead to him.

Chapter 10

I was fighting back tears when the sky exploded. The ground seemed to rock and white light flashed and a noise like thunder shuddered around me. I covered my head with my arms and the noise reverberated in my head, the after-image of the blinding light flickering on the inside of my eyelids, an explosion happening again and again, gradually fading in vividness.

When the echoes dimmed I lifted my head cautiously, my heart thrumming in my chest, my breath coming quick and shallow.

I couldn't hear—my head felt stuffed with wool. Cautiously I snapped my fingers close to my right ear; for a wrenching moment I heard nothing, and then, distantly, as if underwater, I heard a woman screaming.

A wave of smoke and dust drifted across my face and my throat closed up. I fought back a cough, covering my mouth with my sleeve, but I needn't have bothered because no one could have heard me over the next explosion.

That second explosion was loud and bright but not quite as loud and bright as the first—either it was further away or I was still a little deafened.

There was a strange sharp odor now, sliding up under the smell of the smoke, a smell like chemicals. A warden nearby was screaming into his radio. It crackled back at him, but I couldn't make out the words.

Then the strange flashing light was coming right at me. I cowered back into the doorway, trying to shield myself from flying bits of rubble, pieces of rock and wood, sand that scoured my skin raw. The tremendous roar went on for so long I was sure it was the last thing I'd ever hear, and I couldn't tell if I was shaking or if it was the ground coming apart beneath me.

Gradually the ground stopped moving and I choked back frantic gasping tears, forcing myself to be quiet, but Optica was falling to bits and I didn't know where anyone was, or who was alive and who was dead. Trembling, covered with dust and grime, I huddled in the corner of the doorway waiting for another explosion, my eyes closed tight, my arms wrapped protectively around my head.

Minutes passed and no other explosion came. More minutes passed and then voices penetrated my deafness. Men were shouting—wardens—talking about the rebels. I caught Rafe's name, and Farrell Dean's.

"Should have killed them sooner," someone said. "They should have nipped it in the bud."

I didn't move until the voices faded, and then I opened my eyes to a world of dust and ashes. Blinking, half blinded, I pulled up my shirt and wiped my face. I could hear in the distance rumbling thunder that might have been more explosions, or a building falling, or the forewarning of a late autumn storm. The air was thick with acrid, choking smoke.

A group of men ran past just outside the slaughter yard, heading for the gap. Some were wearing black warden uniforms but most were dressed in gray. A few moments later a larger group came by more slowly, and there were no wardens with them. This time I made out a few fragments.

"It's the Guardians, punishing the city for the uprising."

"But the Watcher compound has fallen too. Why would the Guardians destroy the Watchers?"

My heart stuttered. Not the Watcher compound. Not Meritt and Fiona and Michael Alleyn.

Making sure my cap was in place I left the doorway and hurried after the group of people, staying far enough back that they wouldn't think of me as part of their group, but close enough that someone watching might.

We went through the gap and a warden waved us to take up positions along the outside of the wall, in the pale wasteland.

"Yell if you see anything," he said, taking care to stay inside the city wall himself. "And watch that rubble. It's not stable. Things might fall."

They were making regular people stand guard.

I made my way along the outside of the wall with a loose group of people. They were still muttering darkly about the Guardians and the rebels.

Ahead there came a crashing sound, and a yell.

"There goes more of the wall," someone near me said. "They're going to bring the whole thing down!"

When the people around me turned to look at the fallen wall, I took off in the other direction, toward the trees. Seconds later I was in among the tall pines, hidden in the midnight shadows. I stepped behind a wide trunk and looked back at the city.

Across the pale expanse of the wasteland I could see the smoking remains of the wall. To my right was the eastern gap. To my left, almost too far around the curve of the wall to be seen, was a gaping hole and a mound of shattered cinderblocks. As I watched, another portion of the wall buckled and fell, raising a cloud of dust that mingled with the heavy mist, sending debris rolling out into the bare wasteland.

They'd done it. Eric Alleyn and Gabriel—they'd set

explosives between the gaps. If I'd counted the explosions correctly, they'd added six more openings into Optica. And apparently they'd hit the Watcher compound as well. *They strike hard and they strike fast,* that was what Earl had said.

That they were ruthless enough to kill the Watchers without warning or negotiation, I did not doubt. But did they care so little for Meritt, or for me and all my pleas for him? They'd regret it, if they'd blithely sacrificed Meritt, because if he was dead, then Fiona and Michael were dead, too.

Tears were streaming down my cheeks. I tried to ignore what they meant, but I couldn't. I could blame my father and Gabriel for their ruthlessness, but it was my fault Fiona and Michael were in the city. They'd hurried in, without taking time to make contact with the group at the stockade, to try to save me. And they'd done it. They'd delayed my execution long enough for me to get away.

A sudden movement brought me back to myself. Far to my left someone was moving from the tree line out to the wall. I couldn't tell who it was, but he walked right up to someone huddled in the shadow of the standing wall, and then the two of them went back out into the woods.

Who was that, the person who'd gone out? It had be someone who recognized the people standing outside the wall. Not one of my brothers, then, but Harding or Shawna or someone from the city. What was he doing? Collecting allies?

Whoever it was, I was going to find him. I began making my way in that direction, staying in the trees, trying to spot movement in the dark ahead of me. It was impossible— the underbrush was very thick and the night now so dark, the moon buried behind a bank of clouds, not a single star in sight. But I kept pushing along just inside the tree line, not knowing what else to do, keeping the wall in sight, keeping my ears open for any threatening sound.

The brush grew thicker and I lost track of where the figure had entered the trees. I came around a big tree and managed to stub my toe hard against a rock. Stifling a gasp I cradled my injured foot in my hands until the throbbing eased. Then I stepped up on the culprit rock in one last futile attempt to see the person I'd been trying to follow. Where had he gone?

Surely he'd show himself again—I desperately needed him to show himself. The stockade was a long way away and I'd never been there before and I didn't want to try to find it alone, on this dark night, with wild men in the woods and wardens prowling and Sir Tom's traps and the smoke choking my lungs and the mist sliding damp and soft across my face.

Then hands grabbed my shoulders and slammed me back against the tree trunk and held me there. One shoulder suddenly was free again but he wasn't releasing me—he was cocking back to hit me, and if it was a warden I didn't want to announce my name, but if it was a friend I didn't want to get beat up for nothing.

So I said, hurriedly, "Wait! Who are you?"

The hand gripping me relaxed and someone gave a low disbelieving laugh.

"Red?" he said. "It's me, Cline."

I flung myself at him and hugged him as hard as I could. For a moment he just stood there and I thought of course, this was Cline, he'd shove me away, but I intended to hold on until he made me let go, I was so glad to see him, so glad to find a friend, or at least an ally, someone who didn't want to kill me. Then his arms came around me. He had a handgun in his right hand. If I hadn't spoken he'd have hit me with it.

"I thought you were a warden," he said, lifting me down from the rock. "You looked tall."

"I'm sorry," I said. "I'm so sorry."

"It's okay," he said, laughing. "You're okay. I've got you." Only then did I realize I was crying, clutching his shirt.

"I killed a man." I had to say it. "A warden. He was going to—his belt—the chain—the breeding program—we were alone—and I stabbed him and he bled, it spurted in my face. I think he's dead."

Cline held me more tightly. "That's how you got out?" he said, and I nodded. I was shivering so hard my teeth chattered.

"It's okay," he said. "You had to do it. They were going to kill you, you know that. And you're safe now."

He kept hold of my arms but pried me gently away from his shirt.

"Listen," he said, and he spoke calmly but there was underlying urgency in his voice. "Can you listen to me?"

I nodded and then realized he might not be able to see me that well in the dark. "Yes," I said. "I'm listening."

"Farrell Dean just went in to get you."

"But he thinks I'm on the other island—he doesn't know I'm here, Cline, how could he—"

Cline gave me a shake. "Man up, Red. Listen to me. Some strange guy with braids grabbed Farrell Dean and Tor right before the explosions and said you and your sister were in the city. He said you were in the prison and your sister was in the Watcher compound, and your grandfather was pretending to be Meritt, which makes no sense to me, but that's what he said. And Farrell Dean said that gave him an idea but he needed Gabriel, so I found Gabriel for him and now they've gone in after you."

"And Tor went for Fiona?"

"He went after your sister, yeah."

"But the Watcher compound got blown up—that's what people were saying—"

"No, it didn't blow. At least it wasn't supposed to." Cline

paused momentarily, dubious, then hurried on. "Farrell Dean went after you. To the prison, because that's where the guy said you were."

"I was. I was in his cell. Farrell Dean's cell. They put me in the same—"

"That's where he's going, which means, what—will he find that warden still lying there?"

I tried to detach myself, tried to think calmly. "I don't know. He couldn't have gone anywhere himself, even if he wasn't dying, because I locked him in. But someone might have found him and moved him."

"So the problem is—"

A tumbling noise from the city and a startled yell made us turn. More wall must have fallen.

Cline turned to me again. "If Farrell Dean and Gabriel find the warden you stabbed, maybe they'll guess what happened and get right back out of the city. But if someone found him and moved the body there'll be nothing there but blood."

"He'll think it's mine."

"Right. And he'll figure you've been hurt or even killed, and he'll go looking for you. He's not going to come out without you."

He didn't say the rest, but I understood. That city was not a safe place for Farrell Dean—not with every warden out and about, angry, knowing that he was the rebel who got away and then came back to make more trouble. They wouldn't bother to arrest him. They'd shoot him on sight, and expect to be rewarded for it.

"We have to go get him," I said, trying to pull free of Cline's grip on my shoulders.

"Not you. You're not going back in there."

"Yes, I am."

"You just got out."

"I'm going back in."

"It's too dangerous," Cline said, letting go of my arms, and now there was an edge to his voice. "I'll get him. You know I will."

I took a deep breath. I was glad I couldn't see his face, only the pale halo that was his white-blond hair.

"You were right, Cline," I said. "On the cliff. By the beach. But it's different now. I'm going after him. Deal with it." It wasn't a very coherent apology, but under the circumstances it was the best I could do.

For a long moment Cline was silent. Then he reached out and touched my shoulder. I think he was checking to see whether I was still shaking. Miraculously I wasn't.

"All right," he said finally. "But we'd better hurry."

Chapter 11

Farrell Dean and Gabriel had gone into Optica through the western gap, where Warden Karl was stationed. That meant the entire city was between us and them.

We couldn't cut through, not with all the wardens out and about, so we decided to head for the northwest gap. Then we could cut down through the fields to the center of the city.

We felt our way through the dark woods. Once we made it to the pale grass of the wasteland we started running. People were still milling around, most of them staying as close to the wall as possible, one or two venturing a few yards further out. They weren't likely to see us if we stayed close to the trees, thanks to the mist and the dark and the dying smoke which, periodically lit by fitful moonlight, looked yellow and sinister.

"Who built the bombs?" I asked.

"Your dad, and then your brothers placed and detonated them. Your dad wouldn't let anyone else touch the things. Said he didn't want to blow up anybody who wasn't related to him."

Despite everything, I laughed.

"He wasn't joking," Cline said.

"I know—but my father—my brothers—" There was no

way I could explain the intricacies of family life, at least not while I needed my breath for running.

"They sure can shoot," Cline said. "And a sister who looks just like you—that must be something to see."

I expected him to make some quip about the world not needing two of me, but he said nothing more. He was being nicer than I had any right to expect, given our history, and especially given that I'd just managed to endanger Farrell Dean yet again. Maybe I had my bomb-making father and gun-toting brothers to thank.

When we reached the northern slope, behind the Watcher compound, we could go faster because there were no gaps in the wall, no exploded holes, and therefore no people or wardens to avoid.

"Didn't want to risk injuring the old people," Cline said, gesturing toward the intact wall. "Or Meritt." I could have hugged him for that.

"So the compound didn't come down after all?"

"I can't tell. There's a lot of dust here, that's for sure."

For a big guy he could run, but he was finally getting out of breath. When we drew near to the place where we hoped to enter the city, we slowed, dodging back into the trees for cover. A long piece of wall had come down here, worse than at any of the other places we'd passed. Cline eyed the damage and whistled softly.

"Bigger bomb?" I said.

"Angus. He says he has a knack for wanton destruction. Looks like it must be true."

The gaping hole seemed to be unguarded, which was odd. Maybe no one wanted to be that close to the wilderland.

Cautiously we eased forward; no one challenged us, so we picked our way in, through the rubble, to the edge of the fields. There we stopped, faced with blackberry bramble as impenetrable as the wall.

"No wonder there aren't any wardens out here," Cline said.

"There should be paths," I said. "We keep paths cut."

But the paths hadn't been maintained. The bushes had merged together into a massive impenetrable hedge of thorns. I'd been gone less than a month, and already things were falling apart in my fields.

Cline picked a spot that looked marginally less dense and started working his way in. I had more experience with blackberries and didn't even try. When he started cursing I came forward and helped disentangle him from a long cane of thorns.

"We can't get through this," he said, sucking a cut on his hand.

"Can you lift me up?"

Without a word Cline took me by the waist and lifted me over his head so that I sat on his shoulders. I twisted around, looking this way and that.

"They've kept part of the paths cut back," I said. "Just not all the way to the edge of the field. There's one right over here."

"How far away?"

"Three or four yards."

He shook his head. "Might as well be a hundred."

I had Mal's knife, but hacking our way in would still take too long.

"We'll have to go on to the western gap," Cline said.

"There's no time—if we don't catch them at the prison, we won't know where they are. Help me stand up." I was trying to get my right foot up onto his shoulder. "I'm going to jump to the path."

"You'll break a leg," he said, but he grabbed my ankles and helped me balance. "Or you'll come down in that bramble and I'll never get you out."

I didn't answer.

"Get to the western gap by dawn," Cline said. "No matter what, you get there by then. I'll try to find you in the city but if I don't I'll meet you at the gap and make sure you can get out."

"Got it."

"Promise me, Red."

"I promise."

"I can't believe I'm letting you do this. Farrell Dean's going to kill me."

"Not if I can help it. Are you ready?"

"Yeah. On the count of three."

We counted. Cline boosted.

I jumped.

Chapter 12

I cleared the blackberry bramble easily, and landed fine except for the fact that I hit a muddy patch and slid into the next thicket.

"You okay?" Cline called quietly.

"Yes," I said, yanking my clothes free of the thorny canes. I had cuts on my face and hands, and like all blackberry cuts they stung like the dickens, but I was okay.

"See you later," I called. "Be careful." Then I started to run. The moon slid in and out of clouds, lighting my path through the thicket, abruptly leaving me groping in the dark, then taking pity on me once more.

The brambles were taller than my head and if someone stepped out on the path ahead of me I'd have no way of escape, but there was no point in thinking about that now. Surely the wardens were too busy with the chaos in the city to bother patrolling the blackberry fields.

Finally I reached the edge of the bramble. I slowed to a walk, glancing cautiously around. To my left the Watcher compound lay in darkness, parts of it broken and sprawling on the ground, and my heart contracted. I edged closer.

In the darkness it was hard to tell, but from this angle I thought the damage wasn't as bad as it had looked at first. A long section of the privacy wall was down, and the compound's entryway, and it looked like maybe some of the decorative blocks and things. But the main building itself was standing, there was no doubt about that. Maybe Angus had done too good a job with the bomb for the northwest section of wall, and the reverberations had shaken the compound. Maybe that's all it was.

People were moving rubble, trying to clear the entryway. There was a lot to clear—the privacy wall had fallen toward the building. I wanted to edge closer, to assure myself that the damage was mostly external, but wardens holding guns were directing the work and they'd arrest or shoot me on the spot, no question about that.

Turning my back on the Watcher compound I slunk to the edge of the grain field and waited for the moon to reappear, casting anxious glances back at the compound and the work going on there as I waited.

Finally the moon came out and lit the bare fields. I saw furrows, dark and straight, and a few lonely stalks of corn that the combine had missed. I didn't see any people heading toward me, no wardens to prevent me from cutting through the exposed fields to the prison.

The soft tilled ground sank under my feet with every step and dry stalks slapped at my ankles. The moon was still out and if anyone looked across the fields they'd be bound to see me, though they'd only know I was a dark figure running through the field—nothing remarkable, under the circumstances. In any case, they surely wouldn't jump to the conclusion that I was the prisoner who'd missed her execution, especially since I was running toward the prison.

I crossed the hay fields, the dead grass swishing around my legs. When I reached the pumpkin field the moon went behind a cloud and I slowed, afraid I'd trip on a clod or discarded gourd. It wasn't a quick trip—the fields and cattle took up almost the entire top half of the round city, and the moon didn't come out again until I'd reached the bottom edge of the fields. The white spotlight was circling and by then I was in its range, so I hurried forward to get under the reach of its bright finger.

Then I saw them—not two figures, but scores of them, all grouped together in the city circle at the base of the watchtower.

The moon went dark again and I edged forward, straining to see. That mob might have nothing to do with us. Farrell Dean and Gabriel might be already in the prison, or searching the streets for me.

But I could think of no reason for people to be gathered in the city circle after Optica's wall had been destroyed, not when the wardens were pressing everyone into service to guard the city against the rebels in the woods.

Tugging my black cap more tightly over my hair, I crept further forward and hoped no one would spot me. Again I told myself that if they did, they wouldn't know who I was, as long as my hair stayed covered.

Now I could hear the confused murmur of many voices. They sounded anxious, afraid. Now and then a louder, angrier voice rose, and was quickly drowned by a host of nervous mutterings.

As I crept forward in the darkness, the outline of one of the tractor sheds rose up just ahead and to my left. I darted to it as the moon came out again, and slid around the corner toward the crowd, staying against the wall, staying in the shadows.

It was good no one was near me because when I saw what was happening I gasped. There was a large mob—fifty people, maybe more, all in Optica gray—and they formed a rough circle with a large bare center. In the middle of that bare spot stood Farrell Dean and Rafe.

I knew it wasn't Rafe. It couldn't be. Obviously it had to

be Gabriel, dressed in Optica gray, clean-shaven as Rafe had always been, and yet I couldn't make my eyes see Gabriel. Only Rafe, come back again.

Realizing I was in danger of being paralyzed by the sight, I told myself it didn't matter who it was—Rafe, Gabriel—I didn't have to be able to see the difference. I didn't have to keep them straight in my mind.

All that mattered was that he was trapped in the center of that mob, and even as I told myself that I began to panic. They were surrounded—they'd been caught—they were in the city circle.

As I watched more people came, moving in from all parts of the city, surrounding Farrell Dean and Rafe. But I could see no black-garbed wardens, not a single one.

Then the crowd shifted and I saw that Farrell Dean had a faint smile on his face.

For a moment I couldn't get a clear look at Rafe—there were too many people—but then the crowd moved and I saw something dark on his shirt, smears and splashes, and the crowd closed in and I couldn't see, and then it shifted and I saw the awful wound that marred his temple, matted his dark silver-streaked hair, and the world went slantways and I was breathing fast and shallow, hyperventilating.

It wasn't Rafe. Rafe was dead. This was Gabriel, this was Rafe's brother. It wasn't Rafe.

I cupped my hands over my nose and mouth and forced myself to slow down, breathe deeply, hold it, breathe out, easy regular breaths.

Rafe didn't look afraid, any more than he'd looked afraid in the city meeting when he'd died. He didn't look trapped. He was talking but the pounding in my ears kept me from hearing, and I took another slow breath and another, and finally my blood calmed enough that I could hear.

"When they killed me, they said that I'd betrayed the

family." Rafe's voice was clear in the night air. "I never did. But you have."

Someone answered in a blustering, panicky tone. I couldn't make sense of what he said, but I recognized the voice. It was Garry, the bully from my field team.

Rafe laughed. "Is that so," he said. "Then how did you manage to get yourself reassigned to Elise?"

The crowd shifted. Now Garry was the center of another, smaller circle. He raised one arm and swung wide and wildly, and someone caught his arm and another man stepped in, too, and they restrained him as Farrell Dean whispered in Rafe's ear.

Rafe turned to another man. "Genetic Counselor Ray," he said. "Please explain how the genetic counselors decide who to breed with whom."

Ray was standing where I could see his face. He looked disconcerted but not afraid. "I can do that," he said, and turned slightly, facing the bulk of the crowd more fully.

"We're supposed to breed for a healthier Optica," he said. "We're supposed to do that by genetic mixing—you know how mutts are healthier than purebreds? Like that. But only about three-fourths of our people get assigned scientifically. The rest bribe a counselor, or have an in with a Watcher or a warden. Some people don't want to be assigned, and they can get out of it with a bribe. And some people want to be reassigned. That costs more, but it can be done."

A few people in the crowd began to look uneasy; most looked angry.

Garry tried to pull his arms away from the two men who were holding them pinned, but he couldn't.

"I didn't do anything wrong," he said. "It's their word against mine and they're ghosts—you can't trust ghosts."

Farrell Dean turned his head and said something in Rafe's ear, and Rafe looked at someone else.

"And you, Felix," he said. "How is it that you're sleek and fat, when so many are skin and bones? How is it you've never been assigned, and yet you have a house all to yourself?"

Felix was one of my field workers, quite possibly the laziest one of all. I hadn't known that he lived alone in a house.

"I don't have to talk to you," Felix said. "You're dead."

Rafe laughed again. "Only the dead talk to the dead, is that it?" He glanced at Farrell Dean. "Choose your side carefully, Felix, or you'll be one of us soon enough."

How many people had Rafe spoken to, one by one, while Farrell Dean fed him information and scanned the enormous crowd?

Gabriel, that is. It was Gabriel who was talking, and without ever having heard Rafe he was managing to imitate his cadences, the rhythms of Optica. It was so dangerous, what he was doing—if he sounded wrong, if he looked wrong, if he misspoke, he was done for. He and Farrell Dean both.

Farrell Dean wasn't just scanning the crowd, I saw now—he was scanning beyond them as well, watching I supposed for wardens. What would they do if wardens did show up, as they were bound to do, with guns and stunners? They were completely exposed out there.

Then Rafe said, "I'm here to give you a message."

He spoke quietly now, and the crowd leaned in to hear.

"The Guardians didn't destroy the wall," he said. "It was the rebels in the woods. They aren't traitors, no matter what the Watchers might have told you. They want a just Optica, a city that's fair and free. They want a place where you can make your own decisions, live your own lives, where you aren't herded around like dimwitted cattle."

Utter silence greeted his words.

"If you want a better world, a better Optica, rise up with them and fight for it. And be clear about this: if you will not fight with them, you are against them. You are either for the rebels, or for the Watchers."

The crowd began to murmur. People glanced at their neighbors.

"The wardens have guns," one man called out. "And stunners, too," another man said.

Rafe looked exasperated. But before he could reply, someone else spoke up. "Get a spine, why don't you," the man said. "We outnumber them ten to one."

I thought I knew that voice, craned to see, and when I caught a glimpse of his face I felt suddenly proud. It was the farmer in charge of the fields—my farmer. Edgeling's brother.

A man turned to the person next to him and said something I couldn't catch. In response the second man shoved the other one hard, and the first man shoved back. Then the crowd began to move, writhe. Small fights broke out, and noisy arguments. Some people turned, staring balefully toward the dark Watcher compound.

And some people gathered around the farmer. He climbed to a high step in the circle, talking rapidly, and the people in front of him looked angry and determined. One pointed east, toward the slaughterhouse, and made a slashing gesture with his hand, and I knew what he was saying. There were knives there, big knives used to kill and butcher cattle. Weapons.

Behind me a radio crackled. My heart almost leaped out of my chest, but somehow I managed not to flinch, managed to stay pressed into the shadows of the tractor shed. It had to be a warden. A warden had crept up behind me and I hadn't heard.

"I need backup at the circle," a woman said. "Everyone available. Now."

Slowly, carefully, I turned my head.

The warden wasn't looking at me. She hadn't seen me.

She was too absorbed in the scene in front of us, just as I had been. "Got a mob starting," she said. "And some dead men who aren't dead."

Very slowly I inched away from her, toward the front of the shed.

The radio crackled again. "Say again?" a voice said. "Where are you?" Static drowned out the rest of his words.

The warden thumbed her radio. "I said, urgent, we need backup—"

I stepped out into the moonlight. "Hello, Rhoda," I said. "I got loose."

Her eyes went wide and she lunged to grab me, but I darted into the tractor shed. It was dark and crowded and untidy, but this was my territory, my equipment. I skirted plows and hay balers, snagged a shovel from a hook on the wall, and rounded the nearest tractor.

Warden Rhoda didn't fare quite so well. In the darkness I heard her trip over something, stumble against something else, curse.

"Better be careful in here," I said. "There are a lot of sharp edges. And they aren't exactly sterile, what with the manure and all. You could get a bad infection." I felt a little giddy.

"Red?" she called. "Don't be foolish. Come on out."

I laughed.

"I mean it," she said, still groping toward me. "Let me take you back." Her voice turned softer, persuasive. "Meritt's taking care of things. He has a plan to get you out."

I didn't answer.

Rhoda was coming around the tractor, following me, just as I wanted her to do. I climbed up to the tractor seat. In the darkness Rhoda's blond hair stood out dim but clear, a lovely target. For a split second I paused and did a gut check: Was this really necessary, or did I only want it to be?

105

It was necessary.

I slid onto the hood of the tractor and brought the shovel down hard on Rhoda's head.

It only took the one blow. She crumpled and lay still. I slid down and peered at her, keeping my distance, the shovel at the ready. She was breathing, but not moving. Good.

I reached underneath her and grabbed her radio, but it had broken when she fell on it, and it came apart in my hand. Her gun would only work for her, but I didn't think stunners were coded to their owners. It took a moment to get it unhooked from her belt, but finally I wrenched it free and then went through the obstacle course back to the open front of the shed.

The people were talking more loudly now. No one was looking this way. Farrell Dean was still scanning the crowd, scanning beyond them, and I waited until his face was turned my direction. Then I stepped out into the bare moonlight and waved my arms.

He saw me right away—across the wide dark empty space we stared at each other. Then his hand went out and touched Rafe's arm—Gabriel's arm—and Gabriel followed his gaze. I ducked back into the shadows behind the shed, just as a loud popping noise rang out and a dark cloud of acrid smoke rose from where the crowd stood.

The people gasped and swayed back, their faces white and astonished in the moonlight. The smoke thickened, rising in a dense black column toward the sky. It thickened and spread and bit into my lungs and I covered my face with my sleeve, my eyes streaming.

The cries from the crowd grew louder. At first I thought they were cries of fear, but then the sound changed, became louder, deeper, more frightening. A large mass of people gathered and began to run. Some ran toward the slaughterhouse and some ran toward me, and I shrank deeper into the shadows and then they were past me, their faces angry and intent, and still the pillar of smoke grew, and I began to think black acrid smoke was going to fill the whole city.

"Hey," Farrell Dean said softly, and I turned and saw him coming around the back of the shed, and then I was in his arms, holding him as tightly as he was holding me. After a second he pulled back and grabbed my chin, tipping my face up toward his, toward the moonlight, before folding me in his arms once more.

"Just checking," he said.

Chapter 13

Farrell Dean and Gabriel and I had made it to the dark twisted trees of the old orchard and were heading for the western gap when Cline stepped out of the shadows.

"You found them!" he said, giving me an approving slap on the shoulder.

"They weren't exactly hiding."

Farrell Dean laughed. "Gabriel had the whole city eating out of his hand," he said.

Gabriel smiled, but only fleetingly. "Let's save our self-congratulations until we're safely out of here," he said.

"We can't go yet." Cline gestured toward the gap. "Some wardens are out there talking to Karl. We have to wait until they leave."

Gabriel moved toward the gap, checking for himself, I supposed, and Cline followed.

I hung back, in no hurry to run into a group of wardens, glad for a chance to catch my breath. Farrell Dean stayed with me.

The smell of smoke was still strong, even out there in the orchard, but at least it wasn't that terrible choking dust, filling my mouth and nose, blinding me. I took long deep breaths, scarcely daring to believe the truth that was beginning to sink in: I was alive. I was free. I wasn't going to be executed. And Farrell Dean was whole and free and right here beside me.

Still, I agreed with Gabriel. I wanted out. I wanted out of Optica and I never wanted to set foot in it again.

Behind us, in the city, someone shouted and a gunshot rang out. I spun around, saw nothing but dark and twisted trees.

"Hey, Red, here's a question." Farrell Dean's tone was deceptively casual—too easy for that night, too nonchalant ever for Farrell Dean. It was a red flag, and I stopped checking behind us and turned to face him. "How did you end up in prison?"

It was too dark to see his expression, but I didn't need to. He knew—or had guessed—why I'd gone into Optica alone. And I didn't want to talk about it, not now, not here. He would misunderstand—or understand all too well. Either way, I wasn't ready to discuss it.

"Red, I'm talking to you."

He'd never spoken to me like that before, and for a second my temper flared. He had no right to interrogate me, not now. Not about this.

But this wasn't the moment for an argument, not here in the orchard where we weren't entirely safe, still here inside the city wall. And after all, my decision to come into the city alone had almost gotten both of us killed. I wasn't going to apologize for it—I'd had my reasons—but I knew that if things had gone just a little differently, we'd both be dead.

So in an attempt to be conciliatory, I answered him. "Someone had to warn Meritt," I said.

"And I did."

"But I didn't know."

"I gave Karl a message for him last night. It was all under control." Farrell Dean's voice was carefully level.

"But I didn't know," I said again. "And back there—in

Aislin—nobody was listening to me. Nobody wanted to give Meritt a chance. They all blamed him for being Angel's son. They don't trust him."

"I don't know whether I trust him or not," Farrell Dean said, still in that dangerously even voice. "I guess that means I don't. But it doesn't matter. I'd never leave him to die."

I looked down. "I know that."

"No," Farrell Dean said. "Apparently you don't."

For a long moment we stood in tense silence. At my feet shadows sprang into relief as the moon slid out from behind a cloud.

"On the boat you accused me of kidnapping you."

Startled, I looked up at him. In the colorless moonlight his face was hard, his eyes dark with anger.

"Did you think I'd go even further?" he said. "Did you think I'd let Meritt die to improve my chances with you?"

I shook my head, but he kept talking. "Meritt is my friend. And he saved my life. Even if I knew that by saving him I'd lose you to him, I'd save him all the same. Otherwise I wouldn't be able to live with myself."

At that supremely awkward moment Cline walked up. He stopped beside me and though I felt utterly mortified I turned toward him, wanting to escape the look in Farrell Dean's eyes.

"She went in after Meritt," he said to Cline, and the words sounded clipped and final.

"I went in after you, too," I said, but as I turned toward him the moon shone suddenly bright and his expression changed, narrowed.

"Someone hit you," he said. He lifted a hand as if he'd touch my cheek, then let it fall. "What happened?"

My throat closed up and I shook my head. I couldn't talk about the scarred warden. Not now. Maybe not ever. Not to him.

Cline registered my difficulty. "A warden had a go at her," he said, and cleared his throat pointedly. "Wanted to have a little fun. While she was locked in the cell."

Farrell Dean's face turned menacing. For a moment I was actually a little afraid of him.

"Did he hurt you?" he said, and he wasn't talking about a few bruises.

I shook my head, but I still couldn't find my voice.

"She had a knife," Cline said. "She took care of business."

I nodded, verifying Cline's account, intensely grateful that he was saying it so I didn't have to.

"She made it out of the city and then I ran across her," Cline went on. "And don't you even think about giving me grief for letting her go back in after you. I could have stopped her by knocking her out cold, but I don't guess you'd have liked that either."

Farrell Dean half smiled, but his eyes were not amused.

Gabriel walked up. Good—I didn't want to be the center of attention anymore, not the sort of attention I was getting.

My relief was short lived.

Gabriel planted himself in front of me and crossed his arms over his chest. "All right," he said, fixing me with a stern look. "Tell me the truth. If you're here and Fiona's here, then is Rain here as well?"

I nodded.

Gabriel shut his eyes briefly, and then opened them to glare at me. "You're a bad influence, you know that?"

It was so ludicrous that I laughed. "Me? A bad influence on *Rain*?"

Gabriel frowned. "I was thinking of Fiona," he said. "Now—where's my daughter?"

"I don't know."

"But you all came here together. With Mal."

"That's right," I said. "We landed near Sir Tom's cave on

the beach. Where your mother is," I added, looking toward Farrell Dean but not quite meeting his eyes. "That's the last time I saw Rain—there at the cave, early this morning. I know that later Fiona and Michael Alleyn went into the city to see the Watchers—I saw them from the monitors in the watchtower—"

"Michael Alleyn?" Gabriel said.

"He isn't dead. He was pretending, because his twin brother Meritt was watching him—he's the one who did all this, the one in charge—" That was enough summary for now, I thought—"Anyway I saw Michael Alleyn and Fiona on the monitor, telling the Watchers they've been kicked out of power, but I never saw Rain or Earl or anyone else."

"Earl's here too?" Gabriel relaxed just slightly.

"And Will Bright."

Gabriel looked faintly perplexed at that bit of news, but stuck to his primary concern. "Mal didn't mention Rain, when you saw him?" he said, turning toward Farrell Dean.

"No, but he was in a hurry—he'd caught sight of Rufus setting a charge, and guessed what was about to happen, and was afraid we might blow the prison and the Watcher compound too."

Gabriel was silent for a long moment.

"She's bound to be in the city somewhere," he said eventually. "She'd never sit something like this out, not if Fiona was going in."

Cline looked at me. "What exactly did you see on the monitors?"

"Michael Alleyn and Fiona were talking to the Watchers. Michael was pretending to be Meritt Alleyn—the Watchers are all afraid of Meritt Alleyn. Michael pretended he had come from the mainland to shut down the experiment. That's all I saw—it was only a minute or two. The Watchers believed him, but then at the last some of them might have gotten suspicious. I don't know for sure, because the warden in the watchtower started to wake up and I had to go."

"Rain's bound to be with Michael Alleyn," Gabriel said musingly. "To be the least bit credible as Meritt Alleyn, he'd have to show up with an entourage, bodyguards or wardens or whatever, and that would have to be Rain and Earl. They're the only ones the Watchers wouldn't recognize as being from this island."

"They wouldn't recognize Mal," I said.

Cline snorted. "Mal doesn't exactly look like the official bodyguard type."

I had to admit that was true. "I only saw the conference room," I said. "If Rain and Earl were somewhere else in the compound, even just outside the conference room, I wouldn't have known."

Cline shifted. "Did you get a good look at the compound while you were over there?"

I nodded. "It's damaged, but not too bad. It's mostly the outside part, where the entryway and privacy wall are. People are trying to clear the way to get in. Wardens, mostly. There's a lot of heavy rubble in the way."

Without a word Gabriel turned back toward the way we'd come, toward the city.

"No—" I put a hand on his arm. "There are too many wardens."

My uncle shook me off. "Exactly," he said. "There's no telling what they'll do to her. Or to Fiona and the others. We can't let them walk out into that alone."

"But the wardens know that Rafe was behind the rebellion," I said. "They might shoot you on sight. You got lucky just now, but I heard them talking about you and Farrell Dean. And there are at least a dozen wardens at the compound."

"Not all of them have working guns."

"But some do," Farrell Dean said. "Karl couldn't get to all of them. And she's right—getting yourself killed won't do any good at all."

"There's no back way into the compound?" Gabriel said. "A back door, a window, something that isn't blocked?"

"I doubt it," I said. "The wardens would know, and they're not working back there."

"Meritt and I checked it out once," Farrell Dean said, not looking at me. "The back is the same as the front. High, small windows, sealed with those glass blocks. They're for light, not for ingress or egress."

"It's poor planning," Gabriel said. "Anyone with a modicum of sense builds in a bolt hole."

"A bolt hole," I repeated.

"An escape. A secret way out."

"I know. I mean, there is."

All three men looked at me.

"I only just remembered. Meritt told me there's a tunnel from the compound to the stockade. But Jensen's the one who used to know the entry codes."

"What about Sir Tom?" Farrell Dean asked.

"Meritt didn't think the other Guardians had the codes. The Guardians did that sort of thing—division of power or knowledge or whatever. There's probably no way Jensen remembers, though."

"He might." Cline held up one hand and wiggled his fingers. "Muscle memory. And he's at the stockade right now. Sir Tom locked him up so he wouldn't be out and about during the explosions."

Farrell Dean nodded.

"It's worth a try," he said. "We could come in through the far end of the tunnel, get our people back out that way. We'd have the element of surprise on our side."

Even though I was the one who had brought up this

possibility, now that I thought about it I didn't like it at all.

"You don't know what you'd be walking into once you got to the compound," I said. "There are wardens in there, and all the Watchers. It's too dangerous."

Farrell Dean didn't even look at me.

"Go," Gabriel said. "I'll stay here, see if I can find a way to get close to the front of the compound, in case the wardens get them out that way. I'll stay out of sight."

"There's no way to get close," I said. "Not without being seen. You'll be completely exposed crossing the fields."

"That's my concern, not yours. Someone has to cover this end of things."

"Hang on." Cline looked at me. "A lot of rubble, you said? So it'll take the wardens awhile to dig through?"

"I would think so—there's a lot."

"He could cut through the blackberries. It'll be a pain, but it's doable if you aren't in a big hurry like we were before. It's only a few feet."

He was right. Quickly I explained to Gabriel about the path that almost reached the edge.

"We can cut our way in there, near the compound," I said.

"We?" Gabriel said curtly. "You're not invited."

Cline glanced at Farrell Dean, who was half-turned away from us—from me—looking toward the city, pointedly not participating in the discussion.

"You should come back to the stockade," Cline said, turning toward me. "You'll be safe there. And some of your old people are there now, too," he added, as if giving me an incentive.

"They are? Who?"

"Waylon, Bruce, Estelle, Joy. And Tilda and June."

"How did they get there?" Since Cline was the only one speaking to me, I addressed the question to him.

"A few of them managed to escape from the compound a couple of days ago. You knew that, right?"

I nodded.

"They made it to the woods and were hiding out there, near the wall. Some wardens came out, talking about the rebels, and the old people decided to follow them. That led them straight to the stockade. The old folks were hiding outside the stockade, trying to figure out what to do next, when Farrell Dean and all of them showed up. Your brothers picked off that group of wardens, and the old people recognized Ezzie and Farrell Dean and came out and said hello, and that was that."

For a moment I let myself enjoy relief. The ones who had escaped were all right. I was so glad, and I did want to see them, especially Estelle.

But it couldn't be now.

"I'll be more useful here," I said, still to Cline. "If they come out the front, into all of those wardens, I can help Gabriel be a distraction. And that mob—I'm afraid they'll hurt Meritt. They think he turned me in, but he didn't—it was my fault—we were talking and the wardens came, but he wasn't going to do it."

I tried to keep talking to Cline, but I couldn't help myself. I turned toward Farrell Dean. "Meritt tried to make me run. He's been protecting me all along. You—" I stopped, but the unsaid words hung in the air.

You were wrong about him.

Farrell Dean frowned and turned away.

Chapter 14

By the time we made it out of the city the wind was rising, thinning the mist and the suffocating smoke, sending clouds scuttling in front of the moon and then away again.

The first part of our way lay together, so we all headed north, along the perimeter of the city. We kept to the wasteland, where it was easier to run, but stayed close to the protective trees. High above us branches were shuddering, casting strange dancing shadows. Though I tried to watch for wild men, I wasn't sure I'd spot them among the bending shifting shadows in the trees.

I had just opened my mouth to say as much when I heard something. Over the bluster and whistle of the wind, someone was singing. *Singing*—and not too far away.

I grabbed at Cline's sleeve.

"It's okay," he said, but at the same moment a figure appeared, deep among the wilderland trees. He was strolling along in the dark windy woods, casually, his hands in his pockets, and singing at the top of his lungs.

I stopped in my tracks, and the men stopped too.

"It's Ezzie," I said, cold with horror. He'd lost it—he'd gone completely off his head. They should never have brought him back, not when he was still recovering, not back here to the place where he'd been infected.

"He's all right," Cline began, but I cut him off.

"They're after him—it's the wild men—"

And indeed a pack of shadowy figures were loping through the trees, close on Ezzie's heels. Instinctively I stepped forward to call out a warning, but Cline grabbed me and clamped a hand over my mouth. I tried to fight him off, but he held me tight. "Hush," he hissed. "Ezzie's fine. He's doing it on purpose."

I didn't care if it was his life's ambition—Ezzie wasn't going to sacrifice himself to the wild men.

"They don't know what to make of him," Cline muttered. "They follow him around but never get too close."

I still didn't fully understand what was going on, but I relaxed in Cline's grip. He felt it and let me go.

Ezzie started singing a different song, one whose tune I recognized—it was one of the Sunday songs.

"Your brothers couldn't fend them off and set explosives at the same time," Cline said in a rapid undertone, as the figures grew more distant. "And we didn't have enough manpower to send teams. So Ezzie's distracting them, that's all. Keeping them focused on him instead of stalking us and whoever we manage to get out of the city."

"But what if they decide to attack him? They're wild men—you can't count on them always acting the same."

"Sir Tom's with him. Just in case."

"We figured it out right after we landed," Gabriel said. "A couple of them were following us, and Ezzie got fed up and gave them a scolding. They sat back on their haunches and looked at him, just as if they were obeying orders. And they've been trying to get close to him ever since, hanging around the stockade, waiting for him to appear."

"He doesn't really have to do that," Cline said, nodding in Ezzie's direction. "The singing. He must have gotten bored."

The last of the loping figures vanished into the darkness. Ezzie's voice faded and then was gone, lost in the sound of the wind. I never caught a glimpse of Sir Tom, but if he was supposed to be there, he would be. He felt responsible for his wild men.

Cline was looking around. "This is a good place for us to split off," he said. "Ezzie's cleared the way for us, and it's probably as direct a path from here to the stockade as from anywhere."

Farrell Dean nodded grimly. He looked at me, saying nothing, but I knew he was thinking about trying to convince me to go to the stockade.

I couldn't. I had to do my best to help the ones who were trapped—Fiona and Michael Alleyn and the others, of course, but yes, Meritt too. And I wanted Farrell Dean to understand. Anything could happen tonight—either one of us might die. Just in case there wasn't a later, I had to make him understand now.

Taking hold of his sleeve I pulled him off to one side, turning my back to the others. He went with me reluctantly, but he went.

"What?" he said, and though he was looking at me, there was some sort of invisible wall between us, just like in my dream, and I lost the words I wanted to say.

Then he looked away, and that was worse. How was I supposed to make a private declaration when he was scanning the trees, glancing over at Cline and Gabriel, pointedly wishing he were somewhere else, somewhere not with me?

"Thank you for coming after me," I said, just to get his attention.

His eyes met mine and he said, deliberately, "That's what friends do."

"Yes," I said. "It is."

He nodded, then turned and began to walk away.

"Wait," I said.

"Not now." He spoke to me over his shoulder, still moving away. "I know what you're going to say and I don't want to hear it. Not tonight."

"Please, Farrell Dean. It's important. It can't wait."

And he didn't know, that was clear. He didn't know at all what I wanted to tell him, which made it all the more important that I say it.

With a sigh he turned toward me, his face impassive, his hands in his pockets, a heartbeat away from turning and striding off into the dark woods. Behind him Cline and Gabriel shifted impatiently, scanning the trees, the wasteland, the city wall. It was so awkward that I almost gave up. I almost said goodbye.

But if this turned out to be the last goodbye, I'd never forgive myself.

I groped for a way to begin. "Is it midnight yet?"

Farrell Dean stared at me. "No," he said slowly. "It's about ten."

"Good."

In the cloud-scuttled moonlight his gaze sharpened. "Why? What happens at midnight?"

I pulled off my black cap. The rising wind whipped my hair across my face, and I fought it back, wishing I were bathed, clean, dressed in something pretty, or at least in something not smeared with blood. I wished Farrell Dean weren't standing six feet away—I didn't want to have to shout. And I wished we didn't have an audience.

But this would have to do.

Straightening my shoulders, I looked him in the eye.

"Today is my birthday," I said.

Farrell Dean studied me for a long silent moment.

"Tell her happy birthday and let's go," Gabriel said.

Farrell Dean ignored him. Taking his hands out of his

pockets, he came toward me, searching my face. He didn't smile; if anything, the longer he studied me, the more forbidding he looked. "Go on," he said.

I hadn't expected to have to explain; he always seemed able to read my mind.

"On the road to Doria," I stammered. "On your birthday. When we were walking."

He wasn't looking me in the eye. He was examining me clinically, and in the fitful moonlight he looked so grim and dangerous that I almost lost my nerve. But the stakes were high—he might get killed, or I might—so I stumbled on.

"On the road to Doria you said at least now we could choose. I know this is bad timing and I'm not sure if you still—but I do. Choose, I mean. I choose you."

Farrell Dean finally looked straight at me, his gaze quick and direct, and then he pulled me to him and his arms went around me. The tight knot in my chest loosened and spun free, and I pressed my face into his shoulder and just for a moment forgot the impatient men waiting in the shadows, the erratic wind, the woods full of wild things, the wall and the wardens and the Watchers. All I saw, all I felt, was Farrell Dean.

"Well, she did say things were different now," Cline remarked.

Farrell Dean breathed out hard, in what I guessed was a ghost of a laugh.

"I thought you should know." I tipped my head back so I could see his face. "I wanted you to know." My hair blew across my eyes and he reached up and pushed it away, his hand warm on my face. Then he leaned down and kissed me on the forehead, very gently.

Gabriel shifted. "Touching as this is, we've got to get moving."

Farrell Dean nodded and took a step away from me. "If

Jensen can't remember those codes," he said, "I might be able to disable or bypass the locks."

I knew what he was saying; he was the mechanic, not Cline or Gabriel. He had to go the stockade.

"Are you sure you won't come with me, Red? You'd be safer there."

Reluctantly I shook my head. "You have to do what you can, and I have to do what I can. We have to do our best for him. For all of them. But especially for him."

"We do." Shadows from the blowing trees moved across his face, his eyes. "But be careful."

"I will. And you be careful, too."

"We'll all be careful." Gabriel was tired of waiting. "Farrell Dean, Cine, if the two of you manage to get into that tunnel, try to find some of the Alleyn boys to go with you. There's no telling what you'll find at the other end. You might need backup."

"Will do," Cline said.

That reminded me. "Farrell Dean," I said quietly. "If you see Angel, don't tell him about the tunnel. Meritt doesn't want him to know. He said it was a secret, especially from Angel."

Farrell Dean's eyes were curious, but we didn't have time for more. "All right," he said. "I'll keep it quiet. Though I doubt I'll be chatting with Angel."

He touched me once on the cheek, lightly, and turned away.

Cline followed. As he passed he reached out and punched me fondly on the arm—a little harder than he meant to, I think.

Then the two of them vanished into the darkness of the forest.

Chapter 15

By the time Gabriel and I reached the northwest gap, I could barely hear him over the howling of the wind. It blew and then settled, then rose again. The moon shone, then fell dark, then shone, its periods of light growing fewer and farther between. I was glad to have the shelter of the city walls.

"This will take awhile," Gabriel said grimly, studying the wall of blackberry bramble. "Give me the knife."

"Not there," I said. "The path is this way."

I handed him Mal's knife and, when I had shown him the spot, he began cutting methodically at the cane, tossing pieces of it aside in a rapidly growing pile. He didn't have gloves and I knew he was bound to be getting gouged by the vicious thorns, but though he winced now and then, he never slowed.

We could hear shouts from inside the city, and occasionally the sound of gunshots. The smoke, still drifting, made my eyes sting. After awhile the chaos in Optica began to feel like ordinary background noise.

While Gabriel worked, I explained about how I'd come to find Michael Alleyn, and filled in all the other details that he had missed.

I made a point of telling him about how Meritt had tried

to protect me. Gabriel didn't comment; he didn't even turn around.

For awhile we were silent as Gabriel hacked away at the bramble, but there was too much going on for me to keep quiet for long. "Where's my father?" I asked.

"Presumably at the stockade, but only because the boys put up a united front—they weren't going to have a cripple running around in the dark woods with explosives. And Rory pointed out, rightly, that someone needed to stay at command central and keep track of people as they reported back in. So unless Eric has given everyone the slip, he'll still be there." He glanced at me. "Farrell Dean will have the joy of bringing him up to date."

I groaned. Farrell Dean would have to be the one to explain that Fiona and I were here, and Fiona was missing and probably trapped in the compound. Maybe he'd have the sense to tell that part first, and then throw in Michael Alleyn's resurrection as a nice upbeat ending. Except for the fact that Michael, too, was trapped with the Watchers.

A twisted cane broke free and swung out at us, catching Gabriel across the face. He cursed softly and rubbed at the scratch.

"I can cut awhile," I said, but he shook his head.

After awhile I had another question. "I wonder where Mal went."

Gabriel shrugged.

Probably not too far from Michael Alleyn, would be my guess. So if Michael Alleyn was trapped, maybe Mal was somewhere inside Optica, watching the wardens moving debris. Maybe we'd spot him when we broke through.

We'd break through, and then we'd wend through the blackberry paths and see how much progress the wardens had made in digging out the compound. That would be the way everyone came out, because poor Jensen never would be able to remember the code, and what were the chances that Farrell Dean could bypass those locks? So everyone most likely would come out the front, and then we'd know whether the Watchers believed that Michael was Meritt Alleyn. If they didn't, Gabriel and I would have to make a move. We'd have to step out, where everyone could see us, and try to use the element of surprise to get the wardens over on our side, against the Voice and the other Watchers.

That's what I was thinking about when I should have been watching.

"See what you've done?"

I spun around.

Angel was standing a few yards away from us, his pale hair gleaming in the darkness, his knife glinting at the throat of a dark-haired woman who looked spitting mad. Rain.

"Drop that knife," Angel said.

Gabriel dropped it.

"Kick it away."

Gabriel did.

Then Angel turned his attention to me. "I told you I'd kill you if you got him killed," he said. "And I will."

"He's not dead," I said. We're working on getting him out. He's going to be okay." It was the same thing I'd been telling myself, over and over.

Angel didn't answer. Instead, he looked at Gabriel. "You must be the other Drewblood twin."

"That's right." Gabriel's voice was calm though he had to be taken aback, to suddenly see his daughter being held at knifepoint. "And you must be Angel."

Angel gave a mocking half bow, and when he did, the knife pressed more closely against Rain's throat. I couldn't take my eyes off it—surely Angel wouldn't kill her. He had no reason to kill her. But he had a knife at her throat and a gun in a holster on his hip.

"You're slowing us down," Gabriel said. "We're trying to get through so we can help them, once they're freed. There's a mob out there. It's not safe, not for our people and probably not for your son, either."

Angel was unmoved. "He'd never have been trapped in the first place if you hadn't come bumbling in blowing things up."

"We didn't intend to damage the compound." Gabriel still sounded calm, reasonable. "It must have been structurally unsound."

"Collateral damage," Angel said, nodding once. "It happens. And when it does—" The knife shifted, drew a mock line across Rain's throat. "An eye for an eye, a tooth for a tooth, a life for a life, a child for a child."

Gabriel didn't flinch. "Very melodramatic," he said. "But if we can attend to the matter at hand, there will be no need for vengeance. You know the man they call Jensen, I take it?"

I lifted a hand to stop him, but it was too late.

"He knows the codes to a secret tunnel," Gabriel went on. "Have you ever heard him say anything that might give us a clue to the code?"

Angel's face darkened and a sick feeling began in the pit of my stomach.

"How do you know about that tunnel?" he said.

Gabriel nodded at me. "Your son told her. He's been working on breaking the codes from inside the compound."

Without a word Angel shoved Rain away from him and started toward me, the knife glinting in his hand, and abruptly his earlier words—*collateral damage*—called back that first morning I'd spent on Sir Tom's beach, the morning Angel swam out and found us, when Sir Tom told him go away or else.

Or else Jensen would initiate detonation.

That was what he had said, and then Angel said *think of*

the city, and then Sir Tom said *collateral damage*. He hadn't mentioned a tunnel—he hadn't—but Angel said *it would kill Caliban*—

The tunnel was a trap.

Angel reached for me, cold fury in his face.

Maybe it was one of the traps the Watchers had laid for the Guardians, one of the traps that had never worked because Sir Tom's men were trained soldiers, and Meritt had said it was dangerous, and I'd thought he meant telling Angel was dangerous, but he meant the tunnel itself—

Angel's fingers wrapped hard around my arm.

And then the ground exploded.

Chapter 16

It was an explosion like an enormous mole tunneling through the ground just below the surface, spraying clods of earth and tree roots, knocking us off our feet. I landed hard on one shoulder and then was jolted onto my back, then back onto my side. Something struck me on the side of the head. Then the horrible tunneling motion went rumbling away, leaving the ground quivering in its wake.

I opened my eyes and saw Gabriel's boot a few inches from my face. Then it moved away as Gabriel got to his knees.

Behind him Rain was on her hands and knees, her face white and stunned. She reached up and put one hand to her throat. I was lying on my side, my cheek pressed against the cold earth, and I wanted to get up but I wasn't sure which way was up. The earth kept tilting.

Then hands grabbed me and jerked me sideways, set me on my feet.

"Come on," he said. It was Angel. I didn't know what he meant, what he wanted, but it didn't matter. Pulling me after him, he started into the woods, walking quickly at first, then half-running, dragging me beside him.

I struggled to keep up, to not fall, to understand.

The tunnel had exploded. It was a trap.

The woods felt eerily empty and everything was silent. It was only Angel and me, hurrying, but I couldn't hear the pounding of our feet, the rustling of the branches we shoved aside. I couldn't hear the rising wind that blew my hair across my face. And then gradually I did hear everything I wasn't hearing before, the wind and the new screams from the city and the pounding of our feet, but the world was empty because Farrell Dean was gone.

A second explosion rang out, not as loud, but like a painful groan deep in the earth. The ground shuddered with it and I lost my footing and came down hard on a jagged rock that ripped through my pants and into my leg. Blood spilled down my calf, but I didn't care, didn't even know if it hurt. Farrell Dean was dead. He was dead because I'd told him about the tunnel.

Angel jerked me back to my feet. "I told him to stay out of that tunnel," he said, and it looked like he was shouting but his voice came to me as if from a long way away. "I told him it was too dangerous."

"It was Farrell Dean," I said, and I was crying. "It was Farrell Dean and Jensen at the stockade. They blew up the tunnel. It wasn't Meritt. It was Farrell Dean."

"It was both," Angel said. "Both ends of the tunnel blew." He looked over his shoulder, toward the city from which we'd come, where thick black smoke rose over the tops of the trees, obscuring the westerly moon. "The entire tunnel is gone," he said, and now I could hear him too clearly. "The entrance to the compound went first, and then the entrance to the stockade. My son is dead."

They both were dead. I was crying harder, tears running down my face, and Angel grabbed me, shook me hard. "Stop it," he said fiercely, his fingers digging into my arm. "Don't cry for Meritt. He's mine."

And Fiona and Michael and Tor, and Cline, and who

else? Earl? Louie? The other old people? If the whole stockade had come down I could have lost all of them, my father, all of my brothers, and Sir Tom, and who knew how many others—

Angel started moving again, yanking me after him.

"Where—"

"To your father."

"But—" My father was at the stockade. Eric Alleyn was in the stockade and did that mean I'd lost him too?

"I'm going to look him in the eye and kill you in front of him."

But we weren't going toward the stockade—it was back there, it had blown up—we were heading west, toward the beach, toward the sea.

Angel pushed through a thorny bush and a branch snapped back, whipping against my cheek.

"Hurry up," Angel said. "Unless you'd like to die here and now."

I didn't really care where I died, or when. Fiona, Farrell Dean, Meritt, my father, my grandfather—so many people, and it was all my fault. Don't tell, Meritt had said. It's dangerous. But I hadn't understood, and I had told.

Angel dragged at me and I moved faster, pushing through underbrush that scratched my hands, clutched at my clothes, and I didn't care where we were going or why. It was dangerous, Meritt had said, but he had to do it. What was he doing—trying to disable the explosives, trying to clear a path so the old people could get out?

Angel would have stopped him. Angel wouldn't have let his son take such a terrible risk. "I'm sorry," I said. "I'm so sorry."

Angel shot me a look but didn't reply.

We reached a narrow rocky stretch, a little valley that would run with water when it rained. I stepped wrong on a rock and managed not to fall but I twisted my ankle. When I took another step my ankle protested. I could walk but not fast and Angel would probably shoot me now, and he might as well. Why should I drag myself to wherever he was taking me, just so I could die there instead of here?

Angel muttered something that I couldn't hear over the howling of the wind. He pushed me in front of him, propelling me along with an insistent hand on my back, my ankle throbbing at every step. Above us thunder rumbled and a few fat raindrops spattered to the ground.

Then Angel made a strange sound, gave a harsh intake of breath, and his hand on my back was gone and I turned and he was on the ground and there was someone else there, too, on the ground with him.

It was too dark—I couldn't tell who it was—but they were twisting, fighting on the ground, Angel's pale hair telling me that he was underneath the other man, but then Angel made a sharp movement and they went rolling together, elbows and knees flying, fighting for position, and then they broke apart and as they got to their feet I saw that it was Earl. They circled each other, veering toward me, and I stumbled out of the way, afraid to hope because this was Angel, but if anyone could beat Angel surely it was Earl.

Angel's knife was on the ground. I edged toward it, trying to stay out of their way.

"You're out of your league," Angel said, and he was out of breath but he was laughing, I was sure he was laughing, and then Earl brought his bent knee up fast and pivoted and his leg shot out straight and connected hard with the side of Angel's knee and Angel staggered but at the same time his fist flashed.

Earl was too close to dodge away, but he bent his arm up and trapped Angel's arm. Then Earl threw his other forearm across his body and into Angel's elbow and a loud pop sounded and Angel's arm went down, loose by his side, but already he was tilting his head, moving, driving his forehead hard straight into Earl's nose, and blood sprayed and Angel yanked Earl forward and sliced down hard with the edge of his hand, striking the back of Earl's neck and it was dark but I saw, I know I saw Earl's eyes go empty, and I screamed and Earl swayed and, with strange slowness, fell.

Angel stepped back, breathing hard. He didn't stop me when I hurried to Earl, scuttling awkwardly on my injured ankle. I bent and tried to see, through the darkness and the blood, how bad the damage was, but even as my mind registered the smashed nose, crooked on his face, I knew his eyes were blank and would stay blank. Still I rubbed my sleeve gently across his face, cleaning away what blood I could. Not another. Not one more person dead because of me.

"Get up," Angel said. "He's gone."

He'd already caught his breath. His left arm hung limp at his side and his face was twisted with pain, and when he moved it was with an awkward limping stride. I should have tried to run then but I didn't, I guess I was in shock, and Angel snatched up his knife and shoved it in the waist of his pants and grabbed my arm, pulling me to my feet.

"Come," he said. "We'll find your father." And he only had one good arm and his leg was hurt but he was still moving fast, half-pulling, half shoving me forward, and Earl was dead. It had happened so quickly. One minute, maybe less, and he was gone. How could he be gone so quickly? I would have to tell Rain, tell Gabriel, and they'd be devastated—he'd tried to save me and he'd died, and it was my fault because I'd told Farrell Dean about the tunnel. It was all my fault.

I was cold and the wind was chilly but sweat broke on my forehead, and it wasn't only from the pain in my ankle. Branches whipped my face as the wind increased, a strange tense pressure building in my head, in my ears. The sky was growling, black and malevolent, growling and spitting. It looked like the world was ending, and mine was. Everyone I loved was gone.

Without warning a wild man darted across our path. He ran upright, his naked hairy legs pumping fast. Angel pulled out his gun and raised it and fired as the wild man vanished into the trees and yelped and then the gun was pointed at me, and then we pushed through one last thicket of underbrush and we were on the gritty shifting sand of a beach giving way to a cliff, the sea roiling and churning below.

Then I realized where we were. It was the promontory where I'd run from Angel, where I'd gone down the rigged ladder to Sir Tom's hidden boat. Now the sea was wild and high, clawing at the rocks as if trying to climb the cliff and claim me where I stood.

Angel half-pulled, half-shoved me toward the cliff. There was a sudden flash of light, turning the sky above the sea a strange greenish color, and at the same instant thunder cracked deafeningly, and I thought we'd been hit by lightning but then it was dark and I was at the edge of the cliff, Angel's gun trained on me, and lightning flashed again.

Behind Angel the beach was bare and grim, the sand eddying eerily in the wind, something moving in the dark trees, but nothing was there, only the evergreens shifting and swaying in the wind, dark in the coming storm, casting strange shadows in the greenish flickering thundering light.

Angel gestured with the gun. He was hurt, he was angry, and standing there on the bare cliff, the wind lifting his silvery blond hair, he looked every bit as otherworldly as I'd ever imagined the Guardians to be.

"Down," he said. "Get to the boat."

But the ladder was rigged—was it every fourth rung, or every third that was loose? And how could Angel climb with one arm, with a hurt leg? Neither one of us could climb, and

I'd seen the sharp rocks below, the teeth that rose up from the sea, and I couldn't swim.

"We'll fall," I said. "We'll die."

His eyes were cold. "We'll die on the rocks, in the sea, in front of your father if we make it that far. It doesn't matter."

Lightning cracked across the sky, so loud and so bright that for a moment I thought I'd been shot, and then I thought this was how it would end, lightning would flash as I went down that rigged ladder and I'd flinch and then I'd fall and the churning sea would sweep me away and my family would never find me, would never know whether I lived or died, unless they were already dead and we knew each other there.

Then at the corner of my vision I saw something that wasn't a shadow.

Carefully I kept my eyes fixed on Angel's, didn't look again, though not looking felt like the hardest thing I'd ever done, harder by far than forcing myself to put weight on my ankle and move toward the ladder. My vision flickered in and out, threatening to go black with pain or shock, but I managed to get to the edge of the cliff. Getting a good grip on the ropes I lowered myself down, putting all my weight on my good foot.

Angel moved closer, tucking the gun into his waistband, ready to follow me. Lightning crackled again and a strange metallic smell filled the air, a cold smell, and I pushed away the thought of lightning hitting the sea and rushing out to electrocute all the creatures there, electrocuting me if I fell into the rushing grasping waves.

I eased down one rung, two. Which rung was loose?

I couldn't remember, was afraid to step, was afraid for another reason too—Angel was very close now and as soon as I took another step he'd turn to start down the ladder after me, and when he turned he'd see someone behind him, and though he was hurt he was Angel, he was a killer, and so I stood frozen on the shifting rope ladder, staring up at him, afraid to move.

"Go," he said, but then a shadow appeared behind him and I gripped the ropes with every ounce of strength I had because now Angel was staggering at the very brink, leaning precariously over me, about to fall.

But he didn't fall. He twisted to face Farrell Dean—I blinked, looked again, it really was Farrell Dean or his ghost or his soul—but Angel reached out with his right arm, his good arm, and grabbed Farrell Dean's shirt and they staggered sideways and then they were on the ground, level with the top of my head, rolling and kicking, and Angel's gun skittered away over the rocks, out of his reach, out of mine, and I tried to climb back up onto the cliff but the rung collapsed underneath me, almost sent me plunging down, and for a moment all I could do was hold onto the ropes.

Angel was on top of Farrell Dean, his useless arm dangling, and he reached with his good arm and grabbed his useless arm by the wrist, pressing it down across Farrell Dean's throat, putting his full weight on it, but Farrell Dean's hands were up, holding Angel off, and I couldn't see his face, could only see the top of his head, his fingers digging into Angel's arm as he braced and pushed, the cords in his arms standing out, muscles straining against the bulk of the bigger man.

I had gathered myself and was pulling myself back up onto the edge when Farrell Dean reached up with both hands and gouged at Angel's eyes and twisted beneath him and suddenly Angel went crashing off. He rolled back up, to his feet, but Farrell Dean hooked a foot around his ankle and Angel swayed backward, flailing his arms, balanced on the edge of the cliff. He was falling—he wasn't falling—he caught his balance and Farrell Dean was still struggling to his feet. And then I remembered.

I dug in my pocket and, flinging myself up and forward

as hard as I could, I slammed the stunner I'd taken from the blonde warden against Angel's leg.

And Angel fell. He fell with a strange slowness, turning toward the sea as he leaned into the open air, and his eyes went wide at the sight of the churning waves, and then he was gone and there was only the malevolent green flickering light, and then that too was gone and there was only darkness and the hungry gray sea. And I was falling too, sliding, grabbing for the edge of the cliff, my fingers clawing uselessly through the thin dirt on the rocks.

I looked down and in another brilliant flash saw the water pulling Angel out, rushing him away, and I couldn't tell if he was moving or if it was the sea shifting dead limbs. The image of my own body following his out to sea flashed across my mind—my grip was giving way—and then a hand closed around my wrist and I looked up and saw the black ferocious sky.

Then the sky opened and sheets of rain fell and thunder roared, and Farrell Dean lifted me up and stood me on my feet and put an arm around me, supporting my weight, and together we ran toward the shelter of the trees, away from the driving wind and the pelting rain, the rocks and the waves and the thrashing hungry sea, and Angel in the depths.

Chapter 17

I shivered, leaning closer to the fire Farrell Dean was building beneath the crevice he said would draw the smoke upward. Sir Tom's cave was on the sea but its cove was sheltered by the angle of the surrounding cliffs, and though the rain fell and the wind blew and the thunder cracked, inside the cave was dry.

We were alone there—where the others had gone, I didn't know. I couldn't even remember how long it had been since I'd seen them crowded in the small space, exclaiming because Fiona looked like me and Will looked like Louie, while Michael Alleyn tended Joe's injury, and Earl announced that the cave was crowded but would do for a few hours. When had that been? Last night? Surely it was longer ago than that.

And now they were dead, so many of them, or they could be and I didn't know for sure, didn't know anything except that it was too much, it had all been too much, and my teeth began to chatter with the force of my shivering.

Farrell Dean put one more piece of wood on the fire, then sat down beside me and put his arm around my shoulders, twining the fingers of his other hand in mine.

"It'll warm up soon," he said, but I wasn't trembling from the wet and cold. I was sitting so I could keep an eye on the door, the opening toward the sea, and I looked toward it now, seeing nothing but blackness and driving rain.

"He's dead," Farrell Dean said. "He's bound to be dead."

"He's a good swimmer."

"No one could swim in that sea."

Again I saw it churning, wrapping in frothy tentacles around Angel's body, tumbling him this way and that amidst the intermittent flashes of green lightning.

"The water's moving fast," Farrell Dean said. "Even if he survived the fall, he's already been pulled beyond this inlet. There's no way he could swim against that current."

I changed the subject. "Earl's dead," I said.

"I know. I saw him." Farrell Dean's voice was grim.

"I thought you were dead. I thought you were blown up in the tunnel."

He shifted so he could look down into my face. "Jensen couldn't remember the code and I couldn't disable the lock, not mechanically or electronically, so I left, and then there was one explosion and then another. And then I found Gabriel and Rain, and they said Angel had taken you and that Earl had gone to try to get you back."

"I thought you were dead," I said again, very quietly. "Everyone at the stockade could be dead, and everyone in the Watcher compound."

Farrell Dean's fingers tightened on mine. "We won't know until we know," he said. "At the stockade, a lot of people were upstairs, away from the tunnel entrance. Only Jensen was still downstairs when I left. He wouldn't quit trying. He was upset—he knew he ought to know how to open it."

"Maybe he finally did get it," I said. "Maybe he opened the door and that set it off."

Maybe the poor man had succeeded, had felt like his old self, if only for a heartbeat.

But Farrell Dean shook his head. "No," he said. "It started at the other end. There was an explosion farther away that came toward us, and then there was a smaller explosion closer to the stockade. Meritt must have cracked the code on the compound end and tried to come through that way."

"But why would he do that? He knew that tunnel was dangerous. He told me so."

"Maybe he thought he'd disabled the explosives," Farrell Dean said.

"Or maybe he was desperate."

Tears began to roll down my cheeks again, and I didn't bother to wipe them away. What was happening in there, that he had to try the tunnel?

We sat and stared at the fire, flickering warm and bright on the walls of the cave, on our faces.

After a little while Farrell Dean let go of my hand and brushed the tears from my face. "I thought I'd have to tell your father that you and Fiona were on this island," he said. "Funny thing was, Eric Alleyn thought he was going to have to tell me the same thing. When Cline and I got to the stockade he met us at the door, apologizing for not listening to me on the beach in Locria. I didn't want to leave you there, Red. I knew you needed to come back."

"But how did Papa know I was here?"

"My mother got worried and herded everybody here back to the stockade. Shawna and Joe and Will Bright. They thought the rest of us ought to be told what was going on with you, and about the others going in after you. It was too late to stop us from setting the explosions in the city, though. We were already gone by the time they got to the stockade."

"So they were all at the stockade when the tunnel blew, too. Your mother was there."

"They're probably all fine," Farrell Dean said again. "They were upstairs, away from the tunnel. And that was a smaller explosion than the other, and I don't think it blew directly under the stockade. It was closer to the city than that. But Jensen … I don't know. He was right there."

I shivered and leaned closer against Farrell Dean.

"Does Papa know about Michael Alleyn?" I asked.

"I don't know. Everything was a rush. How did you find Michael Alleyn?"

Haltingly, I told him. It took awhile, and the cave grew gradually warmer, and my clothes began steaming gently in the heat. Outside the storm blew on, the rain easing up now and again only to start with new force a moment later. I had never known a storm to fight this furiously, to blow so long. It sounded as if the wind were trying to rip the island out of the sea.

"They were going to kill me at six o'clock," I said. "If Michael and Fiona hadn't done what they did, the Watchers would have made Meritt shoot me."

"He wouldn't have done it."

I looked up, searching his eyes. "It would be better to sacrifice a pawn than lose a knight and a pawn both," I said. "And Meritt always plays to win."

"You're not a pawn. And losing you wouldn't be winning. Not for Meritt."

There was no point in speculating about what Meritt might have done, so we sat in silence, listening to the wind, staring at the fire. My clothes began to dry on my body, sticking to my skin, and my ankle was throbbing. I examined it gingerly, touching the swelling that didn't look as bad as it felt.

"I wish we had some ice for that," Farrell Dean said, gently disentangling himself from me. He got up and poked the fire with a stick and added another log, then handed me another ladle of water from Sir Tom's bucket. "Do you want something to eat?" he said.

I shook my head.

"Then come lie down. You should try to rest. We'll head back to the stockade as soon as this storm lets up."

I had no idea what time it was. Three in the morning? Four? I felt as if I hadn't slept in years, as if I might have forgotten how.

I got to my feet, a little stiffly, and Farrell Dean helped me limp over to Sir Tom's pallet bed. Then he pulled the covers over me and sat down on the edge.

"Looks like you're going to have a black eye," he said, studying the side of my face. For the first time I realized how awful I must look, and I turned away from him, toward the darkness at the back of the cave.

"Hey," he said, touching my chin with his fingertips, gently turning me toward him. "Come back here."

I took a deep breath and held it. Farrell Dean stroked my hair back from my face. I let out the air I was holding, and breathed in again, and focused on doing that again, and then again, and then again.

One breath at a time. I could do that.

I could breathe, and each breath would carry me one tiny step away from the light going out of Earl's eyes, from the scarred warden coming at me, from the gush of warm blood, from the explosions rocking the city and the ground at my feet, destroying too much, too many.

I breathed. I focused on the light from the flames playing on the cave wall, on the feel of Farrell Dean's hand on my hair, of my own breath and heartbeat.

After a few minutes Farrell Dean bent and kissed me lightly on the forehead.

"Sleep well," he said, and began to get to his feet.

Everything came rushing back at me, the sound of the bones in Earl's face cracking, the rush of wind as Angel fell past me, the shuddering earth that killed Meritt and Fiona and who knew who else.

I looked at Farrell Dean, hoping to borrow some courage or some calm, but as he turned to go, his gaze ran over my face once more and his expression shifted, went grim and hard and distant, and another thought struck me. A dark thought, and just possibly a true one. Because—

Before he could move away, I reached out and caught hold of his sleeve.

"It wasn't—" I stopped.

I couldn't say it, and I couldn't meet his eyes. I didn't want to look at him and see that expression, the same one he'd worn in the wasteland when I was trying to tell him I loved him.

"Wasn't what?"

I shrugged, embarrassed to spell it out. Farrell Dean was such a decent person—that was the troubling thought that had hit me. He wouldn't want to humiliate me in front of other people. He'd go along with me when I made my declaration, and he'd save my life and comfort me, and then later, when I was steadier—when the world wasn't falling apart around me, when I could cope with being alone—then he would quietly let me know he'd changed his mind.

"Wasn't what, Red?"

I looked at the sleeve of his Optica-gray shirt, wadded up in my fist. "It wasn't just me, was it, out there in the wasteland? It wasn't just me who chose?"

There was a long silence. In it I saw a future begin to take shape, gray and empty.

I had waited too long.

I had shown myself to be less than he'd thought.

I had gone into the city after Meritt. I had doubted Farrell Dean's integrity. I had been stupid and reckless and blind, and I had endangered other people, and because of me they had died.

I had lost him.

Then Farrell Dean gave a short incredulous laugh. "You've got to be kidding," he said.

I looked up at him. "You were mad at me. Because I went into the city to find Meritt. You were mad."

Farrell Dean's expression darkened. "Yeah, I was mad at you. With good reason. But that doesn't change anything."

"You had this look on your face—in the wasteland and just now, too. You looked—" I hesitated, but it was true and I might as well say so. "You looked like you didn't like what you saw."

That same hard look crossed his face again. "Of course I didn't," he said, and reached out to touch my cheek. "I saw what he had done to you. That warden. Was it the one with the scar?"

I nodded.

"I want to kill him." The calmness of Farrell Dean's voice raised goosebumps on my arms.

"I think he might already be dead," I said.

"Doesn't matter. I still want to kill him." Farrell Dean's gaze went remote. "I want to hurt him for hurting you. I want to make sure he can never touch you like that again. You or anyone else."

"Oh." I didn't want to talk about the scarred warden. "Well, I didn't know that's what you were thinking about," I said. "I thought maybe you didn't want to embarrass me in front of Gabriel and Cline. I thought ..." His sleeve was still in my hand. I let go of it, smoothed it out.

"Red." He waited until I looked at him. "Some things bear worrying about," he said, and his hazel eyes were steady. "This? Never. I chose you, and you're going to stay chosen."

Maybe I still felt the need to justify my worry, or maybe I wanted to clear up every tiny little question. "Even back in Locria you were acting odd," I said. "You barely said goodbye to me when Gabriel and I left."

Farrell Dean looked blank.

"Gabriel said it was because I kept going on about getting to talk to Meritt on the transmitter."

A shadow crossed Farrell Dean's face and I knew he was thinking of Meritt and the tunnel. But he pushed his thoughts back to the sandy Locrian beach, to the day when he and Mal were working on the engine and I was getting crossways with everyone.

"You were excited that the transmitter worked," he said. "I got that. I understood. But I'll admit it wasn't much fun listening to you go on about Meritt."

"I always go on about Meritt. I've done it all my life."

Farrell Dean's expression turned wry. "Yeah, but that particular time you had just told me in no uncertain terms to back off."

I remembered the kiss on the road to Doria. His birthday kiss. "That wasn't all I told you."

"I know. That made it worse."

"So you acted like a stranger."

"No, just like a normal human being who wasn't madly in love with you."

"I didn't like it."

"Good. I don't like pretending," he said, and smiled at me. "I love you, and I always will."

By then there were no shadows in his face, nothing dark or frightening. He looked like his old familiar steady self, and I lay back against the pillow, overcome by a wave of relief and exhaustion.

"I can tell you when it happened," I said. "Or at least when I realized it. When the Watchers were interrogating me, just before they decided to kill me, that's when I realized I loved you."

He was tired and no doubt as worried as I was, but a glint in his eye told me he was about to say something teasing. "Watchers, wardens, interrogations," he said. "It doesn't get much more romantic than that."

I shoved him gently. "They wanted to know why I was a traitor, why I left the island with you, and I didn't want to hurt Meritt by telling him you didn't trust him. So I was going to tell them it was because I loved you, but then I couldn't say it because it was true. It might even have been true back when we left Optica—I'm not sure anymore. I think I've loved you longer than I knew."

I couldn't read the expression in Farrell Dean's eyes.

"Anyway, it was private. It was mine, yours and mine, and I didn't want to use it to try to trick the Watchers. So I didn't say it. But they saw it anyway, and they taunted Meritt about it. About us. And then I told them you were dead, so they wouldn't go looking for you. And the Voice crossed you out of his book." My voice grew thin on the last words.

"Anyway that's when I realized," I said. "You can ask Cline. He knows."

Farrell Dean raised an eyebrow. "I don't particularly want to be thinking about Cline right now."

The cave was warm and quiet, while outside the storm howled. Farrell Dean leaned down over me and kissed me, and I could hear the pounding of my heart over the rushing of the wind outside the cave, over the crashing of the waves along the shore. I wrapped my arms around his neck and felt his warmth and, just for a moment, I felt safe. I forgot death. I forgot all my mistakes and what they had cost.

Then Farrell Dean moved away.

"Sleep well," he said once more, the firelight flickering on his face, in his eyes. When he stood up, again the room went cold.

"It's safe here," he said. "Angel's gone, but I'll keep watch. Just in case."

I didn't want to tell him that I was more afraid of ghosts

that night than of Angel, afraid of seeing Meritt's face in my dreams, Earl's eyes going vacant, Fiona lying crushed and bloodied in some dark and dirty ruin. I didn't say any of that, but he must have read my expression.

"We'll get through this," he said. "We'll get through this, and then we'll go back to Aislin." He tucked the covers more snugly around me. "Rufus has a job for me, and Mick will help me build a house for you, and then we'll marry the way they do over there, with all our family and friends around us. And afterwards we'll walk home together in the dark, to our home, and there will be two candles burning in the window. And we'll go inside and move the candles together so they make one flame."

"Is that how they do it?"

He nodded.

"I'd like that," I said. "I'd like it very much. It's hard to imagine right now, though."

"Things won't seem as bad after you've rested."

"Some things will."

"Some, but right now we're both imagining the worst about everything, and the worst might not come true. So try to rest. I'll keep watch, I promise. I'll keep you safe."

I watched him as he settled against the wall near the fire, pulling a blanket over his legs.

When his face was turned away, toward the entrance to the cave, I edged the Dream Drops out of my pocket.

Chapter 18

I was standing by the sea. It was a gray windy day, and my hair kept whipping in my face, stinging my eyes. The sand was soft beneath my feet, still warm though winter was coming on. I didn't like coming to the sea in the winter. It wasn't terribly cold, but the gray water stretched out flat and melted into the gray sky, and I couldn't tell where water ended and air began. It was unnerving, and depressing too.

Though I didn't like coming, I would come every day. That's what we did, we Alleyns. We went to the sea every single morning, and there we remembered our dead.

I sat up with a gasp.

"What is it?" Farrell Dean said, half rising.

"Just a dream." I lay back down, making sure I could see him. "I'm fine."

Farrell Dean propped his elbows on his bent knees. The cave looked smaller now. The fire was low and cast warm light in the area closest to it. Outside the rain poured down in a solid sheet.

I waited until thunder rumbled and Farrell Dean, listening, turned away from me. Then I opened the Dream Drop bottle and took another couple of drops.

The firelight and shadows moved hypnotically over the

walls of the cave and I began to grow sleepy again. My ankle still throbbed, but my ears had stopped ringing, and the absence of the sound was comforting. In the darkness Tor put an arm around me and pulled me close, and I rested my head against his shoulder and let my eyes close. I was tired, so tired.

After a moment I forced myself to open my eyes, although I knew that when I opened them I'd see only the dark. Moving carefully, groping my way, I found his forehead again. He still feels warm, too warm, but at least he's alive. I had thought at first that he was dead.

That's why I can't let myself sleep. If I sleep, Meritt might slip away.

I saw the look in his eyes when my grandfather and I stood before the Watchers. I recognized Meritt and I saw him recognize me—or my sister, rather. His gray eyes flashed with joy, then darkened as he wondered what my presence there meant. Of course I couldn't talk to him, not then. And once we started to leave, everything fell all to pieces. Rain and Earl weren't where we'd left them, and then the Watchers came pouring out of their room, and the one with the big voice was asking questions, and Grandpa was angry and he was scaring me, and I was thinking that was what his brother was like, this was what Grandpa had been hiding from all of those years, and then Tor came rushing in and the building shook and everyone was screaming.

And then we couldn't leave, even if they would have let us. We all came down to the lower level for safety, in case there were more explosions, all of us down here together, Tor and Grandpa and me, and the Watchers, and Meritt, and some of the old people.

Meritt didn't speak to me then, and I couldn't speak to him in front of the Watchers—I can't imitate Red's voice—but the entire time, Meritt knew exactly where I was. His eyes seeking me out were the last thing I saw before the last explosion, when the roof came down.

He is an enchanter, no doubt, and a powerful one—I felt it when he looked at me—but he isn't indifferent to my sister. I see the way he watches me, thinking I am her. I was annoyed at first, because my sister needs Farrell Dean, not some flighty charmer. Now, though, I think I'm glad. My sister hasn't been played for a fool, which means she has good sense, which surely means she'll have the sense to choose rightly. And she would grieve if Meritt died, and I want to spare her that, and I can't help but want to spare Meritt too, now that I've met him.

So I have to stay awake. I have to do all I can to keep Meritt on this side of the threshold. He mistook me for Red when he was awake, and asleep, unconscious, he will as well. Only my attention—Red's attention—is holding him here.

In the darkness Grandpa speaks. "We've lost another."

"The woman who was bleeding so badly?" I ask.

"That would be Cheryl," Louie says. A disappointed sigh goes around the dark space, and a few old voices murmur sadly. Beneath my hand, Meritt moves.

"May I have the flashlight?" I say.

Tor hands me the light and I flick it on, shine it in Meritt's face. He is still unconscious, but his eyelids are flickering—a good sign maybe.

Maybe the shadows cast by the small light make his injuries look worse than they are. The side of his head is matted with blood. Grandpa tied the sleeve of Tor's shirt around it as a makeshift bandage, but it isn't thick enough and blood is seeping through. Dark bruises are forming beneath his eyes and his cheek has a long gash. We couldn't bandage that, but I held the hem of my shirt against it for a long time, until it finally stopped bleeding. Now it is crusted with dried blood. All in all, he looks horrible.

"Better not waste light, Fiona," Tor says, and I flick the flashlight off again.

Meritt moves again, more than before.

"Red," he mutters, and then again, louder. "Red!"

I don't want to upset him or confuse him, so I try to sound like her. "I'm here," I say.

What does she do, to make her tone level but still lively? Whenever I try I sound flat, monotone. Not like her.

Maybe he won't notice.

"It's all right, Meritt," I say. "You're going to be all right."

"I can't see," he says. "Are you dead? Am I?"

"Don't be silly." I try to put a smile in my voice. "It's dark in here, and we're trapped, but we're fine."

That is stretching matters, but I want to be encouraging.

Louie must have the same thought. Or is it Will? I am so confused. "Hang in there, Meritt," he says. "Sooner or later somebody will dig us out."

I think of my father, digging for Red in the pasture. I hope she's safe. Tor said Farrell Dean and Gabriel were going after her. They're capable men. Surely they've gotten her out of the prison, out of the city, safely back to the stockade. Tor said they would.

"They won't give up," Tor says now. "They'll get us out."

Meritt stirs again. "Who is that?" he says. "I don't know that voice."

I don't want to try to explain Tor, not now when Meritt is already agitated, confused, when it is dark and bound to be frightening for him.

"He's a friend," I say. "How does your leg feel?"

"It hurts." He shifts. "I don't think it's broken, though."

"That's good," I say. "We weren't sure. We didn't want to move you too much."

For a long time he doesn't answer. I begin to wonder whether he's passed out again. Are his eyes open? I feel for his face. If his eyes are open will that mean he's conscious, or could he be unconscious with his eyes wide open? That would be unsettling, though maybe not so unsettling here in the dark where I can't see him staring, blank eyed, at the darkness. And of course I could shut his eyes. Would they stay shut? People put coins on the eyes of the dead to keep their eyes closed. Even if I had coins, I wouldn't put them on Meritt's eyes, not if he is alive. That would surely be bad luck.

But he isn't unconscious. He reaches up and catches my wrist.

"Red?" he says.

"I'm here. I was trying to tell if you'd fainted. Sorry if I disturbed you."

"You sound funny."

"Getting blown up will do that to you."

He breathes a laugh that ends with something close to a sob, and then goes still. After a few minutes his breathing grows even. I hope he is asleep, and not unconscious, but I don't try to feel his face again to see.

Tor speaks quietly. "You'd better rest now," he says. "No telling how long it'll take them to find us. I'll stay awake, and if Meritt needs you I'll wake you."

"Promise?"

Tor kisses my cheek. "Promise."

"All right then."

Then I reach in my pocket and find the tiny bottle I stole from the Dream Recorder's house, after she tried to kill my memories.

I woke with a start, disoriented, my heart pounding.

Meritt was alive. He was alive, and Fiona too.

The cave was as dark as my dream, save for the faintly flickering embers of our fire. Outside the storm still raged, sending a small rivulet of water trickling across the floor. Farrell Dean was a dark shape propped against the wall. His face was turned away from me, toward the opening, but he was awake. I could tell by the set of his head that he was doing just what he'd said, watching, standing guard.

My limbs felt heavy as I moved to sit up, to tell him the news. But then he turned, reaching to put another log on the fire, and as it flamed up I saw his face.

I'd never seen him like this, oblivious to me, unguarded. This was the man I had chosen.

Somehow that finality made him seem less familiar. Or maybe it was because he had been different tonight, earlier, when he was angry. He hadn't seemed like himself. There were things I didn't know about him—some things I knew I didn't know, and other things that I thought I knew but didn't. Things that would surprise me. And there was no telling what might happen to us.

A life was a long time.

The flickering firelight cast unfamiliar shadows on his face, and his thoughts were far away. He looked serious, pensive. Then, suddenly, he smiled—just a small smile, a half smile—and I knew him once again. This was Farrell Dean. I might not know everything about him, but I knew the important things, and we would be okay. He would make sure we were okay.

Still, I didn't want to break into his reverie, especially not with Meritt's name, and besides I felt so sleepy, and he had told me to sleep. Surely I could let him have a little peace, and there was nothing we could do until the terrible storm passed, the woods, in the dark, in the storm.

The new log shifted and Farrell Dean nudged it back into place with his boot, making sparks rise. He was still wearing Aislin clothes. We would go back to Aislin and make a life there. We would have children and they would play with

Fiona and Tor's children, and they would know who they were, whose they were. We would make a good life.

"I'm not an idiot," Meritt says. "Tell me what's going on."

"Nothing's going on," I say soothingly. "You're imagining things."

"No, I'm not. Who is he? I don't know his voice. What is he to you? Why are you acting strange?"

Tor clears his throat. "My name is Tor Van Stavern," he says. "I'm her betrothed. She isn't who you think she is."

"Apparently not," Meritt says.

"We'll be all right," I whisper to Tor. "I might not know all the details of you, but I know you. Sometimes I think I know you better than I know myself."

Tor clears his throat again. He always does when he's uneasy.

"See?" I say. "I know why you clear your throat."

"Of course you know me," Tor says. "You've known me all your life. But why are you talking about this now?"

Meritt moves in the dark. "She isn't talking to you," he says. "She's confused. She's really talking to me. Whoever you are, she's only just met you. I'm the one she's known forever."

"Red has known you forever," Tor clarifies.

"That's what I said."

"Yes, well—" Tor stops because I elbow him. I don't want him to upset Meritt by telling him I'm not Red.

"Well, what?" Meritt says.

Tor has to come up with something to say. "Red has known you all her life, but she's also known Farrell Dean all her life."

I start to laugh.

"What?" Tor says.

"You're standing up for Farrell Dean? You don't even like him."

"I do like him."

"You don't act like you do."

"I do, but— it's confusing, that's all. He looks at her, and then I think what if he gets mixed up and looks at you that way, and—I'll get used to it, I suppose. Eventually."

"What does Farrell Dean have to do with anything?" Meritt says, sounding testy. "Red has spent more time with me than with him. She's spent more time with me than anyone else."

I have an answer for that. "Farrell Dean is keeping watch. He always will."

It sounds rather random, once I've said it. I can't see, not in the dark, but I feel Tor turn towards me in surprise.

"What do you mean?" Meritt sounds unnerved. "I thought you were lying to the Watchers. You mean he's really dead?"

"No," I say patiently. "He's not dead. He's keeping watch beside a fire, because he knows it comforts me."

Tor speaks. "Did you take Dream Drops?"

"Dream Drops?" Meritt echoes. "What are they? And did you take them?"

I nod. Nobody can see me. I'm certain I am awake. Aren't I? Time is standing still in this dust-filled darkness. How long have we been here? An hour? A day? I don't know. All I know is that it's dark, so dark I can't see my own hand if I hold it up before my face, but I can see firelight flickering in Farrell Dean's hair, tracing his cheek with warm fingers. His eyes are far away.

I want to look around, figure out where he is, who else is there, but my eyes stay stubbornly on the boy beside the fire. I can't tear them away. I want to touch him. I want to tell him Meritt is alive, but I won't do that, not yet. I love him, and he is weary and lost in thought, and I will let him think in peace because I love him.

"No," I protest, too loudly. "I love Tor."

Meritt gives an unhappy laugh. "This is crazy," he says. "Maybe I am dead after all."

"You're not dead," Grandpa says, and Meritt tries, unsuccessfully, to sit up.

"You be quiet," he said, and there is a note I don't like in his voice. "I know who you are. You shouldn't be here. You should be dead—this is your fault, all of it—"

"Shhhh," I say. "He isn't who you think he is."

"He's exactly who I think he is, and so are you! You're Red, and you love me, and this isn't a good time to change your mind about that, not if I'm going to get you out of this alive!"

There is a long silence. I can't answer him—I am gazing at Farrell Dean—and nobody else says anything either, which is good because Meritt going over the edge isn't going to solve anything for anyone in this tiny space. "Hysteria uses up too much oxygen," I say. "The fire uses oxygen, too, but Farrell Dean isn't unconscious. He's thinking."

Then Tor speaks. "You did, didn't you? You took Dream Drops. Is that what this is about?"

"I took some, but they can't be working because I'm not asleep," I say. "I haven't been asleep. And it's dark but I can see him. I can see Farrell Dean."

"How many did you take?" Tor says. "You're only supposed to take three, max. And you're small. You probably should only take two. Or one. How many did you take?"

"I don't know. It's dark, Tor. I was guessing."

"What do you mean you can see Farrell Dean?" Meritt says. He is trying to sit up again, and I feel him wince and catch his breath sharply.

"Dream Drops are controlled substances," Tor says. "They're toxic in high doses. You can't slug them down like water."

"Too late."

"What are you talking about? What are Dream Drops?" Meritt's voice changes. "Red, are you hurt? Did you get hit on the head? Hey, you—Tor—is she hurt?"

"Don't shout," Tor says, though he is talking every bit as loudly as Meritt. "She's fine. I hope. Fiona, I'm going to kill you if you die. What would I do without you? Don't take any more. Don't ever take any more."

"Who's Fiona?" Meritt says. "What's going on? Red—talk to me—"

"Be quiet," Tor says. "And please stay calm. I know this is very confusing. It has to do with biological anomalies, with an embryo splitting shortly after fertilization. Eight to twelve days after, to be exact."

"I don't want a biology lesson. I want to know why you're calling Red Fiona."

"If you'll stop interrupting me, I'll explain."

"I'm going to keep right on interrupting until you start making sense."

The air felt stuffy—or maybe it was the ruins where Fiona was trapped—but in any case, I felt as if I could hardly breathe. My chest felt too full, as if two of me were struggling for space inside.

I sat up and swung my legs off the bed, and cautiously put a little weight on my ankle. It held, and hurt less than I expected, so I limped across the cave. Farrell Dean watched me, saying nothing.

The storm seemed to finally be blowing itself out. The wind was high, but the stars were shining brightly.

I scanned my surroundings and then edged around the sheltering face of the nearest boulder. The sea was rippling with still-choppy waves. The wind was cold. I took deep breaths of the damp salty air, but it didn't clear my head.

The moon had long set but in the starlight I could see the dark forms of shells and fish and twisted driftwood, tossed high up on the shore by the violence of the wind and water. I didn't see anything large enough to be a body, but the starlight wasn't bright and I couldn't see far.

It would still be very dark in the woods, under the canopy of the trees, and the wind still rose and slashed, in between moments when it dropped and lay silent. We couldn't leave yet, I thought, but I wasn't sure, and then I realized Farrell Dean would tell me when it was time to go. I didn't have to figure that out myself.

I went back into the cave.

Once again Farrell Dean said nothing. He was hoping I would sleep some more, I thought; he was trying not to stir me fully awake.

How much time had passed since I had seen Meritt and Fiona and Tor in my mind's eye? I felt like I ought to be able to sort out the answer to that question, but my head felt full of mist. What if it had been a long time ago, and they were dead now?

There was only one way to find out—

I sat on the bed and, turning away from Farrell Dean, took another dose of Dream Drops. Then I waited to find out whether my sister was all right, whether Meritt was alive. It was convenient, being able to check in on them.

But sleep didn't come again. I had too much to think about. So I lay there wakefully, waiting for the stars to fade and the morning light to come. Surely it couldn't be much longer.

It wasn't long. The blackness outside thinned, and when it became gray, Farrell Dean stood up. I knew I'd been waiting anxiously to talk to him, but now my mind felt sluggish, and I couldn't quite remember what the rush had been.

He went outside. Pretty soon he came back holding two

fish. "The storm sent us breakfast," he said. "It won't take me long to clean them."

When Farrell Dean went back outside to clean the fish, I was alone in the cave. I followed him out. The air felt colder now than it had earlier, and the chill cleared my head.

"Fiona's alive," I said. "Meritt is, too."

Farrell Dean looked up with a start. I tried my best to explain about the Dream Drops and the ruined building, but Farrell Dean kept looking perplexed and asking questions, so I must not have been being very clear. "Michael Alleyn is doing his best," I said finally, "but he doesn't have anything to work with. No bandages, no medicine. So we need to hurry."

"You're right," Farrell Dean began, but without meaning to I interrupted him.

"I don't know why I keep calling him Michael Alleyn," I said, and my voice came out with Fiona's cadences. "It sounds a little rude, to call my Grandpa by his full name, as if he were a stranger."

Now Farrell Dean looked concerned. "How many Dream Drops did you take?" he said.

I shrugged.

"You'd better eat something and then we'll get going," he said, moving quickly. "It's almost light enough for us to be able to see in the woods."

He cooked the fish over the fire in the cave while I examined the cans stacked against the wall.

Peaches, spinach, lima beans, applesauce, corn and something called spaghettios.

As I studied the cans, my heart stuttered. I shut my eyes and held my breath.

"I talked him into it," Meritt says.

He is sitting up now, leaning toward me.

"I couldn't let him pair you with anybody else, not the way Angel talked about you. Nobody else would know the danger you were in, all the time, day and night. So I talked Rafe into partnering you with me."

Beside me, Tor sighs again. No matter how many times he explains that I am Red's twin sister, Meritt keeps talking to me as if I am Red. I don't know a lot about head injuries, but that doesn't strike me as a good sign. At least he isn't dizzy anymore; he can sit upright without falling over every few seconds.

"And it made Angel happy," Meritt says. "You're ours and nobody else's, so he told me to be sure to get you. It's best to keep him happy if I can, and I thought that maybe if I loved you, if he knew I loved you, he wouldn't hurt you. Maybe I was wrong. Maybe it made him hate you more. I don't know. I've thought and thought about it, and I can't sort out whether I helped or made things worse."

Tor reaches over and takes my hand. It is so odd, sitting here in the dark listening to Meritt talk to me as if I am my sister.

"Is he delusional?" I say, opening my eyes.

Farrell Dean shoots me a look.

The cave is big and open, spacious even, compared to the ruins. "This cave is cavernous," I say. "Am I delusional?"

"Sounds like it to me," Tor says, shifting in the darkness. "And he's probably feverish."

"Isn't there anything we can do?"

From somewhere in the darkness Louie says, "We can hope they find us soon."

"We can go," Farrell Dean says. "As soon as you eat something." And in fact I am ravenous, and have every right to be. I haven't eaten since … I can't remember when. No wonder I'm not thinking clearly. And maybe taking Dream Drops on an empty stomach wasn't a good idea.

Farrell Dean holds out a piece of fish, his face concerned, and I see years and years of moments like this layered together, one on top of another, all those times he's looked after me and I've taken his concern for granted while I longed for Meritt, who was mysterious and beautiful and un-reachable, who loved me or only pretended to, who was feverish and injured and had no water.

"Meritt's very ill," I say. "But Papa will dig us out."

"Let me have the Dream Drops," Farrell Dean says, and I take out the little bottle and hand it to Tor, who puts it in his pocket.

"The sun is rising," I tell Tor. "I can smell fish cooking. I can hear the sea. It's going to be a beautiful day."

"I can't believe you did this," Tor says. "What on earth were you thinking?"

"I was thinking about my sister. She's alive, Tor. She's alive and she's not in the prison. She's thinking about Farrell Dean and breakfast and the blood on Meritt's head and I'm thinking about light. It's dark in here but I can see firelight, and beyond it morning has come."

Meritt laughs. "My mother was crazy," he says. "No wonder I always liked you."

"Stop that," Tor says. "She isn't crazy. She's been trying to save your life. Both of them have. The least you can do is show a little respect."

"Tor says Meritt should show a little respect," I tell Farrell Dean. "He says I'm not crazy."

His look sharpens. "Red, listen to me. Ask Tor where exactly they are."

"Where are we?"

"What do you mean?" Tor sounds tense. "You know where we are."

"But Farrell Dean wants to know."

There is a long silence.

"We're in the basement on the north-east corner of the Watcher compound," Tor says, speaking very slowly and clearly. "When the explosions started some people went outside to see what was happening, and some came downstairs to a protected area where there was supposed to be a secret exit. Meritt came downstairs so we followed, but there were more explosions and it all fell in on us. There's a cavity about twenty by twenty. I don't know how much debris is on top of us, but air's getting in from somewhere. It's stuffy, and we don't have any water, but we can breathe. Say it, Fiona. You too, Red. Say it out loud so Farrell Dean can hear you."

I repeat his words out loud, hearing my sister's voice echoing obediently in my head. Or maybe she is speaking and I am echoing her.

Farrell Dean leans closer. "Ask how many of them are trapped in there."

"How many are you?"

Again Tor speaks very clearly. "There are eight of us alive. A couple of others didn't make it."

"Is Marta dead?"

Meritt speaks. "How do you know Marta, if you aren't from this island?"

"Fiona's not exactly herself right now," Tor says.

"Red isn't Red, she's her sister Fiona. And now Fiona's not herself either? Would somebody please tell me what's going on?"

I pat his arm gently, and I can feel the warmth of his body, the fine fabric of his Watcher clothes—much nicer than the coarse ones Red and Farrell Dean wore—than the ones I am wearing—and at the same time I can feel Farrell Dean's hands on my shoulders.

Somewhere in the darkness Tor laughs.

"You aren't going to believe this. Apparently Red's here, in a way. Inside Fiona's head. The two of them have been taking drugs to enhance their connection. Dream Drops. It only works for identical twins."

161

"Earl's dead," I blurt. "Angel killed him."

Startled silence greets the announcement.

Then Meritt says, clearly, "Are you dead? Did my father kill you too?"

"No," I say, taking his hand. "See? I'm alive. I'm moving. You can feel me moving."

He pulls his hand out of my grasp. "Stop it," he says, and then he shouts right in my ear. "Red—can you hear me? Marta's dead. So is Cynda, and so are most of the old people. I lost them."

"You did your very best," I tell him, patting his shoulder. "Now don't worry your head about it anymore. Just rest, and soon Papa and the boys will dig us out."

"Get out of the way," Meritt says roughly. "I don't want to talk to you. I want Red."

"You're out of line," Tor says. "You can't talk to her like that." He is angry, and he is also afraid. "Don't listen to him, Fiona. Don't go. Stay here. I need you, Fiona. Stay with me."

"I killed the Voice," Meritt says. "Red, are you listening? He's gone. He won't be back. You don't have to be afraid of him anymore."

If he says anything else I don't hear it, but I don't need to. I am remembering it happening, feeling it happen. I see Meritt holding open a small door, starting to go through it, but Marta puts a hand on his shoulder and brushes past him. The very old Watcher says something and she pauses deferentially, letting him go in front of her, and the long-faced Watcher squeezes past her as well, and Marta throws a strange complicated look at Meritt as she's pressed against the wall just inside the tunnel, a look that is somehow pleased and reassuring and resigned and brave, all at once.

It is very crowded and very noisy. Louie is spreading out his arms, trying to stop a handful of old people from rushing toward the small door, but some of them get past him and head for the tunnel. They stream around a heavyset man dressed in white, a man with cold malevolent eyes. He had started to go into the tunnel but now has stopped and is looking at me.

His hand comes up and he says something to Michael Alleyn and I can't hear it over the panicked voices but it's obviously something snide, and then he's pointing a gun at me—at *me*—and I don't have my gun—I gave it to Rain—and I have to get out of the way but there's nowhere to go, I'm blocked in by Michael Alleyn and Tor, and I think, "This is it. I'm going to die."

Then the Watcher's gun flashes as Meritt slams into him and the spray of bullets doesn't hit me, not me or anyone else. They hit the ceiling instead and bits of it come crashing down, crumbling all over the people beneath it, and someone screams, and the white dust fills my throat, choking me, so thick I can barely see, but I see the Watcher raise his weapon at me again, and I see Meritt behind him, grabbing the Watcher's head, twisting, feinting one direction, then twisting hard the other.

The Watcher slumps and Meritt looks straight at me through the ghostly shifting dust and his gray eyes are glad and ashamed and relieved and worried and he doesn't know but I know why suddenly he's looking at me with eyes full of confusion, and he takes a few steps toward me and then the world shudders and I'm flung hard to the ground, and everything goes dark.

"Meritt saved my life," I say. "And he lured the Watchers into the tunnel. That's why he stayed—that was his plan all along." I reach for Tor but I can't see. Everything is black, suffocating.

"What did you say?" Farrell Dean says.

I can see Farrell Dean. I can hear Tor and Meritt arguing. I can hear Fiona weeping, and Tor trying to comfort her and, at the same time, make Meritt be quiet. I can feel my heart beating too fast, because it is two hearts, Fiona's and mine, and hadn't our heart been one in the beginning, before it even became a heart, before we divided, became two of us in our mother's womb?

"Red!" Farrell Dean says, and his voice is urgent. "Red, can you hear me?"

"Fiona!" Tor says. Someone is shaking me, patting my face, and at the same time someone is picking me up, carrying me, moving fast.

"Fiona!" Tor says again, sounding so frightened that I grow frightened too.

Then icy sea water splashes over my face, my body, shocking me, waking me, and the only heart I hear is Farrell Dean's pounding beneath his wet shirt.

When I opened my eyes, the sky was the thin watery blue of early morning.

Chapter 19

"Don't think about it," Farrell Dean said, not for the first time. "Don't think about Fiona. Think about this." He gestured at the beach, dark and pockmarked from the heavy rain, strewn with debris from the sea.

"Think about the way the fresh air smells, about how it feels wet and cold and clean. Feel your ankle hurting. Be yourself, Red. Focus on being yourself, on being *here*."

Here was a good place to be. The sun was out and, late in the year though it was, the rays seemed almost warm. As we made our way into the woods they danced on the mossy tree trunks, sparkled on the wet rocks along the path. It was as if the world wanted to apologize for the violent day before, as if it had looked around at the damage it had done and felt ashamed. Branches lay this way and that, and sometimes they were still caught in the trees and came crashing down as we passed. Here and there entire trees had toppled.

We walked slowly because of my ankle. It was much better than I expected, but still a bit sore. Farrell Dean kept a hand on my elbow, and I wasn't sure if it was because he thought I might stumble, or because he was afraid I'd drift back into the cave with Fiona if his hand wasn't holding me to him. I didn't think that would happen. I felt tired and a little sick, but I knew exactly who I was, and where.

We were about halfway back to the stockade when we came across one of the wild men. He was trapped beneath a fallen tree. His hair and beard were matted with blood, and when he saw us, he started crying. He cried the way small children cry, noisily and unselfconsciously, his whole face distorted.

I inched closer to him, trying to see if there was some way to free him, wanting to comfort him.

"Don't get too close," Farrell Dean said. "Let me try to get this thing off of him."

I was sure the trunk was too big to move, but Farrell Dean bent down and did his best, taking care to stay out of the wild man's reach.

The wild man had stopped crying and his eyes followed Farrell Dean. It had been relief at seeing us, I thought; that was what made him cry. But now he was too exhausted, too injured, to keep on. Under the blood and dirt his face was very pale and his skin had a strange waxy cast.

"He's pretty bad off," I told Farrell Dean, and lowered my voice. "I think he might be dying."

"I can't move this thing." Farrell Dean's voice was strained with effort and frustration. "The roots are still partly in the ground so I can't roll it off him."

He came back from around the tree.

"We'll have to go get ropes and an ax," he said. Then, moving so he was in the wild man's direct line of vision, he spoke to him. "Hang in there," he said. "We're going to go get help."

The man's lips moved. "Help," he said faintly.

Farrell Dean stepped closer to the trapped man, leaned over him.

"Be careful," I said, grabbing the back of his shirt. On the ground the wild man looked up at us. His eyes were blue. His breath was coming in shallow gasps, too far apart.

"Can you understand us?" Farrell Dean said. "We're going to get help. We'll get you out."

The man opened his mouth. His lips moved, but no sound came.

"What is it? What do you want to say?"

With effort he shaped words. "Who," he said, and then his face spasmed in pain.

"Who am I? My name is Farrell Dean, and that's Red. We're going to help you."

The man shook his head. "Who …" He tried again. "Who am I?"

Tears flooded my eyes, stinging, blurring the trees, the man trapped at my feet. Impatiently I brushed them away, swallowed against the lump in my throat. The man was still looking fixedly at me.

"I don't know your name," Farrell Dean said. "I'm sorry. But Sir Tom will know."

The man didn't answer. He looked past Farrell Dean, straight at me, his gaze fixed and earnest.

"You were a Guardian," I said. "Do you remember?"

Farrell Dean reached down and felt for the man's pulse. He was shaking his head. "He can't hear you anymore, Red."

The man was dead, but his gaze was still fixed on me as if he were waiting for an answer.

Hot tears blinded me and this time I didn't brush them away. I covered my face with my hands and wept. Farrell Dean put an arm around me but I shrugged him off. I didn't want to be comforted.

"Don't cry," Tor said in the darkness. "We're going to be all right, Fiona. You'll see."

When I looked up again, Farrell Dean was gathering rocks, piling them over the dead man. I helped, hoping rocks would be sufficient to keep the wild animals away.

It took several minutes to cover him up. Finally, silently,

167

we went on, pushing through the damp, fecund woods, losing our way, finding it again, walking through drifts of mist that rose wherever the sun hit the wet cold earth.

We did not find Earl.

When the stockade came into view, we hurried forward. It was still standing. The ground was disturbed on one side of it, torn and tossed, but the building itself seemed scarcely damaged. It was big and official looking, with smooth unclimbable walls slit with rectangular openings near the top.

As we drew near, one of the big doors opened and Sir Tom came hurrying out to greet us, his blue eyes alight. He was leaning on a stick and his leg was bandaged, and so was one arm, but he moved as if his injuries didn't matter.

"Red Girl!" he said. "I feared I'd never see your face again."

Then he nodded formally at Farrell Dean. "Good to see you, son," he said.

Farrell Dean nodded politely, but didn't waste time. "Who was hurt when the tunnel blew?" he said.

Sir Tom's eyes dimmed. "My lieutenant was killed. Jensen."

"I'm so sorry," I began, but Sir Tom shook his head.

"We were all doing the best we knew how, last night. He was the lone fatality. We had a broken bone or two, a few burns, but most everyone is fine."

Farrell Dean hesitated, and I knew he was thinking of Jensen; then he made himself move on. "There are people trapped in the Watcher compound. We know exactly where they are. We need to go get them out."

Sir Tom didn't ask unnecessary questions. "Right you are," he said, pulling a communicator off his belt. "These gizmos weren't working during the storm, but they're fine now."

He pushed a button and handed the transmitter to Farrell Dean. "Tell Rufus," he said. "He's heading up that team. They're digging."

Then Sir Tom looked at me. "Your father's in the city too. He'll be mighty glad to hear one daughter's safe, though I tell you, he'd have made a fine general, that man. When he heard what had happened to his girls, he didn't panic. He set about dividing us up and giving us our orders, clear and logical as could be, and Gabriel had the sense to step back and let him take charge. It kept him busy, you see. Distracted him from worrying. And he's a fine logician.

"So then he deployed us this morning as soon as the storm weakened. Sent one tactical team to the city to disable the remaining wardens and start excavating that compound, and one team to the woods to track down Angel and Earl and you two. Left me here guarding the injured and the elderly."

Farrell Dean finished talking to Rufus and handed the communicator back to Sir Tom.

"I'll let the search team know you're back," Sir Tom said. "Are you heading straight on into the city?"

Farrell Dean nodded. "I am. Red might stay here."

"No. I'm going with you."

Sir Tom tilted his head and looked at me. "Of course you are. Well, it's safe enough at the moment. But once they get the Watchers out, who knows what will happen. So take care."

"The Watchers are dead," I said, faintly surprised that he didn't know. But he couldn't know, of course. Only I knew.

Sir Tom blinked at me, sunlight glinted silver in his cropped hair. "Are they indeed?"

"They went into the tunnel and it blew up. That was Meritt's plan all along."

"And you know this the same way you know exactly where your sister is, I'm guessing."

169

"That's right. I took Dream Drops."

A shadow crossed the old man's face. "Ah. And has your sister taken them too, do you happen to know?"

I nodded. "She took them. That's how she told us where they're trapped."

"Well." He leaned against the stockade wall and studied me soberly for a long moment. I stared back at him curiously, wondering what he was thinking, too tired to ask and pretty sure I didn't want to know.

"Well, what's done is done," he said finally. "No use crying over spilt milk. But I'd think twice before swallowing any more unknown substances, if I were you. Remember this was a preliminary experiment. Long-term effects are just beginning to make themselves known."

Pushing away from the wall, he turned to Farrell Dean. "None of Red Girl's relatives are here, but your mother is. Before you go, I wish you'd take a minute to get inside and relieve her mind. She's tough, but she's still a mother."

Farrell Dean went in while I stayed behind. I was anxious to get moving, and if I went inside there would be too many questions.

And there were things I had to say to the old Guardian in private.

"Sir Tom," I said, and saw the wariness in his eyes when he turned to me. "We think Angel's dead."

The lines in his face deepened as I described what Angel had done to Earl and had tried to do to me, and what we had done to him.

"It was because of Meritt," I concluded, feeling a surprising swell of pity for Angel. "He thought his son was dead. I think it made him want to die too."

Sir Tom ran one hand over the top of his cropped head.

"I'm sorry to hear it," he said. "Sorry to hear all of it. I never trusted young Angel, and I sure never thought he should be here, but I always hoped he'd eventually get a grip and turn himself around."

"There's something else," I said. "One of the—" I thought of Ezzie and didn't want to use the words wild man. "One of the former Guardians has been killed."

I explained what had happened.

Sir Tom's face was grave. "His name was Jake O'Briant," he said, gazing off into the woods. "Before the ashes, he played the harmonica. He liked whiskey and silly jokes. He was a crack shot. He had a sister in Peoria who prayed for his soul every day, bless her stubborn hide."

He cast a sideways glance at me. "That, Red Girl," he said, "Is what is called a eulogy. Yet another crucial element of civilization of which the good barbarians of Optica have been deprived."

"What's Peoria?" I said. "What's prayed?"

But Farrell Dean came back outside before Sir Tom could answer. In the relentless light of early morning exhaustion and tension were written plain on his face.

"How's your ankle?" Farrell Dean said. "Are you sure you can make it to the compound?"

I nodded. "It's not bad at all."

"Then let's get going."

The path from the stockade to the city was narrow, more of a faint trail than a path. The storm seemed to have hit even more viciously here. The ground was muddy, and wet leaves were plastered wildly against rocks and tree trunks, and now and again fallen limbs blocked our way. At least we didn't have to worry about wild men; Ezzie was out again distracting them, Farrell Dean had learned, with Rory for backup, the two of them clearing the way for the people who were out searching the woods.

"I don't like Ezzie doing that," I said. "The wild men are

the reason he was so sick. Why should he have to be the one out there with them?"

"He's the only one who can do that job. And it's important. It let the searchers move more quickly." He hesitated. "They found Earl," he said. "They've already brought him back to the stockade. So everyone is accounted for now, except for Mal. No one's seen him since he told me you were in the prison."

Mal. And he had less reason to be here than any of us.

"He could be lost in the woods," Farrell Dean said.

I gave him a look.

"Okay, maybe not. But he could be fine. It's just that nobody knows where he is."

Fifty yards or so from the stockade we found the site of the tunnel explosion. Trees leaned crazily around a crater in the earth, their roots exposed. I could see part of an underground concrete wall.

"I bet the Watchers were afraid to come any closer to the stockade," Farrell Dean said, looking it over. "This was as far as they wanted to come in the tunnel, to set their bombs."

"I wonder how Meritt got them to go into the tunnel." I started walking again, not wanting to think about what would have happened if the Watchers had been braver, if they'd crept right up under the stockade with their traps.

"He probably convinced them he'd disabled the bombs," Farrell Dean said. "Listen, Red. I think there might be one little problem."

"What is it?" I said, dread settling over me.

Farrell Dean looked at me, narrowing his eyes against the sun. "I don't think anyone has told Eric Alleyn about his father."

"But—why not? Will Bright knows, Gabriel and Rain know. Surely they told him."

Farrell Dean shook his head. "Just now my mother

asked whether the medical gentleman was all right. She didn't know he was your grandfather, and I guess Will Bright never enlightened her." He threw me a sidelong glance. "Maybe I'm wrong, but I'm thinking if anyone had told Eric Alleyn that his father was alive and trapped in Optica, the entire stockade would have heard his reaction."

He was right, and I had to smile. Then I did my best to pick up my pace. I didn't want my father to be suddenly and unexpectedly faced with his father's ghost. Eric Alleyn was a strong man, but that—well, that could give anyone a heart attack, especially coming on top of the strain of the previous hours.

"That's why they didn't tell him," I said, half to myself, skirting a particularly deep puddle of rainwater. "He was already worried sick about Fiona and me. No one would have wanted to put anything else on him."

"Especially since no one knew whether Michael Alleyn survived the explosion," Farrell Dean said, and helped me over a fallen tree.

We couldn't get into the city on the northwest side. I wouldn't be leaping over any blackberry bramble this time. But that was where we stepped out of the trees, and the sight of the wall made me gasp. I'd known it was broken. I'd seen it in the darkness. Angus had a knack for wanton destruction, Cline had said, and I had smiled.

In the daylight, though, the effect was stunning. The wall wasn't just breached—it was mangled, spilling great ragged chunks of cinderblock and mortar in all directions. Some of the pieces were as big as tables. In the part of the wall that was still standing, rebar lay exposed. Wire mesh, packed with concrete, dangled at eye-level. No wonder it had come down with a sound like the world ending.

We stood there a moment, almost reverentially, and then continued on to the western gap. We went in carefully, but no wardens stood guard; no one was around.

As we wended our way among the old trees, I tried not to think about standing there in the dark with Meritt, trying to persuade him to leave the city. If he had—if he had come with me then—so many things would be different. I would never have been arrested; I wouldn't have killed the scarred warden; Meritt and Fiona, Tor and Michael Alleyn wouldn't be buried in the rubble of the Watcher compound. Earl wouldn't be dead.

But the Watchers wouldn't be dead, either, because Meritt wouldn't have been there to lure them into the tunnel that killed them. And Angel well might have caused his own mischief, if he hadn't been distracted by Meritt's plight; he was so angry with me for coming back, and seemed ready to extend his animosity to my whole family.

"You should probably wear your cap in the city," Farrell Dean said, as we drew near the city streets. "Rufus says it's pretty quiet in there, but you never can tell. And I'm guessing there could be a couple of wardens who might have it in for you."

Silently, I took my cap from my pocket and pulled it on.

Chapter 20

Optica was almost unrecognizable. It looked as if a hurricane had struck, and maybe it had. Surely that crowd, angry as it was, couldn't have done all this. Buildings were crumpled and broken. Some looked as if a giant hand had picked them up and flung them. Others had hardly a scratch, though not a single window in the city was intact, as far as I could see. A tractor was lying upside down in the courtyard of my dormitory. The devastation was enormous.

The cafeteria seemed to be a hub of activity. Groups of people hovered around it, struggling to get in or out of the door. I could hear angry voices, shouts of indignation, now and then a sudden cry of pain.

"They're fighting over food," Farrell Dean said, and I saw that he was right. They were trying to defend their plunder or take someone else's.

Farther away, at the food preservation buildings, a man was handing out jars of jam. Meri was trying to stop him, but he was taller than she was, and making a game of it, tossing jars over her upstretched hands.

"Come on," Farrell Dean said. "We can't do anything about it. There are too many of them."

Nobody paid any particular attention to us, not even the ones who recognized me.

"Hi, Red," Felix said as we passed. He was sitting on the steps in the city circle working his way through a bushel basket of apples. A stack of large round cheeses sat on the step beside him.

"They're eating everything," I said when we were out of earshot. "Don't they understand there's a shortage?"

"That might not be a problem anymore," Farrell Dean said, and following the direction of his gaze, I saw what he meant. The people lying on the ground weren't napping. Lots of people had died. Many were wardens, dressed in black; many more, though, wore Optica gray. I didn't see a red shirt like the one Mal had been wearing.

"How did the wardens kill so many?" I said. "I thought Karl disabled their guns."

"He couldn't get to all of them," Farrell Dean said. "But I don't think the wardens did all of this. Some people were using the chaos as an excuse to settle old scores. Gabriel and I walked into some of that when we came in after you. We hadn't been planning to hold that little meeting—it just sort of happened. We were hoping people would see us and run, but instead they thought the dead ought to judge the living."

A man on a tractor was pulling a flatbed trailer up and down the city streets. He was going slowly, and two men were walking alongside. Every so often they'd bend, pick up a body, and heave it onto the trailer. The man driving the tractor never came to a complete stop.

Mechanic Dane and another man were holding some sort of meeting, taking questions and comments from a small crowd gathered around them, giving instructions. They were standing near the city circle, but not in it.

"Good thing someone's taking charge," I commented.

Dane noticed us, and raised a hand in greeting. Farrell Dean nodded at him in reply, and Dane gestured for him to come.

176

To my surprise, Farrell Dean started that way. To my even greater surprise, he apparently didn't want me to go with him.

"Do you mind waiting here?" he said, a little uncomfortably. "I need to see what he wants, but it won't take long."

"Sure," I said. I stood there on the outside edge of the group, anxious to go on to the Watcher compound, feeling oddly awkward and left out, while Farrell Dean edged between people and made his way to Dane.

One woman did a double take as he passed her. She was plump and gray-haired, and I didn't recognize her from behind. Then she turned—tracing the path Farrell Dean had walked—and looked me straight in the eye.

It was the creepy plump Watcher. She was wearing Optica gray, but there was no mistaking her.

For a moment, I think, she was undecided about what to do. Then she smiled at me and, without looking away, touched the arm of the woman beside her. That woman, too, turned and looked at me. It was the languid Watcher.

They started toward me and I stood there frozen, wondering what I ought to do. I wasn't in any immediate danger—Farrell Dean was right there, and so were dozens of other regular people—but still I took a step or two back as the women drew near, keeping a safe distance away.

"So that boy isn't dead," the creepy plump woman said, just as if we spoke on the street every day.

That boy.

I found my voice. "His name is Farrell Dean, and no, he isn't dead. You aren't dead either."

She raised her eyebrows. "I never said I was. You, however, said that he was dead. You said he died of infection on the other island. You lied."

"Well, I—I sort of had to." Unbelievably, I felt a little guilty.

"One never *has* to tell an untruth," the languid woman murmured.

"They never could be trusted," the plump woman said, looking at her friend. "That's why we always had such trouble with them."

The other woman nodded. "Now they'll see what it's like," she said, and gestured limply back at Dane. "He'll see, if he's the one misfortunate enough to take the reins."

My breathing had begun to quicken.

"After what you did to us, you have no right to any moral high ground," I began. "You killed us. You terrorized us--"

"And there has been no killing and terrorizing on your part?" The plump woman rubbed her hands together. "My dear, those bombs of yours turned men and women into bloody pulp. Did you hear the screaming? The horror and the fear? That was your doing. And tell me you didn't dance a little jig when you thought we all were dead. Tell me you didn't rejoice in the downfall of your enemies. Whereas we? We never thought of you as our enemies. We never hated you. You were our children, our responsibility."

"Your experiment."

She shook her head. "Not mine. Meritt Alleyn. He set all this in motion, he and your grandfather. All we did was try to minimize the damage. Given a set of circumstances beyond our control, we controlled what we could in order to keep you safe. That was our job—to take care of you, to protect you even and especially when that meant protecting you from yourselves."

Over near the food preservation building someone shrieked and someone else laughed, and I heard Meri's voice, urgent, cajoling.

The languid woman sighed. "And now we shall be forced to watch your decline," she said. "One by one you will starve. One by one you will turn on each other, destroy one another in a futile attempt to survive. Independence always leads to chaos, you see." She looked toward the free-for-all at the cafeteria. "Every man for himself means death to everyone else. Only unity lets a people thrive."

In a twisted sort of way, she probably was right. I couldn't even quite put my finger on how she was wrong, not at that moment.

So I changed the subject.

"Did any of the other Watchers survive?"

"Only us," the plump woman said. She attempted to look suitably mournful, but she couldn't quite pull it off. She was too pleased with herself. "Everyone else hightailed it down to the safe room, but I said, how can we deal with a crisis if we don't know exactly what's going on? And with Meritt Alleyn turning out to be Michael Alleyn, obviously we didn't know what was happening in the city. He said rebels were attacking, but he was lying about his identity, so why should we trust his word about other matters?"

"We stepped just outside to check," the languid woman said. "I hadn't set foot outside the compound in years. But when duty calls, we must answer."

"And we were rewarded," the plump woman said. "We lived, and the rest died."

"What are you going to do now?" I said.

"What are *you* going to do now?" The plump woman seemed to think she was being very clever, turning my words back on me. "Are you going to announce who we are? Betray us, expose us, see to it that we're executed? Our lives, you realize, are utterly in your hands."

I blinked.

"No one else knows who we are," the languid woman explained, seeming amused by my bewilderment. "There are so many strange faces right now. They think we came from the other island, with the so-called rescuers." She glanced around. "As far as I know, the only person alive who can identify us is you."

Could that possibly be true? Certainly the Watchers had kept themselves secreted away, tended to by a trusted few wardens and assistants—and maybe all those people were in fact dead.

Meritt could identify them, though, and Fiona and Michael Alleyn. But these women didn't realize they were still alive. As far as they knew, it really did all come down to me. And until the others were freed—if they were successfully freed—I guess it did.

At this moment, I controlled the fate of the Watchers.

The circle near to where Dane and Farrell Dean stood was the same circle where Rafe had died, where the Watchers had killed him and then Petey and Lavinia and the others, where they had tried to kill Farrell Dean, where they had intended to kill me. They had done so much evil, the Watchers. And, worse, they had enjoyed it. They had locked me in a cell and mocked me as I stood before them frightened and alone.

And now here they were, two of them. All I had to do was cry out, and that crowd just a few feet away would turn and finish off the Watchers forever.

Some unfamiliar feeling swelled in my chest.

"Yes," the plump woman said softly, knowingly. "You see how it is."

"Power is very sweet," the languid women added. Their voices were light, but they were watching me intently.

I knew what they were doing. They knew I hated them and were trying to convince me that if I exposed them, I'd become at least a little like them.

Were they right?

"Our lives are in your hands," the plump woman said. "We are helpless now. We are very old and we have no power, no weapons. We don't even have a home. You blew it up."

"All we ask is to be allowed to live out our remaining days unmolested," the languid woman said. "And that is entirely up to you. You have the power to save or destroy."

"Stop!" I said. "Just—be quiet."

The languid woman blinked and the plump woman looked affronted, but they kept their mouths shut.

I wasn't going to play their game. I wasn't going to listen to them, or be hurried or herded. I was going to stand there quietly and think this through, for as long as it took.

I looked at the two women, standing there in the sunlight. Without all the Watcher trappings, the white robes and the luxurious setting, the servants and guards, they looked like nothing but two harmless old women—wrinkled, gray, their bones growing brittle, their muscles growing weak.

But they were still, at heart, the same as before. Their circumstances had changed, but they had not. They had been evil and they were evil still, though now they took an everyday face.

Behind them the crowd of people shifted, talked to each other while Dane was busy talking privately to Farrell Dean. Farrell Dean met my eyes—he was keeping a cautious eye out, I knew, but only just in case. He had no idea that the two elderly women chatting with me were the same women who had tried to kill us.

If I didn't tell on them, they'd blend right in. They'd do some sort of job—weaving, maybe, or laundry if they were strong enough. They'd sit at lunch and visit with whoever sat beside them. They'd make friends. It was quite possible that no one else would ever know who walked among them.

That thought made goose bumps rise on my arms.

Everyday evil is still evil. And even stripped of power, evil is never harmless.

"Thank you for the warning," I said, raising a hand and gesturing to Farrell Dean and Dane. "I don't want to become like you. And I think maybe the best way to avoid it is to not keep dangerous secrets."

"But they'll kill us!" the plump woman said, and for the first time her smile slipped.

"They might. But they might not. And really, I don't think what becomes of you should be completely up to me."

I looked steadily at the two of them. "It shouldn't come down to just one person. Or even to seven."

Chapter 21

"Dane will figure out what to do with them," Farrell Dean said as we moved away from the crowd. "He won't let them get ripped apart. He's okay, Dane is. Really."

Something was going unsaid, and I wasn't sure what.

"You must know him better than I do," I said, groping around, tearing my thoughts away from the Watchers and focusing on Farrell Dean. He mattered more to me than they did. They weren't my problem, not any longer.

Farrell Dean smiled faintly.

"I guess I do know him pretty well," he said. "He's my father. But I'm not sure he knows it. Alice never told him, anyway. And he's never said a word about it to me."

Dane had been in one of the very first city meetings— the one with all the other men who wanted beautiful Lavinia.

Farrell Dean didn't say anything else until we were well out of earshot of the crowd. Then he stopped and glanced back toward the circle, where his father and several other men stood grouped around the two Watchers, shielding them from the crowd and talking amongst themselves.

Dane. I could see the resemblance, now that I knew.

"Just so you know," Farrell Dean said, turning to look at me, "I meant what I said last night. I want to do this the Aislin way. Us, I mean."

I knew what he meant. "Forever," I said.

He nodded. "Happily ever after, no matter what."

I thought about Nana, protected and loved despite her senility. I thought about Carol and her drinking problem, and the way she nevertheless brought something to Gabriel that he very much needed, and the way he protected her and adjusted for her.

Then I looked at Farrell Dean, at his steady eyes, and remembered his easygoing smile. I hadn't seen it much, lately, but it would return once all this was over. He could do it. He could love me happily ever after, no matter what. Could I do as much for him?

I could. I might not always know how, but surely I could learn as I went along.

"Forever sounds about right," I said.

Then he held out his hand to me and we went on, hand in hand, turning toward the Watcher compound, passing the tractor shed that had hidden me while Rafe and Farrell Dean rallied the mob.

That shed was flattened now, its concrete foundation bare. The corrugated steel sheets that had been three walls and a roof were strewn across the pumpkin field. Rhoda was nowhere in sight.

Another of my field workers was poking around in the debris. He looked startled to see me. "Hi, Billy," I said.

"You're supposed to be buried in the Watcher compound," he said. "Before that you were secretly executed for double crossing Meritt, and before that you drowned trying to leave the island. You have as many lives as a cat."

I didn't even try to manage a smile. We went on.

We crossed the fields cautiously. They were blackened as if a fire had run through the stubble, and were still smoldering despite the driving rain of the night before. Ashes floated in puddles along the furrows.

As we drew nearer to the compound we could see a huddle of forms far to one edge.

"They're working in the right place," Farrell Dean said.

The people nearest us were watching the work, their backs to us. We were still a ways away, but I recognized Liza, her frizzy hair standing out in all directions. Will Bright stood beside her, and so did Shawna and my bunkmate Kari.

In fact there were quite a few people, but I still didn't see Mal's scarlet shirt.

Stepping carefully we picked our way over the remains of the privacy wall, finally drawing close to the building itself. Its left side was battered but standing. Its right—the side where Will and the rest were grouped—lay flattened, a heap of rock and rebar. Here and there I saw the dead—an arm emerging from the rubble as if waving, a foot severed from its body, a heap of black rags that once had been a warden.

Rufus shouted, "Now!"

Harding, Angus, and Warden Karl heaved on a rope that was wound around a large fallen section and up over a standing section. Karl was wearing black warden pants, but a gray shirt.

The makeshift pulley worked; the gray slab began to move. Once the slab was partially upright, Rufus and Judd pushed it sideways, and Farrell Dean hurried forward to help them. Together they guided it away from what I now saw was a flat section of flooring, mostly obscured with small debris.

"Release!" Rufus shouted, and Farrell Dean and Judd jumped back as Liza yanked the knot and the slab fell with a crash, clouds of dust billowing, white and eerie.

Eric Alleyn stepped forward with a shovel and cleared away the piles of crumbled rock and mortar. A man in Optica gray—my farmer—stood ready with an ax.

"Get as far away as you can!" he called. "Cover your eyes!" A faint voice from below said something in reply.

"That was Tor," I said aloud, edging a little closer.

Eric Alleyn looked up and saw me and, tossing the shovel aside, moved toward me as quickly as his leg allowed. "My child," he said. "Are all my days to be spent losing you and finding you again?"

Then I was in his arms, hearing the crack of the ax, the splintering of wood, shouts of advice from Rufus and Angus.

"Let me get a good look at you," my father said, pulling off my cap and studying my face, bruises and all. "You're fairly beat up, daughter."

"I'm all right. Did Rufus tell you Fiona is okay?"

He nodded.

"But there's something you need to know," I said.

Eric Alleyn's eyes darkened with concern, and I stumbled hastily on.

"No, don't worry. It's not bad. It's just that Fiona's not the only one down there. The only one of us, I mean. There's someone else—someone you don't expect."

Eric Alleyn's brows came together. He waited, but I fumbled for words.

"It might be a bit of a shock," I said.

"I've survived a few of those already today, Valentina. Spit it out."

I looked him straight in the eye. "It's your father," I said. "He's here, and he's alive."

For a long moment my father's expression didn't change. Then astonishment filled his eyes and he shook his head, as if to clear it.

"He's alive?"

I nodded.

"And he's here?"

"That's right."

"He's been here all along, in Optica? Ever since we thought he died?"

"No—he only came here when I did, last night or the night before or whenever it was." I tried to say it all at once. "He's the one who brought me here—or Mal did, but Michael got Mal to do it, because he's the one who raised Mal while he was pretending to be dead. Not pretending to Mal, but to everyone else."

It was coming out all in a terrible mixed-up jumble, but Eric Alleyn seemed to be following, more or less.

"He wanted to protect you," I went on, and told the rest as well as I could.

My father listened silently until the end. Then, keeping one hand on my shoulder, he turned to face the ruins, where my farmer was prying up splintery sections of floor and tossing them aside.

"So my father is down there with Fiona," Eric Alleyn said, and though his tone was perplexed I knew that he believed me.

Someone appeared at my elbow. I turned and almost stepped straight into Judd.

"I'm getting better at it," he said, tipping his chin down and looking up at me from beneath his eyebrows.

I put my arms around him and hugged him tight.

"Stop it, Red. You're smothering me." But he was grinning as he moved away.

My farmer—Edgeling's brother—had made a hole big enough to begin pulling people out. Everyone edged anxiously closer as he knelt down and reached a hand into the jagged opening. Rufus bent, too, to help him.

Fiona came out of the darkness first. She was filthy, coated in white dust and coughing, her eyes red and swollen, but she was laughing.

"Papa!" she said, flinging herself at him. He put one arm around her, keeping the other around me, and then Fiona let go of him and reached for me. She hugged me so tightly I could barely breathe, while Eric Alleyn kept his arms around us both.

"I'm so glad you're safe," she said in my ear. "And I'm so glad that Dream Drops wear off."

Eric Alleyn held us for a long moment, smiling—I hoped that smile would be more common now than it had been in the past. Then he released us, bent to pick up the cane he'd let fall, and stumped away to try to see into the dark pit without getting in anyone's way.

"You are both safe. That is good," a voice said, and with a start I realized Mal was there beside us.

Quickly I scanned him—no blood or bruises, at least none that I could see. He looked tired and untidy, though. His shirt was torn, exposing a long swath of the design Rose had created for Michael Alleyn; his honey-colored braids were damp and dark, and two or three had come untwined, leaving curls to spring out wildly here and there.

"You're alive!" I said. If it had been anyone but Mal I would have hugged him, but I didn't know what Locrians thought of hugs.

"You are alive, as well," he countered, smiling at me for stating the obvious.

"Thanks to your knife."

As soon as the words were out, I regretted them. I didn't want to talk about the scarred warden.

But of course, being Mal, he didn't ask questions. Instead he merely nodded politely. "I'm glad it was of use to you," he said.

"What happened with his knife?" Fiona began, but then someone put a hand on my arm and pulled me into a hug before I was even sure who had hold of me. It was Rain.

Suddenly I was weeping. "I'm so sorry," I said in her ear. "Earl was trying to help me. I'm so sorry."

She shook her head. "It wasn't your fault. It was mine. I

wasn't watching my back, and Angel grabbed me, right there in the Watcher compound courtyard. I should have been paying better attention. I even had Fiona's gun, but he was so fast I never managed to touch it."

Before I could say anything else, she released me. I caught a glimpse of her face as she turned away and knew she didn't want me to see her cry. She gave a sort of wave over her shoulder and strode away. Mal watched her go, his face thoughtful.

"Should I?" he said.

I glanced at Fiona, who shrugged.

"Might as well," I told him, and he set off.

By then three older women had been pulled out of the debris, none of them people I knew very well. Not Mariella, who had died. Not Estelle, who was back at the stockade.

They smiled at me, though, exclaiming over my resemblance to Fiona as Kari and Shawna hurried forward to help them over the uneven ground, offering them water, wiping at their faces with a damp cloth. Once the older women were taken care of, Kari and Shawna had to hug me, too. "We were so worried," Shawna said.

Kari's hand was on my arm. "I'm glad you're safe," she said in her quiet voice. "And thank you for taking care of Ezzie."

Shawna handed Fiona a cup of water. "You can have more in five minutes," she said. "We don't want to shock your system."

I was still staring at Kari. She had blushed when she had mentioned Ezzie—I was sure of it. It wasn't just her usual shyness making her turn pink.

Now she laughed at my surprise. "He's a good man," she said, and she and Shawna moved on, leading the old women to a place clear of debris.

Tor was the next to emerge from the pit, which wasn't

what I expected. I'd have thought that as an able-bodied young man he'd go last. When they pulled him free of the hole, though, I saw that he couldn't stand.

"He's hurt," I said, surprised. Harding and Angus made a chair for him of their arms, and eased him out of the rubble toward the place where Shawna was tending the old women.

"Yes," Fiona said. "His leg is broken."

And then I was remembering the dark cramped place, shining the beam of a flashlight across Tor's pale face. "Stop pointing that thing in my face, Fee," he says, and his voice is tight with pain. "And stop fussing. I'm not going to die of a broken leg."

"Red?" Fiona was looking at me oddly. "Are you all right?"

"I didn't know about his leg," I said, shaking my head to clear away the belated memory.

"We were more worried about Meritt. Concussions can be nasty things."

Something in her tone gave me pause, though her face was carefully neutral.

"He didn't seem too bad to me," I said. "And he'll be better up here in the light."

"I hope so," she said, sounding unconvinced. "He's lost whole sections of time, Red, and he's all mixed up about things he does remember. Sometimes he knows there was an explosion, but sometimes he seems to be waiting for it to happen. And no matter how many times we explain it, he can't seem to believe there are such things as identical twins."

"Well, it is a little hard to believe, Fiona. I thought I was crazy the first time I saw you."

Fiona smiled, but her heart wasn't in it. "He also keeps asking whether it's getting close to six o'clock."

There was a question in her voice.

"That's when they were going to kill me." I hesitated,

then made myself go on. "Meritt was supposed to pull the trigger."

Fiona studied me gravely for a long moment. Filthy as she was, exhausted and just delivered from a dark pit, my sister still carried a certain self-assurance that made me feel, by contrast, awkward and uncertain.

"He wouldn't have done it," I said.

She shook her head. "No. I don't believe he would. But I'm not sure he knows that. He's confused, and head injuries are unpredictable."

As if to underline her warning, some sort of quarrel seemed to be taking place down below. I could hear Meritt's voice, not the words but the sound of his impatience. Louie answered him soothingly, persuasively, but Meritt had made up his mind about something and wasn't going to budge. Worried as I was, I had to smile; his tones, his moods, were so familiar to me. Even without words I could catch the gist of the argument.

"He doesn't want to go next," I said, guessing. "He wants everyone else out first."

A bad thought struck me; I hadn't heard a word from Michael Alleyn. "Grandpa really is all right, isn't he? I told Papa he was."

Fiona nodded. "He's fine. He's not talking because every time he says a word, Meritt gets all riled up. We kept trying to explain that Michael was only pretending to be Meritt Alleyn, but your Meritt wouldn't listen."

"He's not my Meritt."

"So I gathered," Fiona said, glancing over at Farrell Dean, a faint blush spreading across her face.

For a moment we both watched him. He was listening to Mal, his face intent, while Rain stared blankly off into the distance.

Then, as if feeling my gaze, he glanced over at me and

his face lit up. I smiled at him, and he gave a quick wink and turned his attention back to Mal.

Fiona turned back to face me, her face red, and laughed when she saw that I was blushing, too.

"No more caves," she said, lowering her voice. "It isn't proper. That's why Papa built the gazebo. You can have privacy there, but not too much."

She shot another quick glance at Farrell Dean and I was glad she'd seen only the fire-lit cave, and not the road to Doria on Farrell Dean's birthday, or—my face grew hot just thinking about it—the dark room at Gabriel's house, when Farrell Dean was shirtless and warm from sleep.

"Oh my," Fiona began, turning toward me with a curious glint of realization in her eye, but a sudden flurry of activity among the group around the ragged hole stopped her.

"Look at the two of you!" someone called. "Peas in a pod!"

It was Louie, emerging from the rubble with the help of Rufus and the farmer. The old man looked battered and filthy, but as far as I could see, he was uninjured.

He grinned at me as his feet hit level ground. "I hear I'm a matched set as well," he said.

"Louie?"

He turned. Will was sheet white, smiling tentatively at his brother. Louie went straight to him and hugged him, pounding him on the back. "I remember you!" he said, with a laugh. "You're the one gave me the little scar on my leg when you shot me with our bb gun."

"That was an accident," Will said, and then looked surprised. "I remember. I surely do remember that."

Now Michael Alleyn was being lifted free. Rufus took one look at his face and almost dropped him, but Karl reached across and steadied the older man.

"Grandpa?" Rufus said, frowning.

"Yes. It's me, Rufus," Michael Alleyn said. "Though it may take some doing to prove it."

Leaving Rufus looking baffled, he began carefully negotiating his way out of the worst of the debris, toward Rain, Mal, and Farrell Dean.

"It's him," Eric Alleyn said. "I know my own father."

At the sound of his voice Michael stopped in his tracks, but he didn't turn immediately toward Eric Alleyn. His gaze stayed fixed on Mal, who gave a cryptic shake of the head.

"I am sorry," Mal said. "I looked a long time, but with no luck."

Michael Alleyn's shoulders seemed to slump a little. I barely had time to wonder what that was all about when Michael straightened and turned toward his son.

For a long moment the two men stared at each other. They were only a couple of yards apart, but Eric Alleyn looked as if he were gazing all the way across the sea.

"I shouldn't have left you," Michael said.

Shawna handed him a cup of water, and he drank, then continued his train of thought.

"I'm sorry, Eric. I shouldn't have gone."

"Why did you?" Eric Alleyn suddenly seemed very young.

"I was trying to protect my family," Michael Alleyn said. "From the cameras, the experiment. I hoped that if I left he might lose interest and leave you alone, because he always liked an audience. But I should have stood and fought."

Eric Alleyn gave a short nod. "I'd have liked to have had you by my side, especially when I lost Rachel," he said. "But—stand and fight? How do you fight an enemy you can't see, in a battle that takes place mostly in your own head?"

Michael Alleyn's gaze had gone to the ground, but now he looked up and met his son's eyes. "I don't know," he said. "But I should have tried."

Eric Alleyn stepped forward and, with the hand that wasn't holding his cane, grasped his father's shoulder. Michael reached up with his other hand and grasped Eric Alleyn, and the two men stood there, eye-to-eye, studying each other.

Rufus was still looking utterly perplexed. He glanced at Fiona and me, making sure we saw what was happening, and then turned. "Angus," he called out. "Get over here."

I missed Angus' response to our grandfather's resurrection because then, finally, Meritt was rising from the pit, so covered in grime and blood as to be almost unrecognizable, a makeshift bandage wrapped around his head. He looked far worse than the others, but then he had been closer to the explosion, closer to the tunnel door.

"It's not as bad as it looks," Fiona murmured. "At least I don't think it is. He's really been very lucky."

We had come so close to losing him.

He had more trouble getting free than the others had. His clothes kept catching on the jagged edges of the hole, and he seemed to move in ways that made matters worse rather than better.

Farrell Dean went forward to help, and as he and my farmer finally got Meritt free and lifted him clear of the pit, Meritt's gaze fell on Michael Alleyn. He blinked hard, and frowned, and I saw again the same fleeting expression of dislike that I'd seen before, when they were in the Watchers' conference room.

"You see," Fiona said.

"Mick and Rory are on their way," Angus was saying loudly, and Meritt looked at him. "Looks like Sean was wrong. We all made it. Plus we gained one back from the dead," he added, grinning at our grandfather.

The expression of dislike on Meritt's face deepened to disgust.

Then he lowered his eyes as Farrell Dean helped him over the worst of the debris, watching his footing. Finally he raised his head and caught sight of Fiona and me, and his eyes widened.

"You see? He never truly believed there were two of us," Fiona said, and raised her voice. "It's all right, Meritt. Red's safe. Here she is."

Meritt looked at me. "Red?" he said uncertainly.

I nodded, my throat too tight for words, and hurried forward to fling my arms around his neck, drawing back almost instantly because I didn't want to hurt him.

"I couldn't get you out." His voice was so strained it was almost unrecognizable. He lifted one hand as if to touch my shoulder, but left it hanging there in the air, never touching me. "It was almost six o'clock and I couldn't get you out. I couldn't find a way to keep you alive."

The expression on his face said he still couldn't quite believe I really was alive, and then his gaze shifted to something over my shoulder and his eyes widened again, his face going slack with shock.

"I tried, Rafe," he said. "I'm sorry. I tried so hard."

Then his eyes rolled back and he swayed, and Farrell Dean reached out and caught him as he fell.

Chapter 22

It took awhile to set and splint Tor's leg, and even longer to find a stretcher. Cline and Harding tried the medical center, but it had already been ransacked, everything in it taken or destroyed. In the end they settled for a door.

Meanwhile Mick and Rory and Ezzie showed up, and everyone milled around, hugging and slapping backs and shaking hands, talking excitedly, tending to various wounds, carrying water and food to the people who had been trapped. Clouds were coming in, drifting in front of the bright sun, passing on again. I hoped we could make it back to the stockade before it rained. Meritt had a concussion and needed to rest; everyone needed to rest.

Meritt and I sat off to one side, a little apart from everyone else, near the fallen compound. The gash on the back of his head had started to scab over, so Shawna didn't put stitches in. But she cleaned it and checked for infection, and rubbed on some antibiotic ointment.

"You're going to have a pretty nasty scar," she said, stepping back and checking his pupil size one more time. "At least all that hair hides it. Better hope you don't go bald anytime soon."

He managed a faint smile.

"I don't know how much blood you lost, but judging

from the state of you, probably a fair bit, so you'll feel weak for awhile. And it would be really good if you could manage not to get hit in the head again anytime soon. Even your brains can only take so much jostling around." Taking a step back, Shawna studied him. "Honestly, I'd feel better if Red's grandpa took a look at you. He knows a lot more about this sort of thing than I do."

Meritt's face turned stubborn. "No. I'll be all right."

"He's a physician—"

"No!" He glowered at her. "I'm all right."

Shawna gave me a pointed look. Irrationality and confusion were typical symptoms of concussion, Michael Alleyn had said, during the few moments when Meritt was unconscious. He might be extremely anxious; he might be dizzy, nauseous, have headaches; and he might not remember the hours or even the days surrounding the trauma.

"Well. Keep sipping that water," Shawna said. "I'm off to the next patient." Handing him a bag of dried apples, a hunk of cheese, and a clean shirt, she moved away.

"I saw that," Meritt said irritably, before Shawna was well out of earshot. "I saw that poor-Meritt-doesn't-know-what-he's-saying look. There's nothing wrong with me. I'm fine. I don't know why you're all determined to treat me like an invalid."

"Maybe because you were buried in rubble for sixteen hours," I said, dipping a cloth in a bucket of water. "Take off your shirt and let's clean you up. You're pretty scary looking right now."

He still looked mutinous, but he did as I suggested. Just getting rid of that gory shirt helped, and then while he ate I knelt beside him, sponging the dust and grime from his face and neck and arms, trying to clean some of the matted blood out of his hair without disturbing the injury, rinsing the cloth and wringing it out again. The water in the bucket turned pink and I wished I had fresh water, but that would have to wait until we made it to the stockade.

As I worked I noticed that Meritt kept glancing at Fiona, who was hovering anxiously over Tor while Michael Alleyn and Shawna set his leg, and also at Louie and Will, who were sitting together on a fallen slab of wall and talking nonstop.

"You didn't know about the experiment," I said.

"The twins? No. I didn't know there was such a thing as twins."

If he noticed that I paused for a fraction of a moment, that the washcloth on his neck was still, he made no sign. I recognized, now, his precisions for the evasions they were; but I didn't press him. There would be time later, when he felt better, to ask all my questions.

Instead I started in on the blood that had run down his neck and across his back. When the clouds went behind the sun, chill bumps rose on his bare skin; when the sun came back out, he relaxed and began to look sleepy.

"Talk to me," he said, glancing over his shoulder. "It isn't like you, to be this quiet. I'm about to decide you're your sister."

"Huh. She talks way more than I do."

"So, what are you saying? That there's a third one, a quiet one, and you're her?"

"Nope. Just the two of us. I'm happy to talk, Meritt, but I don't know where to start."

"Start at the beginning. Start with the night you went out into the wilderland without me."

And so I did. I told him about finding Sir Tom, about Ezzie's injury, about going to the other island. I told him about the twins, the Dream Drops, the dreamers and the watched. I told him about the Dream Recorders and the midwife, about the end of the supply drops and the illness that ravaged the Guardians. I told him about my family's life in Doria, and about Tristan, and about Mal and his parents and how Michael had stepped in and raised him. I told him everything, even though he was bound to know some of it already. It felt good. All my life I'd talked to Meritt. All my life I'd told him everything.

"So Meritt Alleyn is the one who's really to blame," I concluded, as Meritt pulled on the clean shirt. "Not Michael. Although the Dream Drops were Michael's idea, which did start the whole thing. He feels terribly guilty about that."

I looked at my grandfather, who had finally finished tending to other people and was sitting down, accepting another cup of water from Kari. Ezzie was standing beside her, watching her proudly.

Meritt was watching Michael Alleyn, too.

"What is it?" I said. "Why do you dislike him so?"

Meritt shifted, looked away. "I don't even know him. Why should I dislike him?"

That was the question. But before I could say so, a shadow fell across us.

"Hi." Rain crouched on her heels beside us and gave Meritt a brilliant if brittle smile. "I hear you saved Fiona's life."

He looked at her, noncommittal. "So they say."

"You don't remember?"

"He's lost a few hours," I said. "But that's normal with head injuries. It might come back to him later."

"Good, I guess. Personally I'd rather not remember being blown up." Rain's eyes glinted. "Red fainted too, the first time she saw Gabriel. My father seems to have that effect on people from this island."

"I fainted," I said. "Meritt has a head injury."

He threw me a sideways look, his gray eyes wry.

"Of course. I didn't mean to impugn his manhood." Rain smiled, again too brightly, and suddenly I was worried that she might blurt out something I'd rather bring up gradually, tactfully, at the right time. You never knew, with Rain.

Fortunately Meritt chose that moment to stretch, wincing.

"Later, Rain," I said. "All right? Let him rest."

"Sure," she said, getting to her feet. "Just wanted to meet the great enchanter, that's all. I'm glad to hear there's more to you than spells and potions."

"Later," I said again, firmly.

Meritt watched her walk away. "Are you going to tell me what that was about?"

Absolutely not. "Just Rain being odd," I said, waving a hand vaguely. "She's my cousin, did you know?"

"On your mother's side."

"That's right. On Rafe's side. I don't have cousins on my father's side—Eric Alleyn is an only child."

As I spoke, though, something shifted in my memory. The words in Michael Alleyn's diary, the revelations the Dream Recorder made when she thought I couldn't move—

"Actually, it's possible he had a brother," I said, half to myself. "Or I guess it would be a half brother. There might have been a son Michael Alleyn lost back when the experiment began."

Meritt frowned. "Pretty careless, to lose an entire son," he said, and then something seemed to occur to him and he turned, scanning the wall behind us, the debris, the blackberry bramble with all its tangled shadows.

My heart sank. I knew who he was looking for.

"I have bad news," I said, because it would be bad news to Meritt, if not to the rest of us. And there was no gentle way to say it.

So I took a breath, and did it. "Angel is dead."

Meritt stared at me blankly for moment, the wind stirring his hair. "Angel?"

"That's right. Angel. Your father. He's dead."

He shook his head, then stopped. "Are you sure? How do you know?"

"I saw it. He fell. He fell into the sea." I wasn't sure I should go into details, not now. I didn't want to upset him more than necessary.

But Meritt made an impatient gesture. "Come on, Red," he said. "Tell me."

I straightened the wet rag on the edge of the bucket, giving myself something to do other than meet his eyes. "When the tunnel exploded, Angel thought you'd been killed, and he—" How to put this? "He was very upset, and he took me with him to that cliff above the sea."

"To kill you." Meritt's tone was matter of fact.

"Maybe. Probably."

"To punish you for living when I was dead. To shoot you on the edge of the cliff. Or to tie you underneath it, where the tide comes in and fills the hollow. Or to set you adrift in a boat, with no water and no oars. Or to make you wade out to the place where the sharks are."

Startled, I looked at him.

Meritt spread his hands. "But he didn't. He could have done any of those things, and he didn't."

"No," I said slowly. "He didn't. But that's only because I got away."

"So he died instead."

I didn't know where he was going with this. "It's not like it had to be one or the other," I began, and Meritt leaned forward, his eyes suddenly intense.

"But maybe it did," he said. "There are choices. Trade-offs. That's what makes it hard. Saying yes to one means saying no to another. So you lived, and Angel died."

I straightened the cloth again, wishing Shawna would come back, or somebody—anybody—who knew more about head injuries than I did. Because even though I didn't have much experience telling people their fathers had died, I was pretty sure this was a strange way to react.

"So you won," Meritt said, and gave a short harsh laugh that made me flinch. "I spent a lot of time protecting you from Angel. It never occurred to me that I might need to protect Angel from you."

He was in shock. That had to be it. And where was Shawna? I couldn't spot her in the group huddled around Tor. Maybe she'd gone to look for something at the ransacked medical building.

"Did he do that to you?"

Warily, I looked back at Meritt. He was studying my bruised face.

"No," I said. "That was a warden in the prison. Angel never actually hurt me. He scared me, that's all."

I don't know why I was downplaying it—because this was Meritt's father, I suppose, and he was dead, and Meritt was all alone now while I had a horde of brothers and other relatives, all here to take care of me, all here to see to it that I was safe and that, safely, I'd make it home.

"Did someone help you get away?"

Before I could reply Meritt gave another sudden bark of laughter, awkward and too loud.

"What a stupid question," he said. "Of course someone helped. Look at you, look at him. You didn't get away from Angel on your own."

As he spoke his voice had grown louder and louder, which wasn't at all like him. He was attracting attention. Rory and Mick turned toward us, their faces darkening with concern and curiosity. I gave them a small shrug, hoping Meritt wouldn't notice.

Apparently he didn't. "Who helped you?" he said, leaning toward me.

"Well, first Earl tried—"

"And got killed. That's what she said—what you said—when we were trapped down there. You said Angel killed someone named Earl. I don't know anyone named Earl so he must have come from the other island. He must be one of your secret allies. Your—" Meritt hesitated, groping for a word, absentmindedly touching the back of his head where the gash ran deep. Then he gave up, gestured. "Go on. Tell me about Earl."

I glanced around for Shawna, but still couldn't spot her. Exactly how upset would he be if I called Michael over?

"There was a fight," I said, while I tried to decide what to do. "Earl injured Angel, but then Angel killed him."

"And you got away while they were fighting?"

I shook my head, but he didn't give me time to explain. "How did Angel get killed if Earl was already dead?" he said. "He didn't just slip and fall off a cliff. I might do that or you might do that but not Angel—he doesn't make mistakes—not like that. And no one walks away from Angel. Not me, not you, not anyone."

"You're right," I said, groping for a way to answer without giving painful details. "Angel was more dangerous unarmed than most people are armed. That's what Sir Tom told me once, and it's true. I wonder how he learned to fight like that?"

For a long moment Meritt was silent. I was afraid to look at him, so instead I pulled up a few spears of dried grass and lifted them, pretending to check the direction of the wind.

"Red?"

I glanced up at him.

"You're acting like me." He smiled faintly. "Only you're no good at it. And this is my father we're talking about. I have a right to know how he died."

It was true; he did.

"There was another fight," I said carefully, glancing across at Farrell Dean as if he could somehow help me with this. "After the one with Earl. It was during the storm and the wind was high and the water was rough, and there was lightning, and Angel was injured and he fell and was swept away in the sea."

Meritt had followed my gaze.

"I see," he said, and his voice had gone hard and cold. "Farrell Dean killed him."

"No! Not like that. Not like you mean. It was like this, Meritt—Angel was upset, and he was trying to make me go down the ladder to the boat, and there was the storm, and we were on the cliff, and we struggled—we all did, I did too—because he really was going to kill me. He told me. So it wasn't like anyone in particular killed him—it wasn't like we set out to kill him. It just happened because I was trying to get away and Farrell Dean was helping me. You understand, don't you?"

Meritt gave a short and bitter laugh. "Oh, I understand. He stole you."

"When I was a baby, yes, but that isn't why we—it wasn't revenge, if that's what you mean, it was only that—"

"Some friend he is."

"He—" I blinked. "You mean *Farrell Dean* stole me?"

Meritt picked up a rock and threw it, hard. "I thought it was a lie, there in the Watcher council when they said you were in love with him." He gave a short unhappy laugh. "I should have known better. I should have known they were right, because they believed you, and you're a terrible liar."

I couldn't meet his eyes. He picked up another rock and threw it.

"I save his life, and what does he do in return? He steals you and then kills my father."

"It wasn't like that," I said.

"It was exactly like that. My best friend takes my girl and then turns around and kills my father. Winner takes all."

"Stop it." I was suddenly angry. "Angel was trying to kill me, and that's why he got killed. And I'm not your girl. You don't own me, Meritt, no matter what your father might have told you. Farrell Dean couldn't possibly steal me from you, because I don't belong to you."

"I never said you did." His gaze was remorseless. "But you loved me."

"I did. But you didn't love me. You liked having an admirer, a pet, and that's different."

He gave me a contemptuous look.

"Don't act like you've been betrayed," I said. "You know you never loved me, not like that. And Farrell Dean did everything he could to help you, and so did I. That's why I was going to get executed, because I risked my life to come into the city and warn you. Remember that? My execution?"

Meritt stared at me for a long moment. Then he pushed his hair out of his eyes and smiled coldly, and his gray eyes turned mocking and distant, and it was like flipping a switch—one second he was himself, angry and irrational but himself, and the next second he was his father. He was looking at me the same way Angel had looked at me, exactly the same way, and my breath caught in my throat and dismay washed over me and suddenly I wondered whether I really knew him at all.

His eyes narrowed.

"You're afraid of me," he said, and though he sounded angry and disappointed, he didn't sound surprised. "After everything I've done for you, you're afraid."

It was true. To hide it I went on the offensive.

"Everything you've done for me?" I said. "You did things for me, sure, but you didn't tell me anything at all. Why didn't you tell me I came from another island? Why didn't you tell me I had a family, that I wasn't a freak? Why didn't you tell me your father was a Guardian who stole me and hated me and was a danger to me? You kept secrets from me all those years, and I was supposed to be your best friend."

"That's right," Meritt snapped. "That's the operative word. You were *supposed* to be."

"He kidnapped me!" I said. "Your father stole me from my family, and gave me to you like a present, and then he tried to kill me. And you're mad at *me*?"

Heads were turning in our direction. Mick and Rory were moving toward us. I waved them off and turned back to Meritt. He was still looking angry and distant, but he looked like himself again, not like Angel, and I didn't want anyone to interfere. I wanted to have it out with him once and for all.

"Tell me this," I said. "Just tell me this much. All those years, when we were partners at school, when we were friends—what exactly did you know about Optica?"

For a long moment Meritt was silent, his gray eyes unreadable.

"Not enough," he said finally, wearily. "Not nearly enough."

He'd never change. This was who he was, an elusive boy running away from me in the dark, the electric blue lights casting strange beautiful shadows on his face, hiding expressions, distorting meanings.

And I was tired of it.

I had loved him, and I loved him still—not like I loved Farrell Dean, but in a way that had something to do with my past, my childhood, the excitement of being out after dark in the big forbidden city, the hope that someday someone would claim me, love me, let me belong.

But I was tired of trying to corner him, tired of trying to understand him, tired of always tagging after him thinking maybe, one day, he'd stop running ahead and slow down and run beside me.

I didn't know, now, why I'd ever preferred him to Farrell Dean.

Maybe he read my thoughts in my face. Maybe he knew the time for questions was almost past. Or maybe he simply felt like giving a straight answer for once. Whatever the reason, just when I was certain he'd never say another word about the things that had happened to us, he spoke.

"I knew Optica was dying," he said, lowering his voice and glancing warily around. "I knew the Watchers wanted it saved and thought I could help them save it. I knew Rafe wanted it changed and thought I could help him change it. I knew Tommy wanted it destroyed and thought I could help him destroy it."

He started to say something else, then stopped, making a frustrated gesture with one hand.

My anger and impatience drained away, and I was ashamed. Meritt was exhausted, concussed, and had just learned that his father was dead. I shouldn't be hounding him, not now.

"A lot of people wanted something from you," I said.

His mouth twisted in a humorless smile. "Of course they did. They all knew who my father was."

His father, the beautiful, powerful Guardian. The man who had known more than anyone else alive about what had happened here, and across the sea, and on the mainland.

"Meritt?"

He looked at me.

"What did Angel want?"

Meritt's expression didn't change. He held my gaze for a long moment, and when he finally answered, his voice was so low I had to strain to hear him. "He wanted to conquer the worlds that had always been his rivals."

Then his gaze went to my lips and lingered there, and though I had chosen Farrell Dean, though Meritt was being once again his maddening cryptic self, I felt a hot flush begin to travel up my neck. I had loved him for so very long.

Something like pain flared in Meritt's face. His eyes met mine and flashed away, and when he spoke again his voice was gruff. "In whatever way was necessary," he said, and the sun went behind a cloud, leaving a dark chill November day.

Chapter 23

I spent way too long pouring out the dirty water and arranging the rag neatly over the edge of the pail. Meritt gazed silently off into the distance.

No one came to interrupt our awkwardness; everyone was busy. My brothers were fussing around Tor—except for Angus, who seemed to be flirting with Liza. Eric Alleyn and Michael were deep in conversation, and so were Mal and Rain, both of whom apparently were oblivious to the faintly alarmed glances Gabriel kept throwing their way.

Ezzie was holding court at the center of a group of Optica females, including Kari, Meri, and the three older women who'd been rescued. He was pointing in the direction of Aislin, no doubt explaining everything that had happened there.

Behind me Karl, Judd, and Harding were moving chunks of debris from the ruins of the Watcher compound, to what purpose I didn't know; and over toward the northwest gap Cline and my farmer were hacking through the blackberry bramble with large hedge shears, clearing the shortest way out of the city toward the stockade.

It took me a minute to locate Farrell Dean—he was down on one knee, talking with Louie, Will, and a handful of Optica men, including Mechanic Dane. They seemed to be diagramming something on the ground, making plans, perhaps. As I watched, Louie said something to Will, who nodded, and then they each in turn shook hands with Dane.

I was seeing the new Optica leadership being formed.

Dane leaned down and pointed at something in their diagram, putting his hand on Farrell Dean's shoulder as he did so. Farrell Dean might not think Dane knew, but I was pretty sure he did.

I couldn't decide whether to be relieved or sorry that Farrell Dean was busy. Part of me wanted him to come over to us, to get his first meeting with Meritt over with, but then again the last thing we needed right now was an argument, or for Meritt to throw a punch at Farrell Dean, or to say something he'd regret later.

Considering all this, I shot a surreptitious look at Meritt, only to find that he was watching me, a sardonic expression on his face.

"Stop it," I said sharply, and to my surprise, he laughed—a normal laugh, his own light laugh—and got to his feet.

"Look, Red, I'm sorry for what I said. Farrell Dean's a good guy. He's always been a good friend to me, and he'll be good for you."

I eyed him suspiciously, but there was no shade of deception or evasion in his face. He let me study him for a long moment; then he half-smiled at me and, moving a little stiffly, turned and began to walk away.

"Where are you going?"

"To look around." He waved a hand south, toward the city streets. "The explosions didn't do all this."

"No," I said, going to him. "I told you, remember—there was a storm."

His face went blank.

Clearly he didn't remember, although I had described

the storm in great detail not half an hour before. That was worrisome.

"It was the worst storm I've ever seen," I said, trying to act as if I were saying something new. "It did a lot of the damage and it knocked out the power. How hard do you think that will be to fix?"

Meritt shrugged and turned away, but not before I saw an uneasy shadow crossing his face. His hand went to the gash on the back of his head, and I thought how hard this must be for someone like Meritt, someone accustomed to relying on a quick clever brain.

"It's normal to be forgetful for awhile," I reminded him. "Michael said so. You'll get better soon."

He shrugged again.

"But probably you shouldn't be moving around too much. We'll be going to the stockade soon, and you can rest, and then you can come back here another day to look around. Tomorrow, maybe."

Meritt shot me one quick irritated glance over his shoulder. "I want to see it now," he said, and gestured toward Cline and the blackberry bramble. "And we can't leave yet anyway."

Without another word he started off.

What could I do, but follow him?

At the edge of the blackened field he stopped.

"What caused the fire?" he said, and then that same uneasy look crossed his face.

I started to reassure him that he hadn't asked the same question before, but decided that would only make him feel more self-conscious; instead I said, "I don't know. Lightning, maybe. Or rioters."

Meritt wandered a few steps farther. I glanced over at Farrell Dean, but he was still completely wrapped up in whatever he was discussing with Louie and Dane.

Well, we wouldn't go far, certainly not out of eyeshot. Meritt wouldn't have the energy.

And so we wandered slowly down through the wrecked city of Optica, through the fields, toward the city streets. At first I kept a careful eye out for trouble, but it quickly became apparent that there was no need. The city felt different. Everyone knew the Watchers were gone; everyone knew Optica was over. No one was wearing warden black, and for the very first time, people were going about their own business. Most were too busy or distracted even to glance our way.

"How many bombs were there?" Meritt said, standing in place and turning to survey the wreckage in all directions. "Five or six around the wall, plus the one at the compound?"

"No—they didn't bomb the compound. They wouldn't, with you in it."

He shot me one skeptical glance, then looked away.

"They knew you were in there," I repeated, "and the old people, and they didn't put bombs there. It was the reverberations from the wall falling that made you get trapped to begin with, and then the tunnel explosion made it worse. Meritt, that tunnel—you were going to lead the Watchers in, if they wouldn't go on their own. That's what you meant, that night in the orchard. You thought you'd be killed in there."

Without answering he started walking again, and I followed.

"You were trying to protect us," I said. "You knew the Watchers wouldn't go down without a fight, and they had the wardens and the guns. You didn't know I'd be able to bring in reinforcements who had their own guns and explosives. You didn't know Michael Alleyn would come and trick the Watchers. You were going to try to do it all alone, to keep the rest of us safe."

"Don't make me out to be a hero, Red."

"Why not? You are."

"I play to win, that's all." He kept walking.

"Yes, but you tried to save the old people, and you tried to get rid of the Watchers in a way that kept the rest of us out of danger, and you saved me. Because you thought it was me you were saving when you killed the Voice. I know. I saw your face."

In a sudden vivid flash I saw it all again, watched the Watcher crumpling to the ground, saw Meritt's eyes meeting mine in relief and then bafflement as he caught some hint that the redheaded girl he'd just saved wasn't me.

"I don't remember," Meritt said, and he stopped and turned toward me, his gray eyes unreadable. "I don't remember anything at all after you walked out of that room."

"You mean the conference room?"

"That's right. When they said I'd kill you at six o'clock." His hand went to his head, as if he had a bad headache—which he probably did—and uncertainty flashed in his eyes. "They were going to make me kill you, Red. I couldn't see a way out of it."

"But you didn't kill me," I said firmly. "You saved my life. I saw you do it."

"I wish I could remember."

"You will. And if you don't, it doesn't matter. It happened, and I saw it happen, and I can always remember for both of us."

Meritt looked at me for a long moment; then he nodded and began walking again, continuing his meandering way toward the center of the city. He looked at the fallen tractor shed, where I'd disabled Rhoda. He examined the table-sized chunk of wall that lay, mysteriously, in the middle of the road. Distant thunder rumbled and he lifted his face to the sky, and I shivered.

"I waited out the explosions at the slaughterhouse," I said, taking a few steps in that direction. "I tried to pretend you were with me, like you usually were, but it didn't work very well."

Meritt was looking at my feet. "Are you limping?" he said.

"Maybe a little. I'm okay."

He didn't ask more questions about that, and I was glad; I didn't want to revisit the issue of his father.

We walked on, more slowly still. I didn't know whether Meritt was being considerate of my ankle, or whether he was simply wearing out. His face was whiter than when we'd started, and there was tension in the line of his jaw. Shawna would probably scold me for letting him be up and about, but I didn't know how to stop him.

I glanced back toward the Watcher compound, spotting in the distance Cline still working at the bramble, people still scattered in small groups. We hadn't been gone long; they probably hadn't even noticed our absence.

Meritt was looking at a tractor that was just disappearing down the southeast spoke of the streets. It was too far away to see clearly—just a tractor, pulling a trailer loaded with something that could have been gray cinderblock rubble. We hadn't passed a single dead body, Meritt and I. They'd all been picked up during the time that had passed since Farrell Dean and I had come this way, and I was glad. I didn't want to see them again, and I didn't think it would do Meritt any good to see them. He'd probably take the losses as some sort of failure on his part.

Maybe I could get him to think about the future, about happier times.

"Will you come back to Aislin with us?" I said, trying to sound casual. "I hope you will."

Meritt threw me a noncommittal glance, but he didn't answer.

"It's a really big island. You wouldn't have to be surrounded by my relatives all the time. Although I think you'd like my brothers, once you got to know them. Some of them, anyway. Cline's going back with us, and some other people too. It would be a fresh start. You could be yourself there, not a Guardian's son."

Meritt still didn't answer, and when I saw the direction of his gaze, I forgot what I'd been saying. We were almost to the prison.

It was no darker here than anywhere else under the gathering clouds, but it felt darker. And though the rest of the city was crawling with people—cleaning, assessing, looting—the prison held no charms for anyone. Its door hung open limply, as if the last warden out hadn't bothered to shut it. They were all busy pretending they'd never been wardens, I supposed. And nobody else had any desire to set foot in that place.

"That must have been some wind," Meritt said, looking up. "The windows are gone—did you see that?"

I couldn't look away from the circle, from the place where Rafe had bled and died. So much had happened since then; so much had changed since the day he walked out of the prison door and down to the circle, alone. But I knew what had struck Meritt. I'd been struck by it myself, when Farrell Dean and I passed by earlier. Nothing else in the ruined city—not the wrecked buildings, the wandering people, the blackened fields—made as definite a statement as the watchtower with its dark and empty eyes.

Optica was over.

"I can't believe it," I whispered.

Meritt's gaze was still fixed on the top of the watchtower, on those dark broken windows, and I supposed that the walk was wearing on him, for suddenly he looked utterly exhausted, as he had every right to be.

"Are you all right?" I said. "We should go back."

He attempted a smile, but failed. "Not yet. I have to go up there."

"What? You mean up in the watchtower? But why?"

The look he gave me was faintly baffled. "To end this," he said. "I have to say goodbye. I have to end this once and for all."

I understood wanting to say goodbye to the city, but climbing all the way up those stairs in his condition wasn't a good idea. Before I could try to dissuade him, though, he spoke again.

"How many days ago did I kill Zee?"

I had to think. "Two days?"

He nodded. "My father showed me how to break his neck." He looked faintly surprised. "It wasn't hard."

The hair on my arms stood up; he'd said it just like that, the night it had happened.

"That's the last time I saw him," he went on, looking back up at the tower. "He isn't there anymore."

"No," I said carefully. "He's gone." They'd carried his body down while I was locked up in the cell—I'd heard them—but that level of detail didn't seem like a good idea, not when Meritt wasn't thinking quite clearly.

But then, I wasn't thinking quite clearly either, because while he was imagining Zee broken and dead in the tower, I suddenly couldn't stop thinking about the scarred warden's body lying in the prison cell, still and silent in a pool of congealing blood. I had done that. I had killed a man. He must be dead, surely, because it spurted—

"Maybe I only imagined it," Meritt said, staring up at those empty windows, at the watchtower that wasn't watching anymore.

"I wish you had," I said, and it was hard to talk with a lump in my throat. "I wish I'd only imagined it, too." Though if I'd only imagined killing the scarred warden, he'd have hurt me. Would I rather be brutally assaulted, or be a killer? Neither choice seemed like a good one.

From the corner of my eye I saw Meritt turn to look at me, and suddenly I remembered that he didn't know what I'd done to the scarred warden. I felt like I ought to tell him—he'd told me about killing Zee—but the words stuck in my throat.

"Red?"

I looked at him.

He hesitated, and then leaned down and gave me a quick kiss on the cheek.

"I'm sorry," he said gently. "For everything. Now go back to your family."

Then he started for the prison door.

Chapter 24

Something in Meritt's tone paralyzed me—something final, something foreboding—and because of that he was halfway to the prison door before I moved, and through it before I caught up to him.

I crossed the city circle without hesitation, but at that dark gaping door I paused. I didn't want to go inside that building ever again. There was death in there. But there was no way I could let Meritt climb all those stairs alone, disoriented, injured.

Cautiously I stepped across the dark threshold, waiting just long enough for my eyes to adjust to the windowless gloom, feeling as if by stepping inside I might find myself thrown back in time, imprisoned, terrified, condemned.

But the long tiled hallway stretched before me bare and dim and hollow feeling, and as I walked its length somehow I was sure no one was alive in its depths, no one but Meritt and me. It felt empty. It felt like Earl when the light had left his eyes.

When I reached the door to my cell I slowed without meaning to do so. I had been in such despair, there in that room; I had been so alone, so certain I was minutes from death. And that had only been yesterday.

So much had changed in a few short hours. I was alive,

and I was free. Optica had fallen. The Watchers were no longer a threat. Farrell Dean and I had a future together. I felt entirely different, and the world was entirely different, and yet the tower still stood, and the prison, and the cell door was bolted, just as I had left it.

Just as I registered that fact and what it meant, a musky, sickly-sweet odor tickled at the back of my nose, so faint that I might have thought I was imagining it, but for that locked door.

Bile rose in my throat. Tears started to my eyes.

"Red?" Meritt was at the end of the hall, his hand on the door to the stairwell. "What are you doing?"

Turning away from the cell door, I started toward him. "I'm coming with you."

Uncertainty flashed across his face. "You can't," he said.

"Of course I can." I hurried to him, away from the locked door and the nightmare behind it.

Meritt stared at me as if he didn't quite understand. He looked very tired, and the bruises on his face stood out starkly against his pallor. He didn't need to be climbing stairs, and he sure didn't need to be climbing them alone.

"I'm your friend, Meritt. If you're going up, I'm going with you. We probably should get someone else to come too, just in case you get woozy again. I don't think I could catch you if you fell."

"No!" Meritt looked truly alarmed.

"All right," I said. "No one else. But I'm coming. You can't stop me, you know."

He stared at me for a long moment, his face so blank that when he finally spoke and his words were rational, I was relieved. "Farrell Dean says I lead you into trouble," he said.

"Farrell Dean will understand. Or not. Anyway, I'm coming."

An echo of Meritt's old grin crossed his face. "All right,"

he said. "And I'll take good care of you. I promise."

Sure. I just hoped he didn't pass out, with only me to catch him.

The stairwell was cold and our feet echoed hollowly on the stairs. Meritt climbed steadily, with determined steps, and I did my best to keep up. He might be concussed, but he'd apparently found some reserve of energy, and of course he'd always been fit. I could see the muscles moving beneath his gray Optica shirt.

"Remember last time we did this?" I said. "It feels like such a long time ago."

The night we'd spied on the Watchers I had never been out of the city. I had never been across the sea. I had run through the dark with Meritt, in the electric blue streetlights, and that had been the widest extent of my world. The night when Rafe had been arrested, when we'd run the streets together, felt like a million years ago and a minute only just past, both at once. Meritt had run so fast, leaving me so far behind—he'd have outstripped me even if I hadn't been dallying, watching the electric blue lights dancing in his hair, making him look strange and mysterious and unsettling.

"Meritt?" I said. "That last night, the night when Rafe got taken?"

He paused on the stairs and glanced back at me, one hand on the railing. "What about it?"

"Did you know the wardens would be waiting?"

I hadn't planned to ask; I wasn't even thinking about asking. The words seemed to come of their own accord.

Meritt gave me one long searching glance, then turned and started climbing again. "Yeah," he said. "Of course. I'm the one who tipped them off."

It felt like the wind had been knocked out of me. The staircase swam before my eyes. I reached out and put one hand on the cold cinderblock wall, bracing myself.

"It was because of Angel," Meritt said, still climbing, his voice echoing in the hollow stairwell. "He wanted Optica to die as slowly and painfully as possible, and it was actually starting to look like Rafe might be able to straighten things out, get rid of the Watchers, improve our circumstances. So Angel had been talking about neutralizing him, and I thought I'd better get Rafe out of the way for a little while, to slow things down until Angel cooled off."

Now he did glance back, and when he saw me standing there, frozen with shock, he turned and came back down the stairs toward me.

"I never thought the Watchers would kill him," he said, looking down at me from a few steps above. "It's hard to believe that now, but then—it never crossed my mind. I thought he'd get thrown in prison for a few days, that's all, where he'd be safe from Angel. Meanwhile I could figure out what to do. It would buy me a little time."

He sat down on the step so that our faces were almost even, and rested his elbows on his knees.

"That was my biggest mistake," he said. "That, and letting the Watchers see that I cared about you."

He was speaking impersonally, as if he were analyzing a chess game.

"I traded out with Cline that night so he wouldn't get arrested when Rafe did, and I took you with me because—" He stopped, and his grin flashed and was gone.

"I actually don't know why I took you along. It was stupid, like Farrell Dean said. He punched me out for doing it. But I always liked having you with me—you were good company—and I knew I could outrun you, there at the last. And I knew you'd hide and not get caught. And anyway I didn't want to leave you alone in your dorm, not with Angel prowling around in a bad mood. He was mostly in a bad mood with Rafe, but when he was in a bad mood with anyone it always put him in a bad mood with you."

The thought of Angel prowling around in my dorm room, while all the girls slept, made me flinch.

Meritt ran a hand through his hair, wincing as he touched the gash on the back of his head. "I'm sorry for a lot of things, Red. I know it doesn't change things. But I am."

Then he got to his feet and started up the stairs again. He didn't turn to see if I was following—I don't think he expected me to. But I did, slowly, feeling old somehow.

It had been Meritt all along. He was the one who had gotten Rafe killed.

Though it could have been Gabriel's fault, as well, for tipping off the Dream Recorder with his recurring dream of a clean-shaven man who looked just like him but was trapped inside gray city walls—a man who didn't like those walls, who was looking for a way out.

Gabriel hadn't known he was giving Rafe away, of course, while Meritt had done it deliberately—though he was trying to protect Rafe, not get him killed. So in a way both were to blame, and neither.

Why was I even trying to sort it out? It didn't matter. Rafe was dead.

At the top of the stairs Meritt stopped, one hand on the door to the Opticon. "You shouldn't have come," he said. "I don't know, Red. I can't think. Go on back."

Mutely I shook my head. No matter what he had done, or why, I wasn't going to leave him, confused and concussed, standing at the top of a long winding staircase.

"Then wait for me here until it's over. Don't come inside." Meritt hesitated. "And Red? Everything will be all right. By my definition, anyway. One way or another, it'll all be all right."

And, turning, he pushed open the door and vanished into the Opticon.

I understood that he wanted to be alone, that he was saying goodbye to our city and to our childhood, and to the person he had been before. But he seemed so stricken, and he had always wanted me with him before. I thought that maybe if I didn't follow, he'd think his confession had turned me against him forever. Me, and all of his friends, because if I couldn't forgive him, who could?

So I slipped as quietly as I could the rest of the way up the stairs and entered the room unobtrusively.

It was dim in the watchtower, with the only light coming from the darkening sky outside. Wind was whistling through the broken windows. The computer monitors were dark. Shattered glass was everywhere, bits of it scattered across the carpet and heaped in drifts like greenish sparkling snow. Fluttering papers drifted across the floor, coming to rest temporarily against a chair or table leg before shifting and continuing on their restless, aimless way.

Meritt was crossing to the northern side, his boots crunching over broken glass. He stopped and looked down at the city circle.

"Michael Alleyn is here," he said, his voice low. "He isn't dead."

What? Alarmed, I hurried across the room to him.

"Of course he isn't dead," I said, putting a hand on Meritt's arm. "He isn't even injured."

Meritt started at my sudden presence beside him, frowned, and then turned back to the broken window.

Following his gaze, I looked down at the city circle. My father stood on the city steps, leaning on his cane and looking up at us—though whether he could actually see us, there in the dark tower, I didn't know.

He probably didn't like me wandering off, not after losing me too many times already, and had come to keep me in sight.

"That's not Michael Alleyn," I said. "That's *Eric* Alleyn. My father."

Meritt glanced at me again. He looked as if he might say something, but instead he merely shook his head repressively.

Then he pulled the telescope toward him and tilted it, pointing it toward the north and the ruined compound.

"You were wrong about a lot of things," he said, speaking in a voice that seemed unnaturally loud, there in the hollow echoing windswept room. "Maybe you were mistaken, or maybe you were lying. I don't know, and really it doesn't matter."

I was wrong? About what? I'd certainly never lied to him. Not to Meritt, not ever. He was off his head.

How was I going to get him safely back downstairs?

I could go get help, of course, but I didn't want to leave the room with Meritt standing there beside the open windows, so high above the ground.

"Let's go back down now," I said, pulling at his arm, but he wouldn't move.

"I've made my choice," he said, still looking through the telescope. "You won't like it, but it's my decision to make. After today, I'll never see you again."

I was speechless.

Then Angel spoke. "You can't possible think I'd agree to that," he said.

I whirled around, papers crunching beneath my feet.

Angel stood leaning against the wall, behind the door that now was closed. I had walked right past him, following Meritt to the shattered windows, never looking back.

He was in terrible shape, bruised and battered, one eye swollen partly shut, his clothes torn and streaked with blood. He was propped against the wall, apparently too weak to stand upright, and in the dim light, looking exhausted, looking so much older than his years—

"You don't get a vote in this," Meritt said, turning and facing Angel. "And I would think you'd understand my perspective. You chose to say goodbye to your own father."

Angel shifted, pushing himself away from the wall, and walked toward us. The way he moved—that odd familiarity I stumbled against every way I turned—the photos in Fiona's bedroom—

"He said goodbye to me first," Angel said.

"No," Meritt said. "He didn't intend to leave you. It wasn't his fault. And even if it had been, you've made him pay long enough. They've all paid enough."

Angel was close enough now that I could see him clearly. "You look like him," I said, amazed, just as the door of the Opticon swung open and Michael Alleyn stepped inside, with Farrell Dean right behind him.

Angel wheeled around to face them and they froze, their faces going blank with surprise. They'd come to check on Meritt and me, that was all. They hadn't expected to walk in on something like this.

"Stay where you are," Angel said, as Michael Alleyn's expression changed, mingling wonder and regret.

Now that the two were facing each other in front of me, the resemblance was too strong to miss.

"He's your son," I said. "Michael—Grandpa—he's your son. The one from before. Angel is your lost son."

Angel answered without turning around, his voice sardonic. "Lost suggests mere carelessness. Discarded would be the more accurate word."

Even from across the room I could see that Michael Alleyn was trembling. He was an old man, and he had been through so much.

But his voice was calm and steady. "I did not abandon you," he said. "Your uncle drugged me and abducted me. I would never willingly have left you, Christopher."

Angel shrugged. "Uncle Meritt told a different story."

"But you know that he lied," Michael Alleyn said. "If you watched us, you know."

Of course. Meritt Alleyn hadn't needed a camera in order to watch his brother; he had the Dream Drops. Someone else had been tending the cameras. At first Angel would have been too young, but later—

"Did you see my confusion, Chris?" Michael took a step forward. "Did you see my anguish as I began to remember what I had lost and could find no way back to? Did you consider, now and then, trying to undo what your uncle had done to us?"

Angel laughed. "The past can't be undone," he said. "That's one of your favorite sayings, isn't it? The moving finger writes, and having writ, moves on. But yes, I studied you. Until you left again, I watched. And when you were gone I watched your other family, the family that wasn't mine."

Abruptly it sank in: Angel was my uncle. He was my uncle, like Rafe, like Gabriel. And yet—

"You stole me," I said. "How could you steal your own brother's child?"

"Half brother," Angel said. "And he had plenty of children to spare."

My mouth went dry. I looked at Farrell Dean and saw comprehension dawn in his face and knew his expression was reflected in my own.

I turned to Meritt. He was watching me, leaning against the window frame, the wind stirring his dark hair. "Meritt," I said, low, just to him. "Did you know?"

The look on his face—rueful, fond—told me the answer was yes.

All those years when I'd felt that he and Rafe were the closest thing to family that I had, I'd been right. They were my own blood.

I was glad and heartbroken and embarrassed, all at once.

"Why didn't you tell me?" I said, stumbling over the words, feeling the blood rush to my face. "We're cousins."

"Half-cousins." Meritt's gray eyes were serious and focused entirely on me. We might have been alone in the room. "It's a genetically negligible relationship."

He lifted one hand and touched my cheek, and my face grew hotter still. Surely he didn't mean—

Then he flashed that familiar grin, and for a heartbeat he looked almost like his old self. "Just teasing, Red," he said softly. "You were always so easy to tease."

Tears stung my eyes. I didn't know what to make of all this—he loved me, he didn't love me, he pretended, he enchanted, he loved me like a cousin or a pet or a friend. *It's complicated*, he had said. He was right.

"He deserved his own flesh and blood."

The voice was right behind me and I flinched and spun around, and Angel was right there, too close.

I tried to move away but he stepped when I stepped, blocking me in, pressing my back against the window ledge, not touching me but bracing his hands on either side of me, trapping me.

Behind him Farrell Dean moved and Michael Alleyn put out a warning hand, restraining him. Then Michael looked at me and made a downward patting motion with one hand, and I understood. De-escalate. Calm Angel down.

So I made myself stand still. I made my face smooth and serene, and I looked up at Angel as if he weren't towering over me, confining me. As if I weren't afraid.

"Your father had plenty and to spare," Angel said, looking straight into my eyes. "And on the other hand, there was the boy with the distraught abandoned mother who overdosed on sleeping pills, the boy with the series of indifferent foster families, the boy who once in a great while received a visit from an uncle who delighted in telling the boy how little he mattered compared to The Cause."

"You were badly wronged," Michael said.

Angel turned, his expression one of cool amusement. In the same moment I glanced down, saw the gun in its holster on his hip, but before I could even start to think to reach for it, Angel had me by the wrist with his good hand.

It wasn't even a struggle for him. He was barely paying me any attention, his hand circling my wrist and twisting my arm up behind my back, pinning me so that I couldn't move.

"That boy was badly wronged," he said to Michael. "But he got over it. Don't think you had the power to destroy an entire life. You aren't that important, not to me and not to the experiment. You never were."

Michael persisted. "I can't make up to you what you lost," he said, and for the first time I heard a trembling in his voice. "But please, son, hear the truth. I have always searched for you in my dreams. And as soon as I heard you were here on this island—when I heard the name Angel and realized who you must be—I came to find you."

Angel ignored him.

"Your father," he said, looking down at me. "He had parents. A home. A wife and family. A father of his own for all those years."

He leaned over me, looking down out the window, pressing against me so that the window ledge cut painfully into my back.

"And now he's out there," he said. "Eric Alleyn, the boy I watched my father raise. He came and destroyed my city, and now he's standing there, irritated that his leg won't let him climb the stairs to my last place of refuge."

For a heartbeat everyone was silent—I certainly didn't know what to say, how to soothe him, and I guess no one else did either.

Then Angel laughed. "It's too good an audience to waste," he said.

Then he was lifting me up, the window ledge scraping at the backs of my legs, and I flailed for balance, reached for the window sill, tried to hold on, and at the same time Meritt grabbed my arm.

"No!" he said. "Not Red!"

Angel tried to shoulder him away.

"I've let you delay this far too long," he said, and the wind grabbed for me with icy fingers, blowing my hair across my face, blinding me, but Meritt held on hard, and then everything happened very fast. Farrell Dean grabbed Angel from behind, his arm around Angel's neck, and Michael was yelling, saying something to Angel, and I was fighting to get free but Angel was too close, too strong.

Then Meritt let go.

He turned loose of me and wrapped his arms around all of us, Angel and Farrell Dean and me, shoving with his whole weight, driving us all sideways, away from the window, and I was caught between him and his father, crushed as they grappled with each other, and Farrell Dean was trying to pull Angel away, and all of us were tangled and too close to the open window, skidding and lurching on the broken crunching glass.

Then Meritt's hands were on me again, holding me, yanking me away, shoving me out of the circle of his arms and Angel's, into Farrell Dean's, and the two of us staggered backwards, off balance, away from the terrible embrace.

And Meritt could have stopped.

He could have let go of Angel then, but he didn't. He held on and kept pushing forward, using all his weight, forcing Angel backward toward the window, and then they rolled and turned and somehow Meritt was on his back against the ledge, off balance, sliding out, and I was

229

screaming and Angel could have let go then but he didn't, he held on to his son, and Farrell Dean lunged forward but he was too late, we were too far away, it was too late.

I caught one last glimpse of gray eyes, dark unruly hair.

Then Meritt and his father were gone.

Chapter 25

I don't know who carried me to the stockade, or who removed my shoes and tucked me in bed, or who sat up with me, taking shifts, all through the long dark night.

All I know is that I awoke in the morning, disoriented but broken hearted, the picture in my mind the same one that had been there when they sedated me, a crystal-clear image of my father cradling Meritt's broken body in his arms, looking up and meeting my gaze as I burst through the prison door, looking straight into my eyes and shaking his head. I remembered that—I would never forget it—and I remembered hearing screaming that wouldn't stop, that could never stop because it was in my own head.

When I awoke that next morning to the sight of Fiona's compassionate face, I turned away from her. I didn't want her. I didn't want anyone who had doubted Meritt. I didn't scream anymore but I started crying and couldn't stop, and everyone who tried to soothe me made the tears flow faster.

My father came and looked at me, shaking his head. Michael Alleyn came and felt my forehead.

"It will always hurt, but not always this much," he said, and left again. Rain came, and told me she understood, that she'd lost Earl, and Fiona said she was upsetting me and tried to make her leave and they got into an argument there in the doorway until Gabriel and Mal came and between them drew Rain away. Estelle came, and I tried to let her distract me with talk of her sister and how wonderful it was to be free of the Watchers, but all I could think was that I'd rather Optica be as it had always been if that meant Meritt would still be alive.

Finally, late in the morning, Farrell Dean came and stood in the doorway, diffident. He didn't say anything, and I didn't either, but a new image abruptly replaced the sight of Meritt's broken body, which, until that moment, had seemed permanently seared into my mind.

Now I saw another vision, a memory, just as terrifyingly clear and vivid, of Farrell Dean lunging for Meritt, leaping headlong toward the open broken window. I saw Michael Alleyn grabbing him at the very edge, holding him fast as Meritt vanished and the window became empty sky and a gust of wind lifted papers from the floor and sent them spinning through the vacant silent air.

I saw what I'd known but not quite realized. I saw that I'd almost lost them both.

From across the room Farrell Dean watched me, his eyes dark, his face grim. Silhouetted in the doorway against the outside light he looked taller, older, sterner than I'd ever seen him. He looked unfamiliar, and the one who was most familiar to me was dead.

Then Farrell Dean reached up and ran a hand across his face, and it was the same gesture he'd made in the boat, when I was hating him and scolding him and trying to persuade him to bring me home, and when his hand dropped and he looked at me again, I knew him.

He was here. He wasn't falling toward a window, saved at the last moment and then turning toward me with loss and horror in his face. He was here, breathing, walking, moving minute by minute into a future Meritt would never see.

As was I.

Shivering, I turned one hand palm-up in my lap. Farrell Dean stared at it a moment, uncomprehending, and then he came and sat down on the edge of the narrow bed, facing me, and took my hand in his own.

"I shouldn't have assumed Angel was dead," he said, tracing my fingers.

"Meritt knew he was alive." Those were the first coherent words I'd said since his death, and they felt awkward in my mouth.

Farrell Dean reached up and brushed a strand of damp hair away from my face, and the feel of his hand on my skin kept me there, in the dim little room, with the scratchy green blanket and the sound of someone talking outside my door.

"He saw Angel," I went on. "He saw him up there, in the watchtower window. That was when he knew Angel was still alive. And he thought I saw him too, but I didn't. I thought he was talking about something else. I thought he was confused."

Farrell Dean's hand tightened on mine. Tears were still running down my cheeks, but I was talking, and I had to keep talking. Someone other than me had to know.

"He didn't want me to go up there with him," I said. It was important that Farrell Dean understand this. "He told me to go back to you, but I went into the prison after him. Then he told me again, but I insisted. And when I followed him up, at the top he told me to wait for him outside."

The light from the doorway darkened as someone came in, but I ignored the intruder.

"I should have let him go alone," I said, looking only at Farrell Dean. "If he'd gone alone he could have told Angel goodbye and walked away. But I didn't listen."

"Don't be ridiculous."

It was Rain again, this time carrying a tray with food

and a steaming mug of tea. "Here. You have to eat." She looked at Farrell Dean. "Make her eat."

Without a word he took the tray from her and set it on the bedside table, then sat back down beside me, leaning against the wall as I was doing, close enough that we touched at shoulder and hip. He was between Rain and me, shielding me with his body, but she moved to the foot of the bed and gazed at me from there.

"Don't torment yourself," she said. "Believe me, it won't do a bit of good. And anyway it's stupid to blame yourself for what happened. Angel was the one who started it."

Fiona was beside her now. "Meritt was fey," she said. "I saw it, that night in the ruins. He didn't expect to live to see Optica free." She moved around the side of the bed, and took my hand, her eyes bright with tears. "But he did, Red, and when he saw there was still more to be done, he did it. Even injured, even concussed, he did what needed to be done. He saved you. He saved us all."

Rain stepped over to the window, yanked aside a curtain, and let daylight come streaming in. "Rufus and Mick are carving a tombstone out in the courtyard," she said, gesturing toward the window. "You can see them from here. We asked them to work where you could watch them."

But when I looked at Rain standing by the window I saw instead Meritt looking through broken glass, heard him say that Michael Alleyn was there and alive.

"Come on," Fiona said, taking Rain by the arm. "There's work to do."

Michael Alleyn is here, Meritt had said, looking down at Eric Alleyn's distinctive red hair. He knew he was looking at Eric Alleyn; he must have known.

Maybe he only meant that Michael Alleyn was in Optica.

Farrell Dean sat on the edge of my bed, feeding me

spoonfuls of broth and bites of toast as if I were an invalid, and I thought it all through, as carefully as I could.

And then, finally, I thought I understood. Before Meritt knew I had entered the room, he had crossed to an open window with a view unavailable to Angel, who was standing over by the door. And then Meritt began to try to lure Angel over to the window, using Angel's lost father as bait.

I have to say goodbye, he'd said. *I have to end this once and for all.*

He knew the depths and determination of his father's vengeance and he tried to protect us, knowing he was no match for Angel in a fight, knowing that he might not make it out of that watchtower alive. He'd even tried to tell me so, in his maddening evasive way.

Everything will be all right, he had said. *By my definition, anyway. One way or another.*

He chose us. He chose the rest of us over his father.

I ran through it all again, everything Meritt had said in those last few minutes. I thought through it and then I said it all aloud.

Farrell Dean listened, and then he nodded. "Angel would have kept killing," he said. "Maybe not right away. Maybe not until his injuries had healed. But he would have come after you eventually, Red. He'd have come after you and your father, and then he would have kept right on killing until someone killed him. He's been nursing his grudge too long to stop. But Meritt stopped him. That's what he went up into the tower to do. Maybe he's been trying to stop him for a long time, and this way was the only way left."

Then I went over every look, every word that Meritt had said to me in the three weeks between the night Rafe was arrested and the day Meritt died. I talked and I backtracked and explained and analyzed, and through it all Farrell Dean listened and nodded and said nothing. He said nothing even when I told him that Meritt had been the one who had turned in Rafe.

"Will you tell Gabriel?" I said. "I don't think I can."

Farrell Dean set the tray aside, then, and nodded. "I'll tell him," he said. "You do realize that at some level he'll be relieved."

"And at another level he'll be furious."

"I'll make sure he understands it was with good intentions. I'll make sure he knows that Rafe would be forgiving."

"Make sure he knows Meritt," I said. I was crying again, but not as hard. By then the heartbreak had settled too deep for tears.

As I was wiping my eyes, Angus and Rory appeared.

"Here you go, baby sister," Angus said, setting a sandwich in front of me with one hand and tousling my hair with the other. "It's good. I made it myself."

A bite had been taken out of one corner.

It didn't make me smile, but something in me loosened just a little.

"You won't eat it?" Angus picked it up and waved it temptingly in front of my face.

"I'm not hungry," I said. "But thank you."

Angus nodded and took another bite.

Rory held up a notebook similar to the ones the Dream Recorders used. "We found some of these in the ruins of the compound," he said, laying it on the foot of my bed. "I thought it might help to write the whole thing down, when you're ready, I mean. That way you don't have to keep it all up here—" he tapped his forehead.

Pulling a pen out of his shirt pocket, he nudged Angus aside and handed it to me.

Earl was buried at the stockade, in the little interior courtyard, but we didn't bury Meritt and Angel there. Instead we buried them in the woods above the promontory where they had stood together the day I first left the island, the day I realized Meritt was a Guardian's son.

Cline and Harding had gone earlier to dig the graves, and we carried the bodies there, a whole procession of us, and laid them beside the holes. The sky was overcast and a stiff breeze was blowing, and beneath us the sea swam dark and forbidding, as grim as even I could wish.

My father put a hand on my shoulder. "Our tradition, on Aislin, is to cut a lock of hair at this time," he said. "I will do that now, to take home and keep with the others."

With my mother's, he meant, and Granny Rose's. Our family.

I nodded, and he bent over the anonymous-looking bundle that was Meritt. Mick came forward and steadied him as he knelt, awkward with his artificial leg. The bodies had been wrapped up in thick cloth—sailcloth, Mal said, from a storage room at the stockade—and stitched securely. Now I saw that Meritt's shroud had not been stitched all the way to the top. My father folded back the cloth, and it really was Meritt's body, Meritt's face.

"Papa?" I said, and he turned, a lock of dark hair in his hand. "Cut a lock of Angel's, too, please."

Eric Alleyn nodded without speaking, and turned to the task; but I saw, then, that my request had been unnecessary. Angel's shroud, like Meritt's, had not been completely sealed.

Michael Alleyn stood by quietly, watching all this, Mal at his side. I went to him, saying nothing, and stood beside him. His grief was different from mine, I knew, but surely just as deep.

After a moment he shifted, his eyes still on the shrouded bodies of his son and grandson.

"Mal searched for him," he said. "While I went in after you, the night the city fell, Mal searched. Because I suspected, you know. When you told me about the Guardian named Angel, I suspected he must be my son."

"Because he'd named his own son Meritt," I said.

"Yes. And because his mother never called people by their given names, but always gave them pet names. And because someone—someone other than my brother, I mean—seemed to have taken a personal interest in our family on Aislin, all those years. A malignant interest." Michael sighed, and squeezed the bridge of his nose. After a moment, he went on.

"Christopher could have chosen another path," he said, and his voice suddenly rang out clear and carrying, and around the graves every face turned toward him. "But when the fathers eat sour grapes the children's teeth are set on edge, and so I pray that his sins may in mercy be laid to another's account. My brother's, or mine. The watchmaker's. But not his own."

"Amen," Sir Tom said. Stepping forward, he raised his arms over the graves. "Dust thou art, to dust returneth, was not spoken of the soul. One short sleep past, we wake eternally, for love is strong as death, as fierce as the grave. Many waters cannot quench love, nor can floods drown it. So death, be not proud. Thou shalt die."

The wind whipped my hair into my eyes, and when I pushed it away the strange tableau remained—two graves, a circle of grim faces, and the strange old Guardian, arms spread, silhouetted against the sea-struck sky.

Then people began to murmur, to talk about Meritt and what they had thought and what he had done, and Rufus and Angus filled in the graves, and the living voices softened the sound of spades and falling dirt.

Gabriel, however, said nothing. He stood a little back from everyone else, his eyes dark, his expression brooding and pitiless, unlike anything I had ever seen on Rafe's face.

But when everyone else had gone, and Fiona urged me at last away, he stayed behind, standing over Meritt's grave; and when I turned for one last look, he was straightening the branch of fiery leaves we'd laid at Meritt's feet.

Chapter 26

Several days passed. We had to let the wounded heal enough to travel, and we had to make sure that those who remained would have resources enough to survive the winter.

Soon, though, the time came for us to leave. Rufus had a wife and children who would worry until he returned, and Sean would worry as well until he saw us all in person. We had no inclination to delay any longer than necessary.

The beach was scattered with people talking and planning, shaking hands and giving hugs. It was early afternoon on a brisk cool day, and someone had dug a pit on the sand and built a driftwood fire. The smoke blew here and there, smelling like winter, tracking the changes of the shifting wind. The water was green and golden, gray and weeping, changing minute by minute as clouds came and went before the sun. Soon the tide would be turning, swimming back toward Aislin once more.

"Half of us bounded by a nutshell, and the others by bad dreams," Sir Tom said, helping to lift baggage into one of the two boats. "That's all over now, and it's a good thing. Although--" he glanced at me out of the corner of his eye— "Some doors, once opened, can never be shut again."

"What's done is done," I said, echoing his own words, thinking of the flashes I sometimes had, the thoughts and memories that were not my own. Fiona and I had an interesting road ahead of us.

Then I reached out and touched the sleeve of his camouflage-mottled shirt. "Thank you for helping us," I said. "You were a good Guardian."

Sir Tom waved a dismissive hand and turned to looking out toward the sea, sparkling and darkening in the ever-changing light.

"There's something wrong with a Guardian who doesn't even notice when the watchmaker comes ashore," he said. "That was some trick you pulled out of your sleeve, Red Girl. I couldn't believe my eyes."

"You thought he was dead on the mainland."

"I thought he was dead," he agreed. "And I had no idea you were his granddaughter. None at all. I knew Angel was his son, and therefore young Meritt was his grandson. But you … you were the wild card. The fairy child. The one who doesn't fit it into anyone's equations. Angel brought about his own downfall, bringing you here."

Then he turned back toward me, opening his arms and pulling me against him, the stubble on his chin rough against my forehead. He smelled of wood smoke and pine trees, of the wilderland, of a wider world.

"You have stories to tell me," I said.

"Yes, I do. Stories a better man than I ought to tell, but since I'm all you've got, I reckon I'll have to do. Treasures in jars of clay and all that. They won't wait forever, and I won't last forever, but they can wait until you've had time to recover." He released me. "She's strong. She'll be all right."

Then, tilting his head, he seemed to listen. "Well, of course I hoped. Though what a thing to hope—amnesia, exile. Better than having you dead, of course, so naturally I hoped. But no one has said a word about seeing you."

Michael Alleyn, standing nearby with my father and

Will and Louie, turned and looked thoughtfully at Sir Tom.

"Sir Tom?" I said, and his eyes focused again. "Are you a twin?"

He snorted. "Better get in the boat," he said. "Time and tide waiteth for no girl."

He wasn't going to answer me—at least not right then—so I didn't pursue it.

"When will you come see us?"

He shrugged. He and a few of the others—Will and Louie, Ezzie—were determined to get a changed Optica back on its feet. It was an enormous task; I didn't envy them. At least they had some good people here to help. Karl and Judd, Dane, and of course there were others. My farmer—Edgeling's brother. Rafe's two sons.

It had taken awhile, but we'd tracked them down. They were soft-spoken men with Rafe's dark eyes, and with children of their own. They were already cutting trees to build houses out in the woods, not content to be inside even fallen city walls. They had promised, some day, to visit us.

A few people were coming back with us—or already had gone, rather, for Mal had made one trip and then sailed back to collect the rest of us. Estelle had already gone to meet Esme and Margo. Alice had gone—she was going to live with my grandparents and help take care of Nana—and so had Cline, who had some cattle scheme, and Liza, whom I suspected had her own scheme involving Angus. Gabriel had escorted them all to Aislin, and stayed to introduce them around and help them begin to get settled.

Harding and Shawna thought they might come later, once Joe was well enough to decide what he wanted to do. Mal had promised to return to Optica now and then, to check on those we were leaving behind, and to carry back and forth visitors who missed old faces.

I didn't know whether I would ever return. I thought I

might, someday. To visit. To see what the others had made of things. To remember.

In the meantime Ezzie and Kari had promised to tend to Meritt's grave for me. *Our Meritt*, his tombstone read.

And the tide turned.

Farrell Dean waded into the cold sea and pushed the boat off the sandy bottom. Then he swung himself up and in, the boat swaying gently as it took his weight. He came and sat beside me, squinting a little as the sun and the waves threw sparkling reflections into his eyes.

The wind kicked up, smelling more of salt and less of the seaweed and smoke from the beach where our friends stood, waiting to say one last goodbye. They had fallen silent now, thoughtful. They stood together, small and few against the long stretch of pale chilly beach, and their smiles fell away until they gazed at us as though we had already passed beyond their reach, and the sun slid behind a cloud and left the waves a flat dull gray, and my eyes were full of tears that didn't quite spill over.

Fiona smiled at me encouragingly. Tor watched with sleepy sympathetic eyes, bracing himself against the rocking of the boat, his leg in a plaster cast. Mal stood at the ready, watching Rufus in the other boat fiddling with the engine.

This was it. This was goodbye.

But after a moment Rufus raised his head. "Go on if you need to catch the wind," he said. "This will only take a second."

Mutely Mal shook his head. He was the sailor, I thought; he wanted to bring up the rear, making sure the rest were safe and sound.

"We'll wait," Rain announced, as if Mal needed a

spokesman.

My heart, already aching, seemed to wither with dread. I was leaving behind everything I had known and loved, and it was killing me, and prolonging the moment was sheer torture. I blotted my eyes on my sleeve and tried not to look at the group standing on the sand, tried not to think about those who should have been standing but were lying in their graves, cold and dark and alone.

Beside me, my father put an arm behind my shoulders and Farrell Dean's.

"You know," he said, "Sir Tom isn't the only one with stories to tell."

Across from us Michael Alleyn looked surprised. The wind stirred his white hair into a halo, and he looked old and tired, but when he spoke his voice was strong.

"You remember my stories?" he said. "After all these years?"

"I'm crippled, not brain damaged," my father said. Then his expression changed. "Some of those stories--the ones I thought you were making up. They were true after all."

"Made up stories can be true," Michael said mildly.

Eric Alleyn breathed in sharply—getting ready to say something brusque, I thought—but then he shot a sideways glance at me and let it out again.

"Tell us one now," he said to his father. "Give us a story to sail away on."

"A family story," Fiona put in. "Red has a lot of catching up to do."

My grandfather looked at me consideringly. He leaned forward and rested his elbows on his knees, clasping his hands loosely in front of him, and then after a moment he nodded.

"Well, Red, I guess you've heard that once upon a time I was a dairy farmer, the finest in the land."

They were trying to distract me from my grief, from the pain of this leave-taking. It was kind but pointless; no one could soften the blow of losing Rafe, losing Meritt, losing the only home I had ever really known.

I opened my mouth to tell Michael Alleyn not to bother, but Fiona spoke before I could.

"That's not how it goes!" she said, indignant. "You were a *terrible* dairy farmer."

Tor made a reproving sound, and she turned on him.

"But he was," she said. "He was simply awful. You know he was."

Michael raised his eyebrows. "You've heard this story before, have you?"

Fiona nodded. "Granny Rose used to tell it. You were a terrible dairy farmer. You didn't know how to do anything properly. She had to teach you everything."

"That's the plain truth. Don't go rewriting history," Eric Alleyn said. "You were a terrible dairy farmer. Without mother we would have starved."

Michael spread his hands wide. "I got better," he said. "And you know, I can't be blamed for a getting off to an awkward start. Telling a man he's a dairy farmer doesn't make him one, and that's what happened to me. They plunked me down in Aislin and told me to milk cows. I was a physician, not a farmer. A research scientist, a city boy. What did I know about cows?"

"You were a terrible dairy farmer," Fiona prompted.

"I was a *new* dairy farmer," Michael Alleyn said. "So, yes. You're correct. Milking didn't always go smoothly. And one stubborn old cow in particular was just as mean as she could be. She gave plenty of milk, and it was the best milk you ever tasted, creamy and rich and smooth, full of sunshine and wide green pastures. You felt all the goodness of the world strengthening you, when you drank a swallow of that milk. I got top price for that milk, and was glad to get it. But I had to fight that cow for every drop."

Fiona leaned against Tor and shut her eyes, listening. Eric Alleyn was smiling faintly. In the other boat Angus and Rory had fallen quiet, their attention fixed on Michael Alleyn.

"Well, one day that cow was utterly determined not to give a lick of milk."

"Udderly determined," Angus inserted loudly, and Mick thumped him on the head.

"Shush," he said.

Michael smiled but didn't pause. "I squeezed and struggled and got stepped on and kicked at, and outside the barn thunder began to rumble and rain began to patter down, quietly at first and then loud on the tin roof, deafeningly loud, the sort of thing Will and Louie used to call a gully washer, which meant I wouldn't be able to finish my outdoor chores in a timely fashion, thanks to that cow."

Across the narrow strip of water Rory was gazing at Michael Alleyn, his face alight. Even Rufus, working on the engine, had one ear cocked to hear his grandfather's tale. Beside me Farrell Dean shifted and threw me a quick grin.

This was what Angel longed for, I thought; this was what he missed.

"So I was angry," Michael said. "Angrier than I've ever been with a brute beast, before or since. And I raised my hand and slapped that blasted cow on her flank, and I cursed her, and just as I did a bolt of lightning struck the tin roof of the barn and went right through it and struck that cow dead."

"The blasted cow got blasted!" Angus said.

"She did. She fell over stone cold dead, and the toes of my socks blew out, but all I felt was a little heat and tingling, because I was wearing rubber mudboots. They saved my life, those boots, and most of yours as well, because Eric wasn't even a babe in the womb. We were hoping for a family, but as of then it was only the two of us."

"Tell what Granny did," Fiona breathed.

This was what Angel had wanted, and what I now had. I had a family. I had history.

"Your Granny Rose—bless her heart, she was a good woman, the best woman I have ever known. But she was not at all sentimental."

"Practical right down to her bones," Eric Alleyn agreed.

"Practical down to her bones. Yet what did she do, when I ran inside through the driving rain and told her how I'd cheated death, how a thunderbolt had come down from heaven and killed the cow? She collected every jar of the precious milk that cow had given lately, milk that was sitting cold and creamy in the springhouse, ready for our customers, and she poured it out, every drop, out of respect for the cow!"

My brothers roared appreciatively; my father smiled and his arm around me tightened.

Across the boat Fiona opened her eyes and looked straight into mine, and smiled as if we had been given a most precious gift.

I could give this to my own children. They could grow up sitting in front of the fire with their grandpa and great-grandpa, with aunts and uncles and cousins. They would listen to stories and know their past and their present and their future. They would know they were loved. They would know that they belonged.

The other boat lurched, its engine suddenly humming.

"Hey!" Angus yelled, and pretended to be knocked off his feet by the movement.

Rory yanked him up and waved reassuringly at us. Angus took a bow. Eric Alleyn eyed them both with a mixture of disapproval and amusement, and Mick shook his head, grinning, looking for a moment very like Meritt.

"Goodbye!" my brothers called to our friends on the sand. "Goodbye until we meet again!"

They called back to us, Will and Louie, Harding and Shawna, Sir Tom, Ezzie and Kari, Karl and Judd, and all the others who had come to see us off. They smiled and shouted and waved, and Judd ran out into the water and splashed it toward us, pretending to wash us out to sea.

Then Rufus opened the throttle and the engine roared and they sped off, setting us rocking in their wake.

Mal turned to Rain. "We're all ready," she said, and he swung the sail around and it filled with wind and pulled us suddenly swiftly out, away from shore, away from Optica, away from the promontory high above the beach where two figures had once stood. One, I'd have known anywhere.

I gazed at the imagined figures on the cliff above the sea until they were tiny specks, unrecognizable, until the sun slid out from behind the clouds and blinded me with brilliance.

Goodbye, Meritt. My first love, my cousin, my friend. I will never forget you.

The waves lifted us, the wind carried us on. The boat bounced with the speed of our passage, but we were safe and in good hands.

I leaned against Farrell Dean, felt his solidness, his warmth. He reached for my hand and twined my fingers with his. Then we and all my family turned our faces toward the west, away from the land and toward the open sun-spangled sea.

Toward home.

THE END

The Red Series

The Watch (Book One)
The Stolen (Book Two)
The Watchmaker (Book Three)
The Forgotten (Book Four)

Visit the author's website
www.amandawitt.com

Acknowledgements

All four books in *The Red Series* were family endeavors:

My husband—a professional writer and editor, and former creative writing professor—provided invaluable editorial feedback, copy editing, and proofreading.

My mother—also an English professor—served as another proofreader. Any remaining errors are ones I probably introduced when I just couldn't stop fiddling around.

My sister—yet another English professor—gave me a much-needed boost of enthusiasm at exactly the right moment, as did my sister-in-law Laura.

My father gave me a collection of Yeats poems for my nineteenth birthday, thus permanently fixing "The Stolen Child" in my psyche.

And my three (then-teenage) children not only talked me into writing these books to begin with, but also offered constant encouragement and insightful feedback every step of the way.

I am grateful to all of them for their help.